RITE OF PASSAGE

I0659312

A SUPERNATURAL THRILLER NOVEL

BY

TENO-E

Published by CaryPress. www.CaryPress.com

"We see what we need to see."

Table of Contents

Chapter 1

THE TWO-HEADED WOLF

Planet earth; beautiful and serene, but only from a distance. The closer you looked the more troublesome it got. The serenity was shattered by wars that were being fought on three continents. All of this was being watched by hundreds of satellites that shared one thing; information. Calls and messages were shared via these satellites, which every so often guided us when needed. The 'eye in the sky' some would say. Satellites were the real information super highway of the planet. They saw, they guided and they watched our every move from miles above the earth. Some satellites stood out from the others; there was one in particular. It was much bigger than the rest and on closer inspection it was distinctively different from the others as well. The insignia on the side said it all. It belonged to the Company with the insignia of a lone wolf with two heads; one head looked up to the sky and the other down to the ground. Every few seconds it broke the silence in space with a bleeping sound.

Its job was to scan the miles of the earth's surface looking for any disruption in the atmosphere. It missed nothing, but some things weren't of interest to the monitors of this satellite. It looked the other way when it came to earthquakes and natural disasters and wars that flattened the wonders of the world...it didn't care about that...it only looked for one thing; for him and nothing else. The disruptions were easy to see, as were the signs of things to come, evil things to be exact. They watched only to be prepared, as these signs were unpredictable and unstoppable. For the past year it had been quiet, but all of a sudden a low frequency alarm sounded in the control room, a room whose location was only known by few, located somewhere secret, as it watched all the way from Europe to Australasia.

However, the latest disruption wasn't in any of the normal places; the satellite zoomed in and confirmed the abnormality. It was a hit, a positive confirmation. Then the controller called the supervisor and shortly after, he grabbed the phone nearest to him, dialled, and waited for the receiver on the other end to be answered.

It was a long distance call to New York City. Someone eventually answered the blue phone as it rang off the hook, but before he answered, the man sighed as he knew it was happening again. There was no need for etiquette; he knew exactly why they were phoning him.

"Where?" he asked as he answered the phone. After a pause, the controller answered back, and confirmed the location.

"Latitude: 33°55'00" S"

A sigh of impatience while the controller the reads the coordinates.

"Longitude: 18°25'00" E"

Then it's confirmed a place where the evil has not yet been, a beautiful place, but where he goes death follows. Cape Town, South Africa

He was born 20 April 1905...

Ferdinand Schultz could feel the pain emanating from his backside. He tried hard to keep the tears from forcing their way out of his fifteen-year-old eyes, and for a while, the tears subsided. He just couldn't understand the unnecessary punishment; he had answered every single question in exam after exam after exam. Each day he wrote about five exams. For him, today's exam had been easy and he was sure that he had passed, but the way the teacher was aiming at his buttocks, it seemed that perhaps he'd been wrong. The only thing keeping him from collapsing was the thought of his family in East Germany. He was born in 1905 in a small town, a truly beautiful town with trees, flowers, and the woods; oh, those woods that he had loved more than anything in the world. The woods had always calmed and relaxed him; they were peaceful with lush greenery, clean water springs and fresh air, right on his doorstep. He really missed it. It had been two years since they came to his house and forced him to attend their school, and although he was in his happy place, occasionally bad memories snuck in.

He remembered the way they took him on that full moon night, gunfire and shouting, and then nothing, just quiet. Ferdinand had hidden under his bed. He was only thirteen years old; what was a boy to do? Moments later, he heard them talking again and then heavy footsteps clomped up the stairs, and stopped in front of his door. Slowly someone opened the door. Ferdinand could see four sets of boots walking into his room, one set belonged to his father. Then his father called to him. His father encouraged him to come out from where he was hiding, saying it was safe and nobody was going to hurt him. So, Ferdinand inched out from under the bed, he had no reason to doubt him. There were three other men standing next to his father, and even then, his father reassured him that nobody was going to hurt him. He tried to see who these people were, but he didn't recognise any of them. They appeared to be very muscular and strong, but something wasn't right, they didn't act normal. Everything they did was abnormal in fact; the way they looked at him, the way they talked. The only normal thing was the fact that they spoke Russian; it was his grandfather's mother tongue.

He had never seen his father so afraid and then he saw that his mother was being held by one of the strange men. And then he saw it - their eyes; there was something very strange about them. With just a quick flicker of perception, he saw that there was no colour in their pupils - just solid and dark; it frightened him. His father had tried so hard to keep them from taking him away; but he was unsuccessful. The men were heavily armed, and his family had no weapons. They were outnumbered.

As they forced him into the car, the Russian-speaking man looked across the field and saw two mysterious men standing at the base of the woods. Moments later, the others also saw them. Then the Russian-speaking man looked over to Ferdinand's father and spoke, "They can't help you; they aren't allowed to." They all got into the car and drove away, as Ferdinand's mother and father gripped each other tightly, and looked on sadly as the cars drove away into the darkness. From that day onwards, Ferdinand Schultz hated the Russian language. These men broke his family apart, and someday, he would make them pay.

He was pulled back into the present; it was two years later and he still had a few lashes outstanding that his teacher was preparing to give him in just a few seconds. He tried hard to be strong. Memories of his family always took him to his happy place. His mind was the only place that nobody could enter. Ferdinand closed his eyes and encouraged himself with thoughts of where he hoped he would be when the school year ended in three months; at his home, reunited with his family. But this wouldn't be the case. A few minutes later, a black car stopped in front of his school. They were coming for him, again. But this time it wasn't the Russian-speaking man from two years prior, it was someone else. Ferdinand was so deep in distraction that he didn't even feel the third lash, and for a brief moment, he actually smiled.

Then a knock on the door made him open his eyes, while the fourth lash connected with his rear, nearly burning a hole in his school pants. This lash was painful, so painful that his face scrunched up in agony as he tried to keep the tears at bay. Then he inhaled. He thought the punishment was over, but as the teacher walked towards the door she reminded him that there was one more left. She certainly wasn't happy, it was written all over her face, and everybody could see it. Lashing was her favourite part of the day, and she didn't like to be disturbed.

Six feet later, she was at the door, and she opened it. Ferdinand couldn't see who it was, but whoever it was frightened her. "Ferdinand Schultz," she beckoned him to the door. At first he looked around, and then walked closer while rubbing his still stinging backside. He couldn't see the man standing outside the door, but he could hear his voice, deep and strong.

The expression on the teacher's face said it all. She was afraid and mumbled apologies for punishing Ferdinand, but she continued to insist that he had cheated. She walked back towards the table, and picked up two tests that Ferdinand had written during an exam and quickly ran back to the man standing in the hallway waiting for her return. Ferdinand took this opportunity to walk closer, as he strained to see who this man was.

He had never seen his teacher so afraid. As Ferdinand inched closer he could see the man standing in the doorway with his cream-coloured suit and shiny black boots. The teacher rushed past him so fast that she almost bumped him into the wall on her way to this mysterious man in the hallway to show him Ferdinand's exam marks. The man took the papers and saw full marks for all three of the day's exams. All Ferdinand could hear was, "He did not cheat." The man spoke very clearly.

Finally, Ferdinand thought, somebody who believed him, and for that he was extremely grateful; he knew that no more lashes would be coming his way. The man then called him over and told him he would be going to University, and in a terse two-minute conversation, he told Ferdinand everything he wanted to hear. Ferdinand didn't think twice. This school was just way too easy for him; he needed more of a challenge. He grabbed his school bag, walked toward the door, and just before he walked out of the classroom, he turned around and looked towards his teacher. He thought of saying something, but his parents had raised him to be polite, so he just walked out of the room, not saying a word, and stood right next to the man in the cream-coloured suit.

Ferdinand had the intelligence to understand he was going to a better place, so he didn't ask any more questions on their walk towards the black car waiting outside. But then one thing came into his mind, which he had to ask, "Who do you work for?" But the man didn't answer; he opened the back door of the vehicle. Just as Ferdinand was about to get in, they both looked towards the woods and saw two mysterious men in long black leather jackets, the same men that had looked at Ferdinand when the Russian man had taken him two years earlier. One was taller than the other; the taller one had a black complexion and the other one had a white complexion. They were just standing there, looking, observing. When Ferdinand got in the car, he peered out the back window, straining to see the two men again, but they were suddenly gone as if they had never been there. The man in the cream suit mentioned where they were going, but he didn't explain what Ferdinand would be doing at the University. As the car drove off with Ferdinand inside, the other students saw what was on the side of the car - a Swastika, placed within a red circle. It was 1920 and the beginning of Germany's Third Reich. This fifteen-year-old boy would play a large part in it.

Ferdinand Schultz matured quickly and he enjoyed every second of it. By the time he turned 25, he was already a Captain in the army, a position offering many advantages, especially the fact that he could visit his family whenever he wanted to. There was one thing however that he found quite odd; he had two soldiers constantly at his side, bodyguards, but he didn't understand why. He studied biochemistry under the orders of the Third Reich, defining cellular components such as proteins and carbohydrates in chemical energy through metabolism in the human body. In short, Ferdinand learned how to make Nazi soldiers stronger and faster.

Everything went better than planned. The Nazi soldiers injected with the developed serum had more energy and stamina. But for the Third Reich, this wasn't enough; in five years' time, it was decided that the serum would be ready to go into Phase Two.

In 1935, five years later, Ferdinand Schultz, now a Major in the army, went for lunch, and returned to find a small box on his experiment table. That was where he saw, yet again, the two mysterious men wearing long black leather jackets. He remembered them clearly. Again, they just stood there, looking, observing. He ordered his two bodyguards to apprehend them, but when they got outside, these men, as before, were suddenly gone.

His attention quickly focused on the small box left for him, a seemingly normal box wrapped in brown paper. But the insignia on the top piqued his curiosity. It was a two-headed wolf, the one head of the wolf looked up at the sky and the other down towards the ground. He carefully removed the wrapping and opened the box.

It was like something he had never seen before. Inside was a large syringe filled with a light green liquid. He knew it was for him as his name was on the box. Then his phone rang; it startled him. He picked up the receiver, answering politely, in an instant he jumped to his feet, and stood as still as a statue saying "Heil Hitler." The call was from him, the Führer himself.

The conversation was brief, "Come see me tomorrow, and bring the box with you," Hitler said in his powerful voice. He put down the receiver. Ferdinand still stood with his phone clutched tightly in his hand. He was astonished. He had never met Hitler, so this must be extremely important.

The next morning Ferdinand dressed smartly; boots polished and was ready to go. This was his big day.

The meeting went well. The Führer was prepared and thorough, and left no opening for questions. However, a large black book lying on the table distracted Ferdinand; it looked old, maybe a thousand years old, he thought. Then before he knew it, the meeting was over. Ferdinand knew what was expected of him, what he had to do; it was time for him to go into the field with his experiments. Regardless, he had his doubts. Then Hitler stood and left the room, and an old man ambled in carrying a briefcase. Just like the book, he was old; he should have been in a wheelchair at his age, as he walked so slowly. He must have had a rough life, Ferdinand thought. He then recognised the insignia on the side of the briefcase; the two-headed wolf again. He had so many questions, but the man, like the Fuhrer, gave him no opportunity to enquire.

The old man explained to Ferdinand what would happen and how it would happen. He was to inject soldiers with the serum just moments after they had died. It sounded idiotic, confusing, and in fact evil. The man explained in more detail; Ferdinand was to take the serum from his laboratory experiments and combine it with the light green liquid that had been sent to him and then watch as the magic happened. However, as the serum had not yet been perfected, it would take a while to work properly - a few men would have to lose their lives in order to make sure it was ready. It was their duty for the survival of their motherland, he was told, and in a certain way he was brainwashed to believe this. He was told, "Kill a few to save millions."

Ferdinand was now ready to embark on his mission. He was walking out the door when the man called him back on this exciting morning in 1938; he had walked into this office as Major Ferdinand Schultz, with a lovely wife and a beautiful daughter. However, when he left the room in a few minutes, he was a General, General Ferdinand Schultz. This was his reward for all his hard work. He would now be ranked number five in the country; glorious Germany! But the old man cautioned Ferdinand once again of what he'd been instructed to do earlier, "Inject *only* when the men are dead!"

On 1 September 1939, the Nazis invaded Poland and World War II began.

Japan had forced America into the war with an attack on Pearl Harbour, on December 7, 1941. It was a Sunday. Four days later the Nazis declared war on America.

Three years had passed and there was still no success with the serum; all the soldiers who had been injected had died. General Ferdinand Schultz was getting frustrated and he was beginning to feel that it was pointless. Somebody had to do something, and somebody did; the man who had made him a General in 1938 arrived late one Friday evening to see him. Ferdinand's wife, beautiful and slender with light blond hair, opened the door.

She was taken aback at how this old man standing before her has passed the armed security. There were almost fifteen guards outside and yet he just sauntered by. None of them had moved a muscle. It was almost as if they didn't see him, and indeed, they had not. The guards looked towards the noises when the old man stepped on crinkled leaves and dry branches. But even with their powerful lights, they couldn't see him as we walked past.

She saw the same two-headed wolf insignia on the side of the briefcase that Ferdinand had seen on a number of occasions; however, she had no inkling of its meaning, she was just a normal housewife bringing up their ten-year-old daughter Maria. She showed the man to the meeting room while he waited for the General, and she made him some American coffee. He said nothing; he only sipped from his cup and gently rested it back on the table as he saw Ferdinand walking around the corner. The man opened his briefcase, removing something shiny; it was a mirror like shape in a canister, with a distinctive metallic shine. He handed it to the General. "This will win the war for us," he said, and then stood and ambled slowly toward the door. But just before he left, he placed a coin on the table, a coin made of solid gold with a few Swastikas engraved into it. At first it appeared to be an insignificant gesture, as Ferdinand had received many coins before. But when Ferdinand took a closer look he saw 1946 engraved on it. "It is the day of our victory," the man whispered, walking out of the door. Ferdinand never saw him again.

Two days later, Ferdinand had his first undeniable success. One of his colleagues volunteered to be electrocuted, then ten seconds later, injected with the supernatural serum concocted with holy water, cyanide and something believed to come from the devil himself, to become the walking dead or 'demon soldier' as some called them. However, when injected, the specimen would only live for two hours, never more, never less, just two hours. Then he would drop dead permanently, his soul trapped between hell and heaven forever. Yet these men did it for their country.

Now it was time to test the serum-injected 'demon soldiers' on the enemy. For the first attack the General only used ten soldiers, a small Nazi troop, to attack an Allied camp of thirty-six, just to see what they could accomplish.

The results proved perfect. The super demon soldiers demolished the Allied camp in forty five minutes. Nothing remained. No one survived. The next morning as General Ferdinand Schultz strolled across the battlefield in his black uniform, he was perfectly satisfied; even with the soldiers who had died, and he had won.

He took out his golden coin, the sun reflecting off it, and smiled.

It was true he thought to himself, "In 1946 we will rule the world." His team were even more secretive than the super Nazi SS soldiers were. They were the pride, and not to mention hope, of Hitler.

The time had come to test the demon soldiers on something far bigger. The Allied soldiers that they had previously attacked had only had small arms weapons, so Ferdinand needed to test them against a full infantry with guns, bombs, and tanks.

On 23 August 1942, General Ferdinand Schultz and his 'demon' soldiers would launch an attack in Stalingrad, Russia. For him this was payback time. He decided to do something different, but in order to complete the mission he needed to go to one of the nearby secret military camps on the outskirts of Berlin. He entered the training ground as if he was a king, waving his arms at the cheering soldiers. Word had spread quickly about the Nazis that would win the war - all thanks to Ferdinand who had transformed some of their troops into super soldiers after the successful attack on an Allied camp in France. Of course they weren't aware of how it was done. His plan was simple; all he had to do was ask them if they wanted to join the secret *4th SS Division Totenkopf*, otherwise known as 'Death's Head.'

Initially there were only three divisions in Totenkopf, so General Ferdinand Schultz decided to form the fourth division, his own. This fourth division was unmistakably superior. It didn't matter what rank the men held, they were respected. Doors opened for them and they received free food and the best beer. They were oblivious, however, to what their actual fate would be.

Their insignia was a blood red skull, unlike the third division whose insignia was only a black skull.

Ferdinand was astonished by the reaction he received; soldiers chanting over and over "Meine Ehre heißt Treue", which meant 'My Honour Is Loyalty'. They chanted so loudly that he couldn't even hear the people next to him. This was exactly what the Nazis needed.

The attack was only two days away. On 23 August 1942, Stalingrad would feel the immense power of the red *Totenkopf*. Finally Ferdinand would be able to carry out his long-awaited revenge on the very people that had split his family in half when he was just a boy of thirteen.

Chapter 2

THE RED SKULL

The war at Stalingrad had already started when the General's black vehicles with the red skull appeared through the mist. It was both mysterious and frightening for the Nazi soldiers; they stood in complete silence, not moving, not even flinching. Hundreds of people had been repeating what the soldiers had accomplished in the first attack on the American camp, rumours spread quickly of the red fourth SS Division Totenkopf, 'The Death's Head,' and when they passed their own troops lining the road, there was a creepy feeling in the air. It felt as if they weren't alone, as if there was something in the mist from which they came, something evil, unseen, swirling around behind them. Even the General sensed something and turned around looking towards the mist out of the vehicle window, making soldiers alongside the road felt cold and afraid of their own people. The General had certainly succeeded in making the masses fear him.

The vehicles stopped suddenly, and an eerie quiet engulfed the camp. Only the bombing and bomber planes flying overhead broke the heavy silence. The red skull showed his superiority; General Ferdinand Schultz got up, raised his hand and shouted "Heil Hitler," followed by the enormous shout of, "Meine Ehre heißt Treue", which meant 'My Honour Is Loyalty', and unexpectedly, the troops on the side-lines started shouting "Heil Schultz" over and over again. In that instant, General Ferdinand Schultz was the most powerful man on earth.

General Ferdinand Schultz then began to engage in war with his full might; the closer they drove toward the border of Stalingrad, the louder the Nazis shouted "Meine Ehre heißt Treue".

Even through the gunfire and bombing, the Russian soldiers could hear the approaching Nazi's who were chanting louder and louder as they moved towards the battle ground. Then suddenly the chaotic noise was silenced by the wave of the General's hand. It was time to unleash his soldiers.

The weeks of planning came down to these two hours. The General commanded the almost thirty willing men into a nearby conquered Russian bunker. It was almost time to inject them. He posted two red skull guards at the entrance of the bunker; not to stop people from getting in, but rather the other way around; to stop men from coming out. While a few of the General's soldiers connected the gas to the bunker ventilation, he walked toward a staircase of a nearby house and gazed towards the horizon, waiting patiently for dusk to settle. During the day, the soldiers were easy targets, but at night, they were unstoppable. He knew a direct hit by a tank would disintegrate the super soldiers. Yes, they were powerful, fast and cold-blooded killers; however, they were still made of flesh and blood.

Dusk fell tenderly over Stalingrad. With a nearly unnoticeable nod of his head, gas was released into the bunker, filling it quickly. It was time for his soldiers inside to die.

The gas made it difficult for the red skull soldiers to scream. Panic spread through the bunker and some of them wanted desperately to change their minds at the last second and tried forcing the bunker doors open from the inside. They were met by a heavy stream of bullets from the other side, as the two guards opened fire on the unarmed soldiers who were intent on escaping. General Ferdinand Schultz knew this would happen, and during the ten seconds of gunfire he turned away, and faced in the direction of Stalingrad.

The gunfire ceased; just as quickly as it had started. The General walked down the stairs toward the bunker. The two guards hesitantly opened the door. Only three soldiers had been hurt by the bullets – but as they'd lost so much blood they were worthless. The General casually walked past them, and followed the two doctors who had already begun injecting the dead soldiers.

They had to be quick. They had only one minute, otherwise the serum would not take effect and the soldiers would remain just as they were - dead meat. Then unexpectedly, the General shouted at one of the doctors to leave those who had been shot dead alone; he was satisfied with twenty-seven super soldiers. He carefully placed the remaining three syringes in the same box he had received years ago; the one with the two-headed wolf. He placed it deep in his jacket pocket, the safest place he knew. The doctors injected the final soldier and stepped back. Now they just had to wait for the effect of the serum to kick in.

Not far from them was a seven-man Allied patrol. They were not there to attack the Nazis; however, they had been assigned to spy on the General. Nobody suspected them of being Allied soldiers as they were dressed in their own attire, and they were one of many Nazi patrols walking the border of the city. The Americans, though, were aware of the power of the serum, and by order of their President, were instructed to find General Ferdinand Schultz and offer him a deal. If that was unsuccessful they were ordered to deal with the problem. However, the emphasis was placed on making a deal as American scientists desperately wanted to get their hands on this powerful serum. As the Allied soldiers made their way closer to the General, the first of the super soldiers awoke; first his arm moved, then the rest of his body, and finally his eyes popped open; eyes dark as night as if there was a demon hiding inside his body.

The injected soldier arose, walked toward the door, and paused in front of the exit, all the while looking straight ahead of him. The General walked toward him and held a piece of cloth in his hand, but before showing it to him, he waited for the rest of the injected soldiers to wake up and join him. The super soldiers were waking from the dead, one by one.

After a few minutes, all twenty-seven stood in front of him, while the two soldiers that were guarding the door handed each one a large sword and an automatic rifle with three full magazines of ammunition. There was no need to show them what to do, they already knew. With death and the injection, only the soul was replaced, the memory and training remained.

Then General Ferdinand Schultz lifted his hand, still tightly clutching the piece of fabric, showing it to the soldiers. They didn't utter a word, but one by one they ran out the bunker door. When the last one was gone, the General casually followed, smiling, dropping the piece of cloth on the floor. Now was his time for payback.

Then from behind the bushes, the Allied soldiers emerged like ghosts, dressed as Nazi soldiers. One picked up the cloth, showed it to the rest, and saw the flag of the Soviet Union stitching on it. He declared, 'It has begun.'

They were too late. There was no way to persuade the General to stop, and soon the Soviets would find out exactly who the red skulls were.

The super soldiers scattered like dogs; they were moving so fast that to take aim was literally impossible for any soldier. They passed their own troops, not harming any of them; their objective was to kill anybody and everybody with the Soviet Union flag on their clothing.

If you had the flag on your uniform, you would die.

The first Russian soldier didn't even see it coming. He heard a noise emanating from the bushes, but he couldn't see a thing in the darkness. His death was instant; the sword sliced through his neck like a gauntlet, and by the time his head dropped to the floor the demon soldier was already attacking victim number seven. It was chaos; the red skulls were slicing and dicing everywhere. There was no stopping them. They killed thirty Soviet soldiers in ten minutes. Then there was a casualty, as the first demon soldier was killed by a tank that accidently drove over him.

One of the red skull soldiers ran past two men who stood right in front of him; the one a black man and the other white. It was the two mysterious men from the woods that Ferdinand had seen when he had been forced from his house all those years ago. The soldier stopped and walked closer to the men, showing his teeth. He was not happy with them being there and quickly ran off into the darkness like a fox.

The two men turned towards each other and agreed the company had made a mistake - the Company *needed* to change this, and soon, by the looks of the damage the red skull soldiers were causing.

The Soviets didn't stand a chance. It was impossible to fight these super soldiers in the dark, even with the full moon shining brightly from behind the clouds. Finally the red skulls switched to their firepower. This was just what the Soviets had been waiting for. As the rifles fired, the muzzle flairs gave the demon soldiers' position away; mistake in judgment made by the General.

Now they could see the super soldiers moving, but again, it seemed easier than it looked. By the time the Soviets opened fire, the evil soldiers were gone and some of the Soviets own soldiers had been killed by their own hands. It was quite by chance that the Soviets had managed to kill a few of the demon soldiers. With every one Nazi soldier that they killed, the demon soldiers took the life of ten. They were getting closer to the embankment where the senior Soviet officers camped; time was running out.

Then a whisper in the ear of one of the Soviet officers gave him a fighting chance. The Soviet officer turned around but saw nothing. The mysterious person who had whispered in his ear was gone, as if by magic. The Soviet officer paused for a moment, and contemplated what he thought he had heard whispered to him; he told himself it could work.

So he decided to try it.

The senior officer shouted towards one of the tanks that were fitted with a hose. At first the soldier in the tank couldn't understand; the command was suicidal. The officer shouted again and this time the soldier obeyed the commander's order; he set fire to the woods. "Everything burns" were the words he had heard someone whisper in his ear; two distinct and clear Russian words spoken by the one of the mysterious men.

When the others saw what was going on, they followed and started burning everything between the frontline and the woods, as they aimed their guns and waited. After a few minutes, they heard gun shots coming from within the fire, getting closer, yet they could still not see any Nazi soldiers only the giant flames licking the sky.

One by one from out of the flames the demon soldiers burst forth, running intensely. They were covered in flames, their clothes and parts of their flesh burning. They all ran in one direction; straight towards the Soviet Army. The Soviet officer bellowed the command; the shooting started and didn't stop until the last demon soldier was dead on the ground.

General Ferdinand Schultz had failed.

In response, the Soviets launched a retaliatory attack on his hideaway. This time General Ferdinand Schultz was the one running.

The Allied soldiers, dressed in Nazi uniforms, were gaining on him, but not to kill him. They were merely forcing him in the direction they wanted him to go, trying to get the General and his soldiers to run into an Allied ambush. They were there on direct orders of the American President and British Prime Minister. They hoped to make him an offer he couldn't refuse.

Chapter 3

IN THE WOODS

The General ran like the wind into an abandoned house two miles from the city border. According to his calculations, he and his soldiers were a safe distance from the Soviet Army, and they were. Nobody knew where they were; they hid like mice in a barn. The house was old and almost shot to pieces, certainly suitable for a hideout. He only had nine soldiers protecting him and two doctors. He felt safe that at least if something happened to them, the doctors could assist.

The General felt uneasy. He looked around, into the bushes, but he saw nothing. Then from around a bend he spotted a few Nazi soldiers approaching, about seven or eight of them. His curiosity moved swiftly from the woods and he informed the men of their good luck; their soldiers were approaching from the north. Relieved, they let their guard down.

Again, he turned toward the side of the house, the quietness still made him feel uneasy. He could not see the second Allied group hiding in the bushes, as men waited for the right moment as they saw the others moving closer towards the house. The General walked casually out of the house, and called them over in German. Then, momentarily, a chill ran down his spine. Something made him turn toward the right side of the house again, as the wind rustled the branches of the trees; the few crickets that still remained through the war fell silent. Even the Allied men hidden in the bushes felt uneasy, as if there was someone lurking behind them. The full moon gave them little comfort. It was as if the sound had been sucked out of world – hollow, slow and empty.

What they didn't know was that behind them, not far from the house, there was movement; someone watched them. This time it wasn't the mysterious two men; no, it was somebody else. At first, it was only one manly figure, and then from behind him, one after the other appeared. They seemed familiar; they were the *very same* beastly men who took Ferdinand Schultz from his home years ago. They just stood there and watched, and then they all disappeared into the darkness; their eyes glowing slightly red as they disappeared. This was not their fight. Moments later, from the hollow dead soundless woods, the chaotic chirping of crickets returned, and welcomed the night again, as the war sounded faintly in the distance.

The General suddenly felt at ease again, and he walked towards the approaching soldiers, he greeted them, and saw them clearly in moonlight.

There was just one small problem; the Allied soldier in front couldn't speak German. English was his only language. The intervention the Allieds had drawn up hadn't given them enough time to find more American German speaking soldiers. Among the seven-man patrol there were only two who spoke German and unfortunately they were trailing at the back.

As the General walked closer, he became suspicious, although the Allied solder in front managed to splutter out "good day" in German. Just as General Ferdinand Schultz realised these were *not* actually Nazi soldiers, the Allied soldiers showed themselves as they came out from behind the side of the house, emerging out of the bushes in a horizontal line. It was too late to do anything. From the back of the seven-man group, a German-speaking soldier shouted, "We are not here to kill you."

There was nothing Ferdinand could do anyway. He instructed his soldiers to lay down their arms. With no other choice, they surrendered.

"We are here to make a deal," the Allied soldier in charge said in English. The General understood perfectly, as he watched the other

Allieds as they came out of the bushes. He knew that if they wanted him dead, he would be dead already. For a brief moment, it looked like a Mexican standoff, followed by a short spell of silence. All except a few Allied soldiers that guarded the perimeter, walked into the house which sat in the shadows of the trees in the moonlight.

Once inside, the Allied soldiers explained the deal and what was expected of General Ferdinand Schultz. The conversation was over in a few moments. The soldiers agreed. Even the doctors agreed. The deal was too good to be true.

As the General and the Allied soldiers walked out of the abandoned house, the Allied soldiers disappeared into the woods as if the meeting had never taken place. The instructions were clear; they were to take a train in two weeks' time, stop near a town called Cologne at a predetermined meeting point, take a boat to a nearby airfield, and fly to America. His family, two scientists and a few soldiers were the only ones allowed on Train 104.

The two weeks passed quickly and the mood on the train was cheerful, but vigilant. After an hour, the train had to make an unscheduled stop as a large tree blocked the track fifty yards from an abandoned train station.

Then all of a sudden it got quiet, the clouds temporarily blocked out the bright moonlight, which made it nearly impossible to see outside. Only burning timber lit up the surroundings. The fire felt warm and inviting on this chilly night. The conductor gazed around. Not even a leaf moved; the only sound they could hear was the crackling of the wood in the fire.

The soldiers were careful, but didn't expect any trouble. Why would they? They had made the deal and were safe from any attacks. It was only their own people that they had to worry about. However, the General was on edge. He knew they had to pass the station and then still go another twenty miles before the extradition.

However, all that planning and all the manpower it had taken were undermined by one giant mistake; another Allied group was there. They had also engaged in weeks of planning to ambush a train traveling to Cologne, Train 329. According to the intelligence, there was only supposed to be *one* train travelling that night and on that train were two Generals who were travelling to an army camp in Cologne. Train 104 was a secret mission; not even the Nazis knew about it.

There was however one man who had queried the fact that the train numbers weren't the same. But, the intelligence had still shown that there was only one train scheduled on this track; this *had* to be the right train. In fact, Train 329 had been delayed at one of the stations, due to the unscheduled yet prioritised Train 104 that needed to travel non-stop.

Train 104 had passed Train 329 a half hour earlier at a railway station; Train 329 had been ordered to hold position for the red skull train to pass. None of the Nazis on Train 329 asked any questions - they wouldn't dare. Train 104 passed them, heading towards the ambush that they were destined for.

Then it began.

The train driver was the first to die.

As he tried to remove the tree from the railway track he realised it was an ambush; a bullet took his head off and anarchy and confusion followed. The Allieds had been trained to never leave a person behind. They were still under the impression that this train carried the two Generals and the hit squad that were on their way to the Nazi war camp near the border of France.

The Allieds were lined up along the side of the train, firing blindly; they nearly shot the wagons in half. They ceased fire after half a minute.

They realised that for some strange reason, nobody on Train 104 was firing back; they were anticipating a return of firepower, a hail of bullets, but nothing.

Then a couple of British and American soldiers quietly entered the train from the last compartment. Only then did they realise they had made a serious mistake.

The four troops lying dead in the last compartment hadn't fired one shot; they didn't even have weapons.

"This is wrong…" the Lieutenant said, not understanding why these troops had no weapons, not even a pistol. *It was part of the treaty, no weapons on the train.*

As the Allied soldiers walked from wagon to wagon it became clear, something was wrong here, very wrong.

They could hear people in the next carriage screaming for them to stop, but the sound of gunfire blocked out the sounds of agony that the Nazi soldiers experienced. It carried on like that for a couple minutes, first the shouting, then the gunfire, and then, finally, silence.

The visibility in the carriages was bad. Newspapers and wine bottles were mistaken for firearms. Some tried to show them the extradition papers, but these were also mistaken for weapons. It was only when the full moon showed its face from behind the clouds that the papers and wine bottles were revealed.

They never had a chance.

It had been impossible to see anything. All they had seen were shadows and that was what they shot at.

The Lieutenant tried to stop the attack from the back carriage, but his screaming was also overshadowed by gunfire. He then strode hastily through the doors separating the carriages, hoping he would be in time. But when he passed through the carriages, he knew without a doubt that he was too late.

Even in the dark, he sensed that they had done something terrible. He couldn't see the bodies, but he knew they were there. As he walked forward the train lights came on, and his fears became reality. He dropped his head in shame as he saw the bloodied bodies on the seats and on the floor, while in the background the echo of gunfire continued to fill the air.

Then in a moment between gunfire, they heard something. They froze and their hearts skipped a beat or two.

They heard something that they never thought they would hear on a train full of hardened war soldiers - *the faint cries of a little girl.*

Her cries flowed through the carriages like a summer breeze. Slowly they all bowed down their firearms to the floor, and felt the sorrow through the stench of burnt gunpowder.

They knew they had done something wrong, something completely unforgivable.

They heard moaning. The sound drew them forward systematically, as they still heard the faint cry of a little girl. One of the soldiers finally repaired the electrical wiring and the lights shone brightly, rather than flickering like a candle in the wind. They needed to see where they were going, and then they saw the figure who had been crying.

It was a little girl in a red dress. She was the sweetest little girl they had ever seen and there she was, lying in the arms of her father, both of them clinging to the little life they had left in them, as they got closer to death with each passing second.

The soldiers took a closer look and saw that the dress wasn't actually red; it was a school uniform that had been covered in blood.

Her father, the Nazi General, was half sitting up, filled with bullets. He found the remaining strength to caress her long blonde hair, as he always did. He loved her so much.

As he caressed her hair blood oozed out of his neck. With his other hand he tightly gripped a piece of paper.

The soldiers instantly recognised the insignia of the coat of arms of the United States. The Lieutenant took a step forward and gently removed the paper from the General's blood stained hand. As he opened it, he saw the pardon letter from the American President. At that moment, the small girl ceased moaning and her neck flopped to the side.

There was no need to declare her dead; it was clear with half her blood spread across floor. The General looked up at the Lieutenant who felt the sorrow of the General, but it meant nothing as his face, too, was dead already. Only his eyes gave away the story - filled with the red blaze of hate. The Lieutenant looked to his side and saw that the General's wife was also dead. The General glared at all the men in the room, nearly dead, but his eyes still showed the unbelievable hatred.

Lying still, he remembered his experiments and frantically darted his eyes back and forth as he searched for the box that contained the serum. His hate was turning him into evil, something he never wanted to become.

Then with the little energy that he had left, he grabbed the small metallic box, and opened it in haste. He knew his time was limited. The Allied soldiers stared at him and slowly lifted their rifles, uncertain as to what was in the box; it could be a gun or explosives. They pointed their rifles straight at him. Their intentions were clear; if it was a weapon, they would shoot.

The General grabbed a syringe and then mumbled in his weak pronunciation, "May God forgive me." He plunged the syringe filled with the watery liquid into his arm, and injected every last bit into his veins. This was the first time the serum had ever been injected into a person that was still alive, but he had no choice, it was the only way. He recalled the witch doctors warning; "If not dead, the soul is lost." That was the only warning she had issued, yet she was very persistent about it.

General Ferdinand Schultz could feel it working, as his flesh pulsated from the inside. The Allieds no longer regarded him as a threat as he was almost dead, however they wondered what he had injected inside himself as two more syringes remained inside the box. Before they could ascertain what it was, the General quickly jabbed one into his daughter and then his wife. The empty syringes dropped to the floor, and shattered into tiny pieces.

The Lieutenant bent down, setting his handgun on the seat, and picked up part of the broken syringe. He turned his head slightly backward to the medic in a gesture asking for assistance. The medic might know what the syringe contained.

The medic shook his head; he had no idea what it was. The Lieutenant turned back as he found himself staring into the barrel of his own gun. "I'm coming for all of you!" the General yelled. Those were his last words. He said nothing else before being filled with Allied bullets which splattered his blood everywhere.

Then the shooting stopped. They knew they had made a grave mistake; they were all to blame for the murder of nineteen people on that train. They felt slight remorse for what they had done, but decided to burn the train to the ground to hide the evidence.

The train burned quickly; the wooden panels fuelled the fire intensely. Some of the soldiers grabbed souvenirs like a Nazi hat here and a uniform or two there, as they stripped them of their Nazi insignia. Little did they know that those souvenirs would haunt them down their bloodlines forever...

They looked on as the train started to burn violently, as it filled the night with light, and created an inferno. They hoped that all the evidence would be destroyed.

Twenty miles away the fire attracted the attention of the government members in charge of the extradition. They didn't even have to ask, they knew it was the General's train. However, they thought something entirely different had happened to the inferno of the train; they thought the Nazi soldiers had found out about the extradition and killed all the defectors. They weren't going to take a chance and investigate the fire. It was too dangerous.

Back at the train, the soldiers started to move away from the scene. It wouldn't be long before the Nazi soldiers moved into the area to investigate the fire. They were right. As if reading their thoughts, they saw a scouting plane flying overhead and the Allieds disappeared into the countryside, and assumed that nobody had seen them disappear; but someone had.

They were being watched from inside the burning inferno by three figures that moved toward a large opening on the side of the carriage that had been created by the fire. Everything was vague, but as they moved closer to the edge of the wall, things became far clearer. The vibrant red dress of the small girl had caught the eye of one of the Allied soldiers.

He thought he was seeing things, but when the Lieutenant saw the same image of her father and mother next to her he knew something was terribly wrong. Then, in an instant, the images disappeared into the out-of-control inferno.

The two soldiers looked at each other, not saying a word.

They never uttered a word about the incident until the first killing happened two years later. They had heard rumours about a ticket and a little girl in a red dress. Some called it an urban legend, while others knew exactly what was going on.

There was nowhere to hide. Seven of the Allied soldiers who were involved in the carnage all died over the next ten years. And then it just stopped.

The Lieutenant thought it was all over, their plans to send the evil back to the next world; the one they belonged in hadn't worked.

They were wrong; they had only postponed it.

Twenty years after the seemingly successful attempt to end it, he returned in 1964. By that time all had been forgotten about the incident, but those who were still alive were haunted by the image of the girl in the red dress. So when a ticket arrived for them, they knew what was coming and in a way felt relieved as they knew it would end soon.

Those who came willingly died in a respectable way; suicide the police reports detailed.

Those who didn't want to go, and those who didn't even know that their fathers and grandfathers were involved in this misconduct were reported missing...they were sent to dwell in the realm of insanity for eternity, stuck on a train as forgotten souls.

It was their punishment – there was no way to get away from it and no way out. It was the end for them.

Chapter 4

THEY ARE WATCHING US

Planet earth; beautiful and serene, but only from a distance. The closer you looked the more troublesome it got. The serenity was shattered by wars that were being fought on three continents. All of this was being watched by hundreds of satellites that shared one thing; information. Calls and messages were shared via these satellites, which every so often guided us when needed. The 'eye in the sky' some would say.

Satellites were the real information super highway of the planet. They saw, they guided and they watched our every move from miles above the earth. Some satellites stood out from the others; there was one in particular. It was much bigger than the rest and on closer inspection it was distinctively different from the others as well. The insignia on the side said it all. It belonged to the Company with the insignia of a lone wolf with two heads; one head looked up to the sky and the other down to the ground. Every few seconds it broke the silence in space with a bleeping sound.

Its job was to scan the miles of the earth's surface looking for any disruption in the atmosphere. It missed nothing, but some things weren't of interest to the monitors of this satellite. It looked the other way when it came to earthquakes and natural disasters and wars that flattened the wonders of the world...it didn't care about that...it only looked for one thing; for *him* and nothing else.

The disruptions were easy to see, as were the signs of things to come, evil things to be exact. They watched only to be prepared, as these signs were unpredictable and unstoppable.

For the past year it had been quiet, but all of a sudden a low frequency alarm sounded in the control room, a room whose location was only known by few, located somewhere secret, as it watched all the way from Europe to Australasia.

However, the latest disruption wasn't in any of the normal places; the satellite zoomed in and confirmed the abnormality. It was a hit, a positive confirmation. Then the controller called the supervisor and shortly after, he grabbed the phone nearest to him, dialed, and waited for the receiver on the other end to be answered.

It was a long distance call to Building Number 8, New York City. Someone eventually answered the blue phone as it rang off the hook, but before he answered, the man sighed as he knew it was happening again. There was no need for etiquette; he knew exactly why they were phoning him.

"Where?" he asked as he answered the phone. After a pause, the controller answered back, and confirmed the location.

"Africa."

However, the Company had nobody there. It was time to call them. They had been chasing this abnormality for a long time and meanwhile, back in Cape Town, it had started. It crossed the Atlantic Ocean with its sights set on Table Mountain. Just before the base of the mountain, it dipped and the sight of the railway station welcomed it. Soon it would begin.

It began exactly four days later ...

It had been a long day and he was too tired to care about anything. Most people were already at home enjoying a well-deserved rest. But then there were the poor souls who had to work all day, and took the only transport available to them - the trains. This was where his evil deeds would begin. The trains were cold and the seats hard; this was certainly no five star hotel. These steel wagons, the only transport that didn't cost a day's wage, were always uncomfortable.

The station was now in chaos, people ran up and down as they tried to catch the last trains to anywhere, anywhere but here. All of them were tired, wishing they could have taken the earlier train or called in sick for this Saturday, but the world wasn't perfect. At least the station was safe with security and police patrolling the platforms regularly and for those who wanted a snack or a drink, the station shop would deliver and fulfil their needs.

However, if you were after a pack of cigarettes, it was too late. The owner also thought it would be better closing up sooner tonight. '*Come back tomorrow*' the sign read with a smiley face on the door; a happy face you would just like to punch. There was no time to be friendly tonight, with some fighting to stay awake for the 3535 train to Wellington.

The day had been way too long for most of them, the poor feeble-minded souls. It just made you feel sorry for them.

There was no place for feeble minds tonight...a stiff, cold darkening feeling was filling the station. If you were a pathetic soul it would be best to just stay away from here. This was no place for wimps.

Well who believed in these urban legends, as he looked at the poster on the wall? No really...vampires? "You have got to be kidding me," said Johannes who was standing on the platform. The poster was really causing a buzz. Everybody had been waiting for this movie for a while, and they stared at the poster on the wall. "I've heard of sequels, but you've got to be kidding me -'*The Return of the Vampire 5*'," Johannes said out loud.

Johannes tried ignoring the movie poster and shuffled onward; he had a train to catch and he unintentionally bumped into one of these feeble minded people. Some would call them ignorant, but Johannes stole a glance at the poster again and then looked around at all the other people who were waiting for the last train. If they missed this train, they'd be stuck there till morning, waiting for the next one.

"No way in hell…" Johannes shouted, as he tried to buy a ticket at the only open kiosk. As he'd attracted too much attention, the ticket sales assistant decided to issue him a ticket.

She was not supposed to give him one. In his haste, fuelled by greed, he dropped the ticket and his wallet on the floor.

He bent down, picked up his ticket and his office identification card that had fallen out of his wallet. 'Johannes Roland', the card read.

He felt better now that he had a ticket; that is all that mattered. The ticket sales assistant only gave him a ticket due to the extreme rudeness he exhibited towards her. She was not supposed to give him a ticket, but who was going to explain if he had smashed the window?

It was the almost empty bottle of rum that was responsible for him almost breaking the window. It was his own fault that he was late for the earlier train. If he had not flirted with the woman at the corner pub earlier, he could have made the earlier train, *and he would have.*

His only option was therefore Train 3535 from Cape Town to Wellington. He watched the information board that displayed all the trains and he was confused. He walked towards the board and searched for his train. The man at the turnstile said that the train was departing from platform 10, but there was no train there yet. He checked the time on the clock next to the train schedule, which confirmed that it was scheduled for 19:00. He walked back to the platform.

The train was supposed to depart in ten minutes. He felt frustrated and uneasy while he looked at the other people also waiting for the train. He decided to sit down somewhere and walked over toward an empty seat. He quickly stole another glance at the other people waiting for the train. These were not the people that he normally travelled with. The train he normally took was full of black suits and the smell of expensive perfume that always welcomed him; this smell, however, was stale and unwelcoming.

There weren't even twenty people on the platform, including a couple of suspicious onlookers. Johannes might be drunk, but he forced himself to be alert. "Let them try," he mumbled, hoping to sound aggressive while he hid his wallet with twenty bucks in it and some small odds and ends buried deep in his sock.

He bent over and dropped his almost empty rum bottle on the floor, smashing it into sixteen pieces; then again, he wasn't sure. The rum was obstructing his senses, making him see double. He focused and recounted – right, only eight pieces.

He didn't even bother to pick up the pieces. Why would he, he thought to himself, as cleaning the train station created a job for someone.

"Finally," said Johannes, as he saw the train approaching the platform at last. "It's about bloody time…" He tried feebly to make conversation with the person next to him, but she was clearly not amused.

She had to clean up the broken bottle pieces. He hadn't even realised that someone was sitting next to him. She just shook her head in disgust.

She wouldn't have minded pushing him in front of the tracks; it did, in fact, cross her mind for a brief moment.

"Asshole!" she hissed, hoping he'd hear her. But she was already out of his hearing range, as he strode toward the first class compartment to try his luck with his third class ticket. He knew there were no ticket verifiers on the trains this late at night on a Saturday, and the police patrol weren't worried about it. Why would they? It definitely was *not* their job.

He regarded his third class ticket - it felt *unusual*. It wasn't the normal paper, he pondered, as he rubbed the ticket with his finger. And then he took a closer look at it.

He distinctly remembered asking for a third class ticket, but nothing about third class was actually printed on it. It only said 'Admit One'. For a moment, he thought he'd gotten the wrong ticket. He looked at the woman leaning against the pillar and saw that she had the same one; he disregarded the notion. He could hear the train approaching now, but it felt like hours before the train arrived, and to add to the confusion, there was no number displayed on the front of the train where it should have been. It only had four zero's.

They were on the correct platform; Platform 10 at 19:10. He checked the information board yet again.

As he tried to figure out whether he was on the right platform or not, he saw that he was the only one left; the others had boarded already. He wanted to be sure so he waited for the numbers to change. He didn't have to wait long, as he saw the digits appearing one by one.

Train 3535 was now ready to depart.

He boarded and made himself comfortable, as he heard the train doors slam shut. He quickly scanned the compartment to see if he was alone; it wasn't a good place to be alone. He felt relieved once he saw the priest as well; though he wasn't sure whether it was a man or a woman. At least there was someone he thought to himself. It was the first time he'd taken this late train; he normally took the earlier one brimming full of commuters. He rubbed his tired eyes, as he tried to stay alert and awake. This helped through the first two stations, but his eyelids got heavier and heavier and he couldn't help but dose off.

He woke up to the sound of an enormous smash. "Asshole..." the person cleaning the platform grumbled. This time he didn't hear her and he looked down at the rum bottle lying broken on the floor. He looked around and glared down the platform at Train 3535 that was parked on the line and he rubbed his eyes a couple of times, "It was just a dream." He saw the train was one minute late and he walked towards the first class compartments, as he passed an open window where he saw the priest. A man bumped into him as he tried to get on the train. He recognised this man from the dream he'd just had.

"It was a man," he said, and then stopped walking. He could feel someone standing close to him. It sent shivers down his spine.

"Sir, are you sure you want to take this train, you are not on the list," someone said.

He turned around and saw it was a small girl; this certainly wasn't the place for a young girl alone, regardless of the time of day. "What are you doing here? Where are your parents? What list?" he asked, as he looked at her.

He could see she was young. He noticed her dress, a school uniform, which he thought seemed odd as it was a Saturday.

"You mean a ticket, I've got one." He showed her his ticket; she looked, but seemed confused.

"You should not have got one...Daddy won't be happy."

"What?" He had no idea what she was talking about.

"Where are your parents?"

She glared at him for a moment and then answered.

"They are coming; they are waiting for the train to depart." She didn't seem worried or scared.

He looked around. *"Her parents must be nearby,"* he thought.

He opened the train door and entered the compartment, the smell made him flinch. He stopped and turned around thinking that the girl was also going to get onto the carriage, but she just smiled at him and ran towards the next carriage. He quickly peeked around the corner and saw her getting into the next one, helped by some woman. *"Probably* her mother," he thought.

He felt very sober now; it seemed as if the rum hadn't poisoned him this time. He scanned the carriage for somebody else. He didn't want to be alone. He read the information on the side of the carriage wall - *travelling alone is dangerous* – he instinctively knew the sign was right.

He gazed through the window that separated the carriages and saw the woman who had helped the young girl onto the train, and then he heard something behind him.

"It was just his luck," he thought. He felt around to make sure all his belongings were well and truly hidden from sight. He could hear by the way they were speaking that they were part of a local gang, so he decided to move off to the next carriage. He heard the train guards' whistle, the sign that the train was ready to depart, and the train doors closed.

He knew he wouldn't be able to open the train doors, so he decided to walk to the door that separated the carriages. However, when he tried to open it, it was stuck. *"It's okay,"* he thought, *"people walk through them regularly, but it truly is stuck."*

There was no need to fight it; he had to stay in the carriage he was on.

"I'll jump over on the next station," he decided, while he looked towards the far side of the carriage where the three gangsters walked through the door separating the carriages. They noticed him staring so he quickly sat down and looked at them through the corner of his eye. "Shit," he exclaimed, as he saw them walk towards him. He knew he was going to be a statistic and he quickly took the wallet out of his sock and hid it in the side of the seat. However, he realised that they would know he was hiding it, so he quickly took the wallet out from the seat and removed his money and credit cards, and placed the empty wallet in his pocket. The train, however, was already stopping at the next station and so were the gangsters. Something had frightened them. The doors of the carriage opened and four cops climbed in.

Twelve hours later...

Now an uncomfortable chair had replaced his comfortable seat and he could see in his view that a detective stared straight at him. Every so often, the detective looked towards the two-way mirror. Something had happened on the train. What exactly had happened is what the cops were trying to determine.

This was a place Johannes didn't want to be, but it was unavoidable.

Something had happened on his train, and he was the only witness, or perhaps even 'suspect', if you looked at it from a police officer's point of view.

He had been pelted with questions for hours and the police refused to stop until they got the 'right' answers.

"Okay, the four cops climbed into the carriage, and then what?" the detective asked. He really needed to know what happened.

"I then promised never to say anything bad about the boys in blue ever again," Johannes was relieved. He could feel his stomach melting away. They had wasted no time in searching the hooligans and a couple of knives had dropped onto the floor.

"The pigs...I mean the officers...did find a couple of grams of cocaine on them," Johannes said.

"Cocaine...how did you..." he stopped, as this question wasn't important.

He continued.

"What about the girl?"

"She came out of nowhere; I almost died of shock! She looked almost saddened that the police took them away. She started talking about the list and their names were on it. I then asked her…"

"Who, the gangsters?"

"No, 'all of them', she replied," Johannes explained.

As the police escorted the gangster troublemakers out of the train, Johannes had walked towards the door trying to see where they were taking them, but he couldn't see anything, and when he turned around, the middle door was open and the little girl had vanished.

"I have answered all your questions twice. When can I go home?" shouted Johannes.

The detective stood and stretched, then walked towards the office window and stared outside.

"Four police officers are missing…**you are not going anywhere!**" He didn't mention the hooligans. *"It seemed like they'd made it after all,"* Johannes thought to himself.

He had to ask. "You haven't mentioned the gangsters?"

The detective walked back to the table and opened a file that contained large pictures. He couldn't make out what it was, but Johannes didn't have to wait long to find out.

"We found them. Their bodies are the only ones we could find," the detective said, as he placed the pictures one by one on the table. "Well, we found parts of them in the last two carriages," the detective said, as he watched Johannes' reaction carefully. The detective's plan worked; the pictures made Johannes sick to his stomach. He wasn't used to this kind of brutality! At that moment, the detective knew for sure that Johannes had nothing to do with the murders.

The detective walked back to the window and mentioned the others to Johannes.

"What others?" asked Johannes.

"Nobody made it out alive," the detective replied, as he glanced at the door and nodded at the commander. The detective understood what the commander wanted to tell him.

"Your lawyer is here," the detective said. He walked out of the room abruptly without speaking another word. Johannes tried to think what could have happened, as he replayed the night in his mind over and over again.

"You are not on the list." The media had mentioned that a serial killer was on the loose; a serial killer who used a young girl to lure people in.

"It's not possible." He closed his eyes, and drifted off to sleep on the cold hard metal table. The past 24 hours had been way too much for him!

Chapter 5

TWO MYSTERIOUS MEN

"No, all of them," the girl's reply echoed over and over in Johannes' head until he was sound asleep, his head on the table. His lawyer decided to give him a couple of minutes. It gave the lawyer a bit of time to read through the dossier while Johannes rested.

It wasn't long before Johannes started dreaming of the events that had unfolded on the train. Even his eyes told the story of the ordeal, as they reacted spontaneously while he slept.

The uneasiness ran through his entire body like the blood that pumped from his heart. It was something bad, something his mind, while not wanting to recall, forced him to remember.

"No, all of them," the little girl whispered. She then turned around and walked over towards the door separating the carriages; she opened it easily, as if it was never locked.

She walked a couple of feet further and sat down on the edge of the seat facing away from Johannes. Johannes could only see her dress sticking out from the edge of the seat. She was just sitting, staring silently down towards the far side of the carriage, as if waiting for someone. He walked towards her and tried to open the door, but he couldn't. He tried to turn the knob. He pulled hard on the handle, but still the door refused to open.

He realised he still had time to get out of the main door, onto the platform and run around to the carriage in which she was sitting.

He ran towards the door. He jumped off the carriage, and then quickly ran to the next carriage. As he ran he looked through the window in the next carriage. Then something, a shadow of sorts, caught his eye where she was supposed to be sitting, but now there was nothing, no one, she was gone. He just glared at the empty seat as he passed the window. He was certain that she had been on the second seat from the door.

He remembered part of her school uniform sticking out from behind the seat. *"Maybe she moved,"* he hoped, as he ran into the carriage.

And there she was sitting quietly playing with her doll. He wondered why he couldn't see her from the outside. However, he dismissed the idea thinking it was because of his view into the carriage.

 He was in bad shape, so he took a few seconds to catch his breath and then sat in front of her, smiled and took a closer look at the doll. From where he was, it looked like a doll dressed as a police officer.

"So you want to be a police woman one day?" he asked, but she didn't answer and continued to play with her doll.

Then the wind blew the door open that separated the carriages, and filled the carriage with a gust of freezing air. He instinctively got up, walked to the door and forced it shut. He looked into the carriage he had come out of.

"Spacesuit?" he mumbled in surprise. He was *sure* he had seen someone in a spacesuit, but it was difficult to tell through the fogged-up windows. He wiped the window to see into the next carriage while he called back to the young girl.

"Come and see something funny…" he said, but the space man was gone, so he turned around and walked back to the seat on which the girl had been sitting.

Now she was gone. *"Why would she leave her doll,"* he wondered. He picked up the police officer doll and then saw it wasn't a police officer at all.

He recognised the red material with the swastika easily. He shook his head. This was not a toy for a young girl, or as a matter of fact, for any child.

He picked up the doll. It looked old. "An antique," he mused. It could be worth something; he put it in his pocket, and then checked the time. This trip was taking extremely long, longer than usual. "What the hell," he saw it was nine o'clock. He flicked his finger on the face of the watch, trying to determine whether the wristwatch was still working. It was working, except the time was an hour ahead.

He felt a cold gust of air filling the room again and it started to get really cold. He closed all the windows near him, but it didn't help.

It felt like he was turning into an ice block, as he rubbed his hands together and tried to warm them up. He got the feeling someone was watching him. He turned around, but there was no one there. He glimpsed at the young girl running on the platform past the open door, he quickly ran towards the door and saw her disappear into the next carriage.

"She can move fast for a little girl," he said, smirking. Suddenly he heard a commotion which sounded almost like a party carrying on in the next carriage. He wanted to go and see what was happening, but the train started to move. So he walked casually towards the door that separated the compartments and wondered why the train safety guard wasn't blowing the whistle.

This time he succeeded in opening the door. As he stood in between the carriages, he saw the girl run and stand next to her mother. He waved to them, but they just stared at him not responding to any motion or sound, almost if they were in a vacuum. The mother, without emotion, turned around and walked towards the door on the far side of the carriage and pulled the young girl by the arm, almost dragging her away, but this didn't stop the little girl from staring at Johannes.

The little girl's mother was not happy with her. He remembered her saying that her parents were waiting for the train because she was late.

If this was so, where was the father? The little girl shook her head, but not at Johannes. It seemed almost as if she was communicating with someone behind him.

He didn't want to turn around; his gut was telling him there was someone behind him. It crossed his mind that it could have been those gangsters again. He could swear he felt someone touch his shoulder a moment before. It was a faint touch, but yes, definitely, someone touched his shoulders.

He squinted more closely at a dim reflection against the window that separated the carriages. Now he knew there *was* someone behind him. Or maybe it was just his overactive imagination. While the lights dimmed momentarily, the image he saw disappeared and the coldness he had felt for the past couple of minutes disappeared at the same time.

He turned around quickly. He had to be sure. But there was nobody.

He sighed in relief, but again he was alone in the compartment. But he wasn't quite alone. He still had the girl's doll. He looked at it again and put it away in his pocket, then he sat down and took out a small bottle marked 'aspirin'. Opening the bottle, he removed two tablets to alleviate his headache. He could feel that the headache was getting worse, so he popped an extra two pills and swallowed them.

"Why didn't I take the early train, I'm such an idiot!" he chastised himself while trying to relax on a comfortable seat. He thought of the young girl. "Why did she disappear so quickly?" he wondered, trying to decide if he should get off at the next station or not. Bellville was a big station and there was a police station near the platform, so he knew he would be safe there, but he wondered where he would find a taxi. The police wouldn't give him a ride home; it wasn't protocol for them. He sat discreetly, and relaxed for the moment.

He rubbed his eyes. The sound of the door opening behind him sent his heart rate sky high, it felt as if his heart was about to burst out of his chest. He looked around the corner cautiously, not wanting anyone to notice how scared he was. But his nervousness diminished to relief when he saw it was only the young girl. Then she said something out of the ordinary, not a hello or a smile, just a straightforward instruction, "You should get off at this station." She compelled him to get off the train.

Johannes frowned slightly. How did she know he wanted to get off, or was it just by chance? He noticed she was wearing a red dress and wondered what had happened to her school uniform. It wasn't important, he decided.

He looked to the left as something had caught his attention. He looked closer, just to be sure of what he saw – it was a hand radio lying on the floor - where moments before there had been nothing and then, as if by magic, there was nothing again. It disappeared into thin air.

He didn't feel so well. There was a bad smell in the train, a dead decaying smell. His stomach turned and he felt as if he was about to vomit at any moment.

And then all of a sudden, the spaceman was there again. He looked straight at Johannes.

"Who is that?" Johannes asked. She looked to where he pointed but saw nothing.

He wasn't sure. He wanted to investigate, but the small girl pulled his arm and walked in front of him. "My daddy is angry. You should get off here!" He yanked his arm away from her and caressed his wrist. She gripped so tight that his arm was bruising. But as he examined the bruises closely, he saw that they resembled burn marks.

"My daddy won't allow me to help you again."

That's it he decided...it was time to confront this 'daddy' that she had been talking about.

"Where is your DADDY?" he demanded furiously. Just at that moment he realised that she was probably not even 8 years old; there was no need to attack her. His jitters were making him a bit crazy; like seeing a spaceman. He didn't know what to think. He looked back again to where he'd seen the spaceman, just to calm himself, just to make sure. He realised that taking four pills for his headache was really a stupid idea, but there was nothing he could do about it now. The little girl's father wasn't far from them when she made the request; he appeared behind her dressed in a black military uniform. Just as suddenly as he came, he disappeared, as did the rancid smell. It was if the smell of death followed him around. Johannes started to feel better, now that the bad odour was gone.

He looked back down the carriages; he saw a frightening figure, someone he had dreaded seeing on the train; the ticket verifier. He wasn't scared, and couldn't help but stare. "That must be her father," he said. It was. This time he was dressed in a conductor's uniform and Johannes wondered how long he would take to reach the first class compartment, looking at his third class ticket. For the first time he took a closer look at the ticket the young girl had been rambling on about.

"What an odd ticket," he muttered, as he examined the ticket again. It looked old and used, almost like paper out of an antique book. It also had a funny smell, not a bad one, it was almost like perfume. He rubbed his eyes. He was really tired now. Again he glared towards the ticket verifier, and stood like a statue, staring straight at him. He sat down, still gripping the ticket in his hand as he read the printed letters, growing even more confused.

"Admit One," he read again. He just couldn't understand why the ticket was different. He took out a real train ticket that he'd used the previous week, and compared the two. The ticket he had now, looked more like a movie ticket than a train ticket. He put the ticket away in his wallet. He could feel the train stopping so he read the name of the station 'Muldersvlei'. There was only one more stop left until his destination station in Paarl. He looked out the window and saw the mist from the farms over the fields, almost engulfing a couple of houses. He remembered the jokes people made about this station when they travelled on the earlier train; that if you were left stranded there after midnight the locals would eat you alive! "What nonsense," he said, but he had to admit that the mist was freaking him out, making him uncomfortable. The train was taking too long to move again.

What had happened to the girl? She had disappeared again. He got up and closed the door to try and stop the cold breeze from whisking in, and then sat back down facing the windows.

He remembered there had been a murder at this station the previous week and just the idea of it was making his uneasiness worse. He heard footsteps on the platform, but he was too scared to look outside.

A dark figure passed his carriage. He could see the figure clearly but only in silhouette. He couldn't see his face from where he was sitting. But then it stopped right in front of his carriage door. While Johannes looked at the silhouette, he saw the sign at the same time. It was the same sign he'd seen when he'd departed Cape Town; *it is dangerous to travel alone in a carriage.*

The 'thing' that was standing outside the door just stood there. Then he heard more footsteps, as if someone was running down the platform towards the silhouette, but these footsteps sounded lighter, smaller, like that of a young person. He was right. It was the little girl, dressed in her red dress.

The air got cold, very cold, almost freezing. It was even colder than before. He rubbed his hands together to warm them up. Outside the running had stopped right next to the silhouette figure and it was quiet for a moment. Then he recognised the voice of the girl, but he couldn't make out what she was saying. He inched closer to the window to hear what they were talking about.

One thing was clear; she was trying to stop him from entering the train carriage. Johannes caught a glimpse of her father again, and he wasn't what he expected at all.

He was dressed in a fine looking suit now; it looked a bit old fashioned, but expensive. *"Someone should tell him the eighties are over,"* Johannes criticised in his mind. Then her father turned his head and looked straight at him.

"Impossible," he thought.

He couldn't have heard what I was thinking.

The little girl's father looked angry, terrifying even.

The two walked away, and moved out of his sight. Johannes quickly got up, walked towards the window, and tried to watch where they were going, but they disappeared in the mist, which had snuck up against the train.

He didn't want to stay alone in the carriage anymore, so he ran towards the door. He'd make a run for it and would try and make it to the next carriage before the train started on its journey again. But as luck would have it, he took two steps and the train started to move. Disappointed, he walked down to the other door on the far side that linked his carriage to the next one. The closer he got the more relieved he became as he saw people!

"Finally," he thought, *"I would prefer not to be alone."* He opened the first door. The cold air was almost refreshing, but the wind almost blew him away. Only the rubber restraints and a steel plate platform kept him from falling onto the tracks. Just one more door and then he would be with other people.

He struggled to open the next door and despite all his efforts, it refused to open. He saw another ticket verifier and shouted as hard as he could to attract some attention, but it was as if they couldn't hear him. He banged against the door window. This should get some attention his way! Not even a flinch from anybody. "Hey, are you deaf or something?" He banged even harder against the plastic window and his fist cracked it slightly. The ticket verifier looked straight at him in anger. This was no normal anger; it was almost like a possessed anger. The verifier stormed towards him and the broken window.

Strangely enough, he wasn't angry about the window, it was something else. He bumped past people in the carriage to get to the window. It was only then that Johannes looked closely at the people in the compartment.

They looked different somehow, almost as if they were high on something. They just sat there, not moving an inch. One was knocked down while the ticket verifier stormed towards the broken window. The guy, who'd been knocked over, literally just got up and took the exact same position he had been in before he'd been steam-rolled by the ticket verifier. He showed no remorse or pain even though blood poured out the wound from where his head had smashed against the steel doorframe.

The closer the ticket verifier got to the door, the more his rage built. He was only a couple of feet away from the door, when he stopped suddenly and turned his head to the left where someone was hidden away, behind one of the seats, gazing with angry tired eyes.

It was as if he was waiting for a command from someone. Then a small arm appeared out from behind the seat, took hold of the ticket verifier's hand and calmed and reassured him.

It was only then that he recognised the ticket verifier. He had been the one that had walked with the girl five minutes earlier. *"How is this possible? They'd walked the other way!"* The train slowed down as it approached the next station, Klapmuts, and a gust of air forced him back into his carriage, almost if he'd been pushed backwards.

Johannes was extremely confused about what had just happened in the other carriage.

The door nearest to him opened and he could see the platform floor, but nobody was getting on the train. He walked closer and glimpsed outside. He heard a car hooting and it flashed its headlights towards him.

He could see it was a taxi. He certainly wouldn't mind taking a taxi now, but he didn't have enough money for the trip; he was ten bucks short and only one station away from where he stayed. Suddenly, he was startled by something flying past his face against the side of the door. He took a closer look.

"No way!" he exclaimed as he saw a ten rand note forced against the doorframe by the wind. He couldn't believe his luck. He took the note and shoved it into his wallet. The taxi driver got out and waved to him, calling him over.

Again, Johannes thought of getting off the train, but for some reason, he decided against it.

"I've got better things to do with the money," he said, as he walked back into the carriage and closed the door behind him. Out of his line of sight, someone was extremely sad; it was the young girl as she gazed back through the connecting door window. She looked very disappointed, dropping her head downwards slightly. Johannes sat down; chuffed with the ten bucks he'd just scored. He didn't have a care in the world, and he forgot about what he'd just seen in the carriage next door. Then he started to laugh, a weird kind of laugh, almost as if he'd been drugged.

She tried to help. If he only knew what was waiting for him. But she tried one last time to get him off the train.

"Hello, I said hello. Wake up man," he looked up and around him. He was still in the interrogation room at the police station. "I'm your lawyer," a man said with a perfect American accent. He walked around the table, set his briefcase down, opened it and took out a file with a few papers in it.

"Where's Peter, my regular lawyer?"

"I'm David Thomas his replacement; he's in Dubai on holiday," he answered, as he placed the file on the table, right next to the file that the detective had left. He stood, walked towards the coffee tray for some bad coffee, and then asked, "Are you Johannes Roland?" Johannes paused for a moment. *"He's my lawyer, so he should know my name I guess,"* he thought to himself.

"Just call me Johan or John whatever is easier for you," he answered while the lawyer took out a second cup and poured some coffee. "Sugar?" he asked Johannes, as he took a small plastic bag out of his pocket with a fine white powder in it. He hid it in front of his body, out of the line of sight of Johannes.

"Five please," Johannes requested, pausing for a few seconds. "Are you American or Canadian?" The lawyer looked up into the mirror seeing Johannes clearly.

"American, from Florida," he replied. Seeing Johannes was distracted, flipping through the file the detective had left on the table, he took the opportunity to pour the fine white powder into Johannes' cup of coffee, followed by seven teaspoons of sugar.

Johannes turned towards him and in curiosity remarked, "I didn't know the legal company had any foreigner's working for them." The lawyer quietly stirred the coffee. "The Company wanted the best, and we are the best," the lawyer said, as he stared at Johannes in the mirror.

"So what can you tell me that you didn't tell the police?" he asked, placing the doctored cup of coffee on the table, stirring it one last time to hide the powder residue left on the cup.

"There is one thing I didn't tell them," said Johannes as he drank his cup of coffee non-stop, until the last drop was finished.

The lawyer was pleased. He glanced at his wristwatch and started the stopwatch timer.

It became clear that this David Thomas was not who he said he was. Johannes became disorientated and wobbly. Whatever the lawyer had put into his coffee was beginning to work.

"You said, 'There is one thing I didn't tell them'. What was it that you didn't tell them?" the lawyer asked hastily, speaking into a small microphone by his wrist. He waited a moment while he received a message from a small device in his ear.

"Two minutes to evacuation..." someone said through the device. He looked at his wristwatch which showed that there was one minute and thirty seconds remaining.

In his wobbly-drugged state, Johannes answered the question. He had no doubt in his mind as to why the lawyer asked the questions, "She told me her name."

"Who...the young girl? What is her name?" the lawyer asked, standing near the table, waiting and wanting answers. Johannes, in his drugged state, heard him speaking to someone and he looked around the room, but couldn't see anybody that he could be talking to.

"Who are you talking to?"

The lawyer was getting frustrated with Johannes. "What was her name?" he demanded, as he took the file that the detective left on the table and put it in his briefcase.

"Evacuation in thirty seconds" an instruction blared in the lawyer's ear and he confirmed this by looking at his wristwatch, the seconds ticked away. He was still waiting for an answer. "She said her name was Maria...Maria Schultz." The lawyer sat dead still; he had heard this name before.

"What else did she say?" He looked at his watch. There were only ten seconds remaining, and he was waiting for something more. Then came the answer he had been waiting for; "She said I was not on the list!" Johannes answered as his eyes became heavy and his head collapsed on the table. At the same time, the lawyer's alarm sounded while down the hallway a device planted on the fire extinguisher clicked to zero and exploded, a gust of powder filling the hallway. Then the 'so-called' lawyer disappeared in it, leaving no trace that he was there, as the police officers were trying try to get rid of the fog by opening some windows.

By the time they had opened the windows and cleared the air, the lawyer had already made it out the building. The lawyer looked up to the second level, and saw powder billowing out the windows. He climbed into a sleek black vehicle with tinted windows and drove away, undetected, down the busy street, and disappeared between the side streets.

Back in the interrogation room, Johannes was still sound asleep, dreaming of better days. He forgot that he was in trouble. The case against him grew as each hour passed. The police cordoned off the train in a secluded secure location.

The press were camped out in front of the police station, wanting to witness the whole ordeal as they saw smoke escaping from the windows. They were waiting for information about the serial killer, Johannes Roland, the only suspect the police had and the only lead to any of the murders. But, the four missing police officers remained a secret. This was kept out of the press for the privacy of the families of the police officers involved. However, they knew it wouldn't stay out of the press for long.

Chapter 6

DAVID THOMAS

"Hey, Johannes...wake up!"

Johannes lifted his head, and screwed up his eyes, gazed around, and saw that he was still in the interrogation room at the police station. But where was David Thomas? Johannes glared at the person who had woken him up and now he saw a familiar face.

"Peter, I thought you were in Dubai?"

"What?" Peter asked, somewhat confused.

"Your replacement, David Thomas, said you were in Dubai on holiday."

"What are you talking about? I'm right here," Peter walked closer to the table, placed his briefcase down, and then opened it as he always did. In it were only a few blank papers, a golden-coloured pen, and a magazine about holiday resorts in Hawaii, which was stuck in one of the side pockets.

"Going on holiday?" Johannes asked when he saw the book through the transparent plastic cover.

"Yes, or anywhere," Peter replied half-heartedly. Peter needed a holiday and he needed it desperately. In a few days he was going to lose his job, he already knew about. He was only postponing the inevitable. He was saddened by it, but not because he was going to lose his job; rather due to the fact that his boss had been involved in embezzlement, money laundering and murder, which meant he was going to struggle to find a job after the fiasco, as nobody would be inclined to hire him.

Peter had no part of it, but as one of the trustees, he stood to lose everything.

Peter changed the subject and read the copy of the dossier...

"You are in deep Johannes, real deep...anyway what are you talking about? You didn't phone for a lawyer."

Peter was right. Johannes didn't phone for a lawyer. "Who is David Thomas then?" Johannes confusingly mumbled then shook off his insecurity.

Peter looked towards the door to see if anybody was listening.

"What happened on that train?"

Johannes shut his eyes; he needed a moment to find his bearings.

Then it **all** came back to him.

"Wait a minute...what is going on here, where is David Thomas," he said a bit frantically, and then explained everything that had happened before Peter had woken him up, but only everything before he drank the coffee. He remembered the accent; Peter himself had a slight accent that he got from his father who moved here from South Carolina before he was born. Peter's father, however, never indicated why they moved to Africa.

Johannes denied that he had anything to do with the killings on the train, but Peter didn't think they were going to believe a word of what he said.

"What coffee?" he asked, seeing no cup on the table.

The ill-mannered American had apparently taken both cups with him; he was clever, and extremely well-trained to leave no evidence behind. Or perhaps it was all in Johannes's imagination? But he had not imagined it.

While the two were talking, someone was watching them, recording everything, every move, every gesture that Johannes made.

David Thomas had taken the opportunity, while he made the coffee, to bug the room with cleverly planted cameras and microphones. They were looking for something, something only Johannes could help them with. But while they observed Johannes and Peter on their monitors, a problem arose! After retrieving the file on Peter, they found that he was not all he made out to be.

Peter had a secret past, one that he'd been hiding for over twenty years!

It was all there on the monitor; the border war, the Russian KGB and the South African Defence Force.

"Peter Richards…" David Thomas, the 'so-called' lawyer who sat behind a monitor looking through Peter's file, stated aloud.

"So he was part of Koevoet," someone said, as they read the file signed 'Top Secret' with the old South African insignia on it.

"Koevoet?" David Thomas asked, "but that's his alias, as his real name is Josh Williams, Special Agent Josh Williams of the Federal Bureau of Investigation, part of the FBI's top-secret investigations known as the….well, nobody really knows what they are called. They are too secretive - not even the Central Intelligence Agency of America knows their names." Special Agent Martin Davis, who was in charge of this mission, repeated slowly, "Koevoet."

Martin Davis, an ex-army Major, seemed to recall some knowledge of this elite unit and he walked closer to Agent Williams.

"Coin…," he reflected, while he looked at his file and enlarged a picture.

Peter was part of the Counter Insurgency Team or 'Coin' for short.

"This is a problem...or not," the Major contemplated aloud, still staring at the top-secret file, looking at the picture of Peter Richards, thinking silently for a solution. He then turned towards the live feed from the monitor that was linked to the cameras in the interrogation room, and saw the two discussing the case.

"He is going to figure out that we used sodium thiopental."

Williams, finding this discussion interesting, walked closer to the Major, and took a seat next to him.

"How will he know we used the truth serum?" Williams asked, as he turned his head slightly towards Major Davis expecting an answer.

"Because I gave it to them," the Major said, as he stared straight at the monitor and at Peter Richards. He decided to explain to the rest of his team precisely what was going on.

"In 1988, they needed something 'extra' during 'Koevoets' counter-insurgency, and Major Martin Davis was the one who gave it to them - it was necessary."

"The war had to end. It was interfering with the Bureau's investigation in Angola. They were so close that time, but unthinkable circumstances were responsible and the Bureau couldn't continue their investigation. They were forced out of the country by the United Nation's special unit to Angola."

"They had no way of staying - political 'red tape' they called it - and they decided from then on, that no government would know about the existence of the specialised unit."

"Five Angolan Defence Force soldiers died two days after they pulled out. The only thing the investigation unit could uncover was that each one of them had a ticket with a perfumed smell, an easily recognisable smell like expensive perfume that filled their nostrils - a fresh summer fragrance with a hint of apple."

"There was one thing for sure; the tickets weren't meant for them. In the last days of the war, the soldiers boarded the train, robbing and terrorising unarmed people, taking what didn't belong to them - the tickets. In so doing, they had taken the place of those who should have been killed."

"Then he mumbled again, but they couldn't understand him."

"The girl's father still looked towards the floor. He wasn't worried about the four soldiers pointing their automatic weapons at him. Then he said it again, this time in English, so they understood him clearly; 'They're not yours to take.'"

"They started to laugh. And slowly but surely, they made him angry. The harder they laughed, the angrier he became."

"The girl's father looked up at the four soldiers, and then turned his head towards the side of the carriage, out of their sight, looking at his daughter standing nearby. She was looking back at him. She turned around and walked in the other direction, and disappeared from his sight."

"The four soldiers had enough of this ignorant person. It only took one shot to his head to make him drop to the ground."

"They started to laugh again and while they walked past him, each of them fired a couple of rounds into him, to make a statement, and to make sure he never got up again. The firing got so intense that one soldier had to jump out of the way of the squirting blood as the bullets ripped his body apart. When they thought he'd finally had enough, they walked away into the next carriage, still laughing as if it was a game to them."

"And when the last soldier entered the next carriage, the little girl's father opened his eyes. While still on the floor, his clothing changed to a General's Nazi uniform, the one uniform he felt comfortable wearing."

"He got up, not even using his arms, but it was almost as if he was erecting himself as a ghost out of the ground. One of the soldiers said it got cold. Then moments later, he was facing the floor from the roof. An excessive power had forced him against the ceiling, cracking his skull, and his lifeless body dropped harshly to the floor. He died in a 'sensible' manner - the other three didn't have the same luxury."

"The second soldier felt a force burn through his body; he was the cocky one, the one that had the most to say when the little girl's father had mumbled the words, 'They're not yours to take.'"

"He certainly didn't expect that he would burst against the wall, squirting and pasting the light green wallpaper with his blood, while his right hand severed and stuck, holding the AK-47, as it still fired rounds in the carriage, aiming at nowhere until the last bullet left the barrel."

"This confused the other two soldiers; they had never seen anything like it. The man that they had horribly killed in the next room now stood tall, and looked straight at them. They began begging for their lives!"

"He stopped and looked at the two for a moment; this had never happened before. They tried to give back the tickets after they'd seen him collecting them from the two already dead soldiers. They thought that if they gave back the tickets he would spare them their lives. It didn't even cross his evil mind to save them; they had been very much mistaken."

"He reached behind his back, and held his hand behind him for a few seconds. First the barrel of a rifle appeared. It looked old, like an antique. As soon as he pulled the trigger they fell to the floor, quick and clean, leaving the remaining two tickets next to their bodies.

"The locals who discovered the bodies destroyed the evidence, but before they burned the train, they removed the two recognisable soldier's bodies."

"They said it was an evil train and blamed the South African Defence

Force for the attack, but after all they had done to cover-up everything, one ticket had survived. It was stolen by one of the men responsible for burning the evidence, as he wanted to keep something for himself. The little that was left of the bodies on the train was burned, and then what was left was buried in shallow graves near the Namibian border by Angola where they still lay today."

"The problem was that the Angolans were not the targets, they were only killed as they had killed the intended targets, and one of those men who was given a ticket, didn't die on the train…he survived, and observed everything from afar."

"He decided to give his ticket to someone else to see what would happen, but his plan backfired. He thought he would be free, but that never happened."

"The little girl's father still carried on looking around on the train…he was looking for him, he was looking for the man who had been watching from a distance. He was the man who knew exactly what was going on. His name was Martin Davis, Marine Major Martin Davis, in charge of the mission. He had been hiding the fact that he had received a ticket two days earlier, though at that time he wasn't surprised that he got it; he always knew he would get one."

"The stories his grandfather told of the days of the big war burned in his mind."

"And every day since his grandfather had disappeared, he knew his day would come. He had been running from his own death ever since, trying to stop the attack on the bloodline of the people responsible for his family's death on the train in 1943."

"In this world, he was sure of one thing: evil doesn't forgive or forget. So far, every attempt at getting him into the next life had failed."

"They had tried so hard, but each time they failed. So, for Major Martin Davis it was extremely important to find a cure for this evil."

"The Major had lost his grandfather and then his own father due to the evil and for him it was getting closer. Since his father had disappeared, he had been receiving tickets. He had four tickets in total."

"He slipped the ticket into the unsuspecting traveller's pocket and when the train stopped, he jumped off, and ran as fast as he could to find a place where he could watch everything."

"He was alone at the time that his team were forced to leave the country after they disclosed to the Angolan Government why they were there."

"When Major Martin Davis saw that his plan didn't work, he returned home and in a private meeting with certain secret role players, that included a major church organisation from around the world, a top-secret agency within the American Government was established. And because of the agency's contacts, their funding was immense. The churches protected their heritage. People *must not* know about these attacks."

"The ticket that disappeared from the train belonged to Major Martin Davis. He tried to get the ticket back, but was unsuccessful on numerous occasions."

"His ticket sold on the black market for five hundred thousand United States Dollars and the person that tried to sell the ticket ended up dead alongside the one who had bought it, killed by an unknown assailant who after successful recovery contacted the Company organisation in Italy."

"His report was short and clear for the receiver; 'It's done.'"

"And shortly after they had received the call, they informed Major Martin Davis."

"The church had to act; the ticket was believed to be a ticket to the underworld and sought after by disturbed rich and famous people around the world. The person who purchased the ticket was exactly that - rich, powerful, and dangerous."

"The church knew that he was going to use the ticket to gain incredible power, the power to control other human beings."

"This idea was a possibility, but the Company could not take the chance. So they did what they had to do."

Back at the FBI field office in Cape Town, Major Davis had now established that Peter Richards was a threat to their investigation. The FBI agents in the room turned up the volume on the monitor to listen to what advice Peter gave to Johannes.

Peter got up from his chair. He was uncertain as to what was going on.

"I'm telling you the truth; I even asked him about his accent," Johannes stopped talking and bowed his head slightly downwards.

"He said he was from Florida," Johannes said, as he rubbed his hand against his head. It felt as if his skull was about to explode.

Peter paused.

The headache and lack of memory seemed all too familiar to Peter, and he had only one conclusion. Peter doubted himself for a moment, and then decided that there was a possibility.

He looked around the room and saw what he was looking for. He got up, walked towards the water dispenser and took out a plastic cup, handing it to Johannes.

"What?" Johannes asked confused, looking at the empty cup.

"Fill it!" Peter insisted, forcing the cup back into Johannes' hand. He knew it was the only way to prove that what he was saying was true.

It was the only thing needed to confirm his suspicions. After a bit more convincing, Johannes reluctantly filled the plastic cup. First Johannes wanted to go to the toilet, but Peter convinced him it would be better to do it here, so as not to attract any attention to his investigation.

Special Agent Josh Williams of the FBI looked at his monitor. He knew this was what Major Davis was talking about; this inquisitiveness of the lawyer would hamper their investigation.

He turned around and saw Davis walking up to him.

"That sample must not reach the lab, intercept it by any means," Special Agent Martin Davis gave a clear, indisputable order.

The specialised unit had already bugged the lawyer's vehicle so there was no need to follow him; they knew exactly where he was going - to the one man Peter knew was qualified to help him, Charles le Roux. His name stuck out on Peter's top-secret file like red tape on white paper.

It was only a fifteen-minute drive from the city centre and there it stood on the slopes - the Department of Chemistry of the University of Cape Town.

The only person Peter knew who could help him and would, was his old friend, Charles le Roux. It had been twenty years, but Charles le Roux would remember Peter Richards. He would never forget the man who had saved his life.

At the university Peter wanted to park his vehicle close to the entrance of the building, but part of the entrance area had been blocked by road works, so he parked further away at the bottom of the huge stairway. As he walked up to the building, he looked up the stairs and at the building behind it. It was his first time here and he was amazed at the building structure. The stairs led up to the main building that looked like a replica of pillars in front of the Whitehouse in America.

"Why do there always have to be stairs," he grumbled, shaking his head, and then he started to climb them, holding the urine sample in his hand. He was watched closely by the agents who were already there. Peter noticed them following him.

He was absolutely sure that they weren't students or even teachers. Peter had been trained by experts and the one thing they'd taught him was to always look behind you. He noticed not one, but three so-called 'specialised agents' tailing him, and then he knew with certainty that the cup with the urine had some importance.

He had to be sure, so it had to be tested.

He could see that one of the black sets of clothes following him was very persistent, but Peter knew the modus-operandi like the back of his hand.

Some would call it the 'rat race' or 'procedure', or 'method of operating' as translated from Latin. From what he'd learned years ago, he didn't even need to concentrate.

He had already identified them. Then again, he *could* be mistaken. It had been twenty years but it could only be FBI or KGB. But the KGB was no more, having disbanded years ago. He could think of no one else. He wanted to know why in the world they were after Johannes. He had never hurt a fly.

"Back in five minutes."

Peter read the sign on the door; he knew that he probably only had one minute before they found him. He tried to open the door. "Locked...!" He saw someone coming around the corner. He stopped dead in his tracks, but was relieved; it wasn't one of them.

It was a student and in a moment of desperation, as he looked at the tray the student was pushing, he had an idea. "It will work."

Peter believed that these people, the ones in the black suits, were after the urine sample. It couldn't possibly be anything else.

They looked 'book smart' and it was time for them to meet up with his 'street smarts'. He walked by and bumped the tray purposefully. He did it so quickly that the student didn't even see him take something from the tray. He was just in time, as he saw the man running towards him from down the corridor. They knew their cover was blown so all that remained was to intercept the urine sample.

It was all they needed, and if they got the evidence now, the trail ended.

Who would believe a lawyer working for a company involved in criminal activities? If he told the police his story, they would never believe him.

So he needed proof.

They stopped running halfway down the corridor and started walking casually towards him, and when they were a couple of feet in front of him, they stood still.

Peter took a good look at them — it was almost like a Wild West stare-down - and then in his peripheral vision, he could see one of them approaching him from behind. However, this man wasn't intending to attack Peter; he wanted to get a better handle on the situation.

They all stood quietly and waited; like alpha males ready to attack.

Peter grinned and nodded a few times and the one standing across from Peter did the same.

He glanced at their suits. He could see they were expensive designer suits, definitely not government-issued.

"Stylish..." Peter let out a wise-crack, that was just who he was. In part, he was luring them into responding. If they did, he could pinpoint who they were. But it failed to work and they just stood there and stared at him, their eyes never leaving the cup that contained Johannes' urine.

Peter knew these were tough guys, not the normal cheap-suited FBI agents, and like clockwork, the one agent lifted up his jacket and revealed his pistol to intimidate Peter. It usually worked, but not this time.

Peter was expecting a Glock-9mm, but now he was staring into the back of a Walther-P99 magazine clip. The nonchalant way the agent revealed his firearm gave Peter enough time to gather some information from the firearm and belt. Even the inner linings of the jacket gave him some information. Peter wasn't a customary criminal. As a matter of fact, he wasn't a criminal at all; he was a forgotten war hero who had some secrets.

Peter was confused. The man in the black suit had given him a hint as to who they were. The weapon was not a standard FBI-issue, more MI-5 or probably MI-6 British Military Intelligence. They said nothing. The one pointed to the cup and with a hand gesture which instructed Peter to give it up; his body language suggested that they meant business.

"No getting out of this one," Peter thought as he accepted the fact that he was trapped. But there was one thing he was certain about; they wouldn't kill him as doing so would attract too much attention. They weren't murderers, just investigators, or so he hoped.

But that didn't mean he would come off scot-free; he'd probably come out with a couple of cuts and bruises.

This was their way of showing him they were in control, but still they stood there, not saying a word.

"You want it, come get it…" said Peter as he stepped forward, and lifted up his fists, laughing.

"Just kidding…" he said as he placed the cup of urine on the floor and stepped back. He carefully watched their reactions, but there was nothing. The one closest to him picked up the cup and walked away as if nothing had happened; very professional and covert at the same time.

He decided not to even try and follow them. Why would he? That would be a stupid idea and by the time the door closed behind the three, they were gone in any case.

"Peter?" a surprised voice called from behind him. He instantly recognised the voice. The accent was distinctive - not many 'Koevoet' members were born in the United Kingdom, and after twenty-five years in Africa, he had never lost his accent.

He turned around. It had been twenty-years since he had last seen Charles le Roux, but Charles has not aged one bit. He looked almost exactly the same as he had twenty years ago, barring the little bit of grey hair sticking out underneath the New York Police baseball cap that he'd bought when he was on holiday there years ago.

"Hey Prof...How are you?" Peter asked politely.

"Coffee?"

Charles unlocked his office and the two walked in. Peter recognised himself standing next to Charles in pictures that were hanging against the wall. There were no names, just faces, but they knew who they were.

There was no need for anyone else to know what had happened. What happened in Angola stayed in Angola; this is what they'd agreed all those years ago.

"It's been a long time. To what do I owe the pleasure?"

"Sodium Thiopental!" Peter said as he took a sip of his coffee, waiting for a response. Charles got up and closed the door then turned slowly towards Peter.

"We said we would never talk about it."

"And we won't, this is something else," Peter reassured him, as he put the coffee cup on the table. He put his hand in his corner pocket, and took out a syringe filled with a light yellow liquid. Charles knew exactly what it was.

Earlier he had used his quick reflexes; stuck the needle in the specimen, and withdrew some of the fluid. The rest he gave to the influential agents. He'd taken a big chance, pure genius on his part, and it had worked. By the time they figured out that he had outsmarted them, he would have the results.

Peter smiled and nodded, looking at the urine. Charles also smiled and jokingly thanked him for the gift after twenty-years of not having any contact.

"Yours?"

"A client. Can you?"

"Certainly. Could it be something to do with those guys in the black suits?" he said with his back turned to Peter, snapping on a pair of rubber gloves. Then he turned back to him, and took the syringe with Johannes' fluid.

He didn't answer Charles, and in a way Charles was grateful; too much information. Peter took a business card out of his pocket, and gave it to Charles, who instantly spotted the company name on the card.

"I saw it on the news...loads of money went missing, are you a part of it?"

"No...just bad timing from my side," that was all Peter had to say. Charles believed him. There was no reason for them to doubt each other.

Peter finished the last of his coffee and said goodbye, while Charles assured him that he would have the results by that evening.

He was pleased that the results would be back so soon. He decided to go back and check on Johannes who was still locked in the interrogation room. In the back of his mind he felt stupid, now that he'd had time to think everything through. The possibility that those guys in the black suits could have killed the cops was absurd...they wouldn't be so careless.

And this is why he thought the cops were missing, and not dead. If they had been killed, the whole of Cape Town would be after them. There were too many angry and stressed cops in this town, who would rampage everything in their path to try and find the killers. And if they found the killers they wouldn't survive to tell the tale. "Street smarts!" It was almost like in Angola. But Peter had not uttered a word about this in twenty years.

"But why kill the people on the train?" He was still trying to understand why they would leave so much evidence behind. But they'd obviously been cleaning up the crime scene, as the last two carriages were spotless and reeked of ammonium.

"What are they trying to cover up?" he wondered, and then he heard police sirens behind him while he was driving.

He could see it was a cop car in his rear view mirror, but why would they want to pull him over? His speedometer gauge showed that he was within the speed limit. "Why now?" He looked at his watch. Time was running out. He had to get to the police station before 5:00pm; otherwise he was going to miss the detective with whom he'd made an appointment earlier in the day.

The cops were taking their time, the just sat and looked at him but didn't get out of their vehicle. It was almost if they were waiting for something.

Peter could see the passenger talking on a cell phone, but still no movement. Then, as he looked in his passenger side mirror, he saw the door opening.

He instinctively knew something was wrong. He had been stopped by the police before and this wasn't normal. The glimpse that he'd caught of them had made him unsure as to whether they were even real police. Then again, they had the car and the uniforms, so he blamed his overactive imagination and the fact that he felt paranoid about the black suits following him. He'd been daydreaming for just a second and then realised that the officer who'd got out of the car was nowhere to be seen. Hastily, but without seeming paranoid, he carefully tried to locate him by looking in the rear view mirrors.

Then suddenly, standing right next to him, was the cop in his full uniform. Peter felt stupid as this guy was clearly a real cop; he had his name badge and everything!

"Everything okay?" the cop asked politely, seeing that Peter was quite jumpy. This type of behaviour would normally result in the vehicle being searched - he should know, he was a lawyer. Suspicious behaviour, they called it. But they weren't interested in the car. They didn't say anything except for the, **everything okay**. Peter gave him his driver's licence, even though the cop hadn't yet asked for it. This showed respect and cooperation, from the '101 manual' when pulled over by the cops.

He had to ask, "Did I do something wrong?" but the cop didn't respond.

"Sorry, we thought you were someone else," the police officer said, and strolled away as if nothing had happened. Peter was relieved that he hadn't been given a fine, and drove away in direction of the police station. He still had time for that appointment with the detective.

Peter glimpsed towards the far side of the road. There was a man staring straight at him, not towards the cops, definitely straight at him.

It was warm outside so a man wearing a large black coat and sunglasses was highly likely to draw attention, but nobody seemed to be looking at him, and then like mist on water, he just disappeared. Peter quickly forgot about the weirdo and drove away.

The driver of the police vehicle got out and joined his partner; both of them watched him as he drove down the highway. The cop on the passenger side turned towards the other one.

"So what do you think, my German friend?"

"*Was darfichhoffen...es muss sein?*" (What may I hope...it must be?) he answered nodding. The passenger shortly followed his nodding. "I think you are right, *it must be*." The two got back in the vehicle and drove in the opposite direction, careful not to attract any suspicion as to who they really were. They weren't just two ordinary police officers; in fact, they weren't police officers at all. They were those mysterious men that seem to be everywhere.

When Peter arrived at the police station he realised that the cops hadn't returned his driver's license; he was disgruntled, but there was nothing he could do.

The two suspicious police officers drove back to where they'd come from fourteen minutes earlier...

The police car was stolen exactly fourteen minutes before they stopped the good lawyer Peter, and exactly five minutes prior to stealing the car, they had got off the train and walked toward the main road, waited two minutes and twenty seconds for the lady to be mugged by a couple of hooligans, and then waited calmly for twelve seconds for the two police officers to stop the vehicle, in an attempt to stop the hooligans. The two police officers were unsuccessful.

The two robbers ran into the alley followed by the two cops who left the police vehicle exactly where it was supposed to be, in front of two onlookers, unattended, engine still running.

All they had to do was get in and drive away.

Everything was timed to the second, and when the two police officers returned with their suspects, they found the vehicle exactly where they'd left it, not suspecting a thing. Except there was one small thing; the satellite-tracking device fitted on the police vehicle had switched off the moment the two mysterious men had got in the vehicle, which had activated an alarm at head office. The signal disappeared from their monitors, and all communication with the vehicle was cut.

Sixteen minutes later after the vehicle was 'taken' the signal returned the moment the two men got out of the vehicle and walked away, unnoticed except for a young boy who had seen them.

They stopped when they saw him looking.

The one glanced over to the young boy; they could feel him staring at them. They looked at each other and nodded in agreement. Then they walked towards him.

The German speaking one took something out of his pocket, bent over and gave it to the young boy - something shiny and extremely valuable - followed by some very confusing words.

"If not in your hands...*given to those which value the past,*" he said, and then walked into the alley and disappeared among the crowd.

It would take the young boy a few months to understand what the weirdo had said while he watched a history programme on the Second World War and the lost gold coins from Hitler's bunker, presumed to have been a gift to his generals as a token of appreciation for their good work after the war.

There were twelve coins in total made by a master coin maker in Berlin, and then secretly transported with Hitler's private plane to one of his hideouts, *the Führerbunker,* where he placed his signature on the one side and the date - 1946 - a year ahead of the planned victory.

Only six coins were found near Hitler's self-inflicted body at the end of the war in 1945.

It was said that it was by chance that this young boy was given the coin, but nothing happened by chance, and the connection between the boy and the two mysterious men went back sixty years. It was the day his grandfather had helped a man that was trapped and left for dead underneath a collapsed building. A reward was coming to his family and all they had to do was be patient. They never knew about the reward; they would never know where it came from, all hidden among secrets. These two men were the only ones that would know for now.

Chapter 7

THE TICKET

The meeting that Peter had with the detective went very well. It seemed as if the evidence against Johannes Roland was drying up as was the case that the police had stacked against him.

The police certainly weren't amused, but they told Peter that Johannes would be released before the end of the day. Even if they protested, he would still be set free. Peter was happy with the good news. He greeted the detective and walked down the corridor towards Johannes' holding cell, stopping momentarily to recall what the detective had said; *"The train driver did not get on the train."*

Then who drove the train? He was still confused as to why Johannes was the only survivor.

"Seven dead found, four cops missing and one survivor..." Peter mumbled to himself, but one thing was not clear, one small thing, and it was making him uneasy; "Who drove the train?"

The detective made it very clear that Peter was not to mention the missing police officers to anybody. He readily agreed as nobody really wants an angry cop breathing down their neck.

He walked down the passage, just as he was about to pass the investigation office, he saw something in the office that made him stop it was a picture.

The picture on the wall was unclear, but he recognised the picture of Johannes that was right next to the blurred picture.

He took a step back. "This is a stupid idea," Peter said to himself, wondering whether he should or he shouldn't.

He knew the case against Johannes as redundant; but his curiosity was killing him about the other picture. He hesitated but decided to go in. He quickly looked around to ensure that the coast was clear, walked into the office and quickly shut the door behind him just in case someone was watching him. He wasn't concerned about whether the police would find him; he was more worried that the people in the black suits would.

He opened the door to the hallway again, and glanced out towards the hallway making sure no one saw him. He then shut the door and locked it. He needed to take precautions, as he certainly didn't need any surprises as this point.

He walked closer towards the picture on wall, recognising some of the pictures the detective had shown him earlier. However, there are also pictures that the detectives weren't allowed to show him. These were truly gruesome; only a severely troubled person could have committed such horrifying acts. Peter came back to reality and remembered the reason he was there in the first place. He walked towards the rear wall of the office, where he had seen the picture of Johannes and the one next to it which he was unable to make out from a distance.

"This is it!" he exclaimed, "the ticket," realising that this was exactly what Johannes had been talking about! This was why the cops didn't believe him! All because of a ticket. And printed on it were the exact words that Johannes said; 'Admit One.' Now the ticket was staring him in the face and he realised that everything Johannes had told him was true. Peter leaned forward and read the investigation information carefully, but all of it was useless information to him, except one thing; "He did say the ticket looked old, about seventy years old," Peter mused, examining the ticket.

He couldn't believe this; he took the enlarged copy out of the plastic protection and quickly made a copy, folded it up and put it in his pocket. Then something startled him, there were voices, people were approaching.

He could feel his body tensing up as he waited for the person to enter. He was relieved he'd locked the door earlier as it had bought him some time.

And there it was...*the sound of a set of keys being taken out of a pocket, clinking outside the door.*

The sound made him jumpy. He quickly ran towards the door and positioned himself behind a bookshelf. He bumped it slightly with his shoulder, and it wobbled a bit to the side. An off-balance book dropped to the floor. The bookcase had moved enough for the police officer to notice it and push it back again. He didn't suspect anything as he walked in the door.

He picked up the book. *"Who reads this rubbish?"* he wondered and set the book back on the shelf. As he walked towards the corner desk, Peter scanned the room for a possible exit, but found nothing. He just had to wait. Luckily for him, the bookshelf was fairly secluded; it was a good place to hide with only a couple of empty boxes lying around. He looked around and tried to make himself comfortable; a bit of a challenge when you're sitting on a box!

Peter didn't have to wait long; the phone on the desk rang. The police officer was hesitant to answer it, but eventually he did, purely because the noise was annoying him.

"Jacobs..." he answered. Nothing - just static followed by a high-pitched sound which forced him to put the phone down. He rubbed his ear to get rid of the ringing noise, but then it rang again.

"What?" the police officer shouted annoyed with the interruptions, his work was already behind and his captain was breathing down his neck results.

But this time the line was dead - not even static - just dead silence. He listened again and looked at the phone. Then there was a knock on the door.

Peter glanced around the corner, trying to see who was knocking on the door, but his view was blocked by the books on the bookshelf. He slowly and silently pushed a couple of books out of the way, but it didn't really help. When he got a clear view of the door, the sandblasted glass window concealed the person. All that he could see was a dark silhouette.

"Yes?" the cop answered, setting the phone down on the receiver. The person behind the door didn't answer back.

"Kan ek help?" he asked politely, assuming the person was Afrikaans. But again he didn't answer. Peter then saw something moving behind the door, and then a hand appeared, stretching out from beyond the doorframe. The hand was holding a brown envelope.

The police officer stood up from his chair and walked towards the door, the envelope carrier was still silent.

Peter shuffled to the side, straining to get a better view, and he saw something familiar. He had seen that marking before, but where? Ah, then he remembered.

The cop that stopped him on the highway when he was returning from his meeting with Charles le Roux had the exact same marking on his ring; it was an odd symbol, but very distinctive.

"It's for your captain," the deliverer finally spoke.

He decided to stay put and not take the chance. He waited for the cop to leave the office. A few moments later the detective was also ready to leave the room, and as he was so stressed out already about the investigation, he dashed out, leaving the door open again. Peter casually walked out from behind the bookshelf, as if it was his office, thinking at the same time that he would probably never have his own office again, and he stopped at the wall he had been looking at earlier.

This job was just to help a friend, a pro bono job. "For the good of the public...when will it be for my good?" he whispered.

Johannes was not the best friend a person could have, but he was a friend at least. For a few seconds Peter stared at the picture and looked around. The office still smelt fresh, another reminder that he would never see his office again. His office had been closed down after his boss had been arrested; he had been caught with illegal narcotics in his possession a week earlier and was linked to a money laundering syndicate.

At the wall, he took one final look at the picture of the ticket, and in the corner of his eye, he saw his driver's license. *"But how in the world?"* he thought to himself. Then to his surprise, something he thought he would never see was also lying on the table, still sealed in a forensic evidence bag.

"The ticket!"

It was just lying there, almost as if someone had intended for him to find it, almost as if someone *needed* him to find it.

And then he saw something that made things even clearer for him; the symbol – for the third time! The second time had been moments earlier on the envelope, and then an hour before he'd seen the same symbol on the ring that the cop was wearing, and now it was on the ticket.

He startled; there was someone at the door again. Peter checked out the man's business insignia on his pale blue jacket and was relieved to see that it wasn't the cop, only the phone company guy. He sighed silently.

"I'm here to install the phone lines, are you Warrant Officer Jacobs?"

"Uh…no, I'm…" he stopped and threw in, "Phones lines…?"

"Yes, new office - new lines."

That explained the empty boxes he had been sitting on earlier, as well as the fresh smell. He turned away, ready to walk out the door, and then turned back, looking at the phone on the desk that had rang only minutes earlier. He walked a step closer. He looked over his shoulder at the electrician, curious, like a cat scoping out its prey.

"That one working?" Peter asked.

"Can't be. No wiring connected," the technician said picking up the phone, but Peter didn't hear him. He was already halfway down the corridor with his license and the train ticket in his hand. He hoped for some answers. Then from behind the shadows, were the two mysterious men who had stopped him on the highway dressed in police uniforms. However this time they were dressed in silky black suits, both wearing a ring with that same mysterious insignia on it. They looked pleased about something; almost as if they were pleased that Peter had snatched the ticket from the office.

They nodded and turned towards each other.

"Soon," the one said. As if by magic they disappeared, just as quickly as they had appeared. They both knew there was one more thing they had to do.

Rite of Passage

It was not something they particularly wanted to do, but it was necessary. Then again, this was the second time they had encountered Peter in twenty years, and as we know, things happen for a reason. However, twenty years ago was not Peter's time.

Six months from now, it would be his time, and failing then <u>was not</u> an option.

This would be their last chance to complete their mission as seventy odd years was a long time for trial and tribulation. They had tried, and each and every time had failed.

The attacks happened in London and in New York; the Big Apple was the worst hit out of the two.

Special Agent Martin Davis and his team were in charge of that mission. It all went well until the fourth day of the mission. They nicknamed it the *'New York City massacre.'*

Chapter 8

NEW YORK CITY MASSACRE

One year earlier: 7 June 2009, 17:40, New York City

Nine minutes before the *'New York City massacre'*

"We move in seven minutes."

"Copy that Major," Special Agent Josh Williams of the Federal Bureau of Investigation said, confirming the time on his watch and understanding what Major Martin Davis wanted him to do.

If everything went according to plan, it would all be over and the world would never see this evil again. But they were wrong; five minutes into the mission, someone overstepped the boundary.

If you don't have a ticket, you must never overstep the boundary, never.

Never - even with the agency's so-called 'protected camouflage' that made them invisible to those who had not yet stepped over to the other side - anything could happen.

Using a ultra-violet beam light which made the dead visible to the human eye without detection had its complications. It took time to set up the lights and the mirrors, and mistakes could certainly happen.

Who would have thought that one small rip in the special material would have a disastrous aftermath? But the moment the clothing ripped, *he* knew.

Not much was known about **_him_**... as he'd died in 1943. According to stories from 1943, **he** was leading top secret experiments for the nationalists, even more secretive than the Super Nazi SS soldiers; and they were the real pride of Hitler.

The most feared man was not Hitler himself; it was the one who always looked on from afar, Doctor Death. His real name was known only by Hitler, but after an attack on his bunker the alias stole the valuable documents and his name was spoken aloud for the first time since the war started; Ferdinand Schultz, General Ferdinand Schultz. He was the reason that over one hundred of his own soldiers were killed through experiments; experiments that only started showing results after two years of repeated failures.

The Allieds called them **_'poltergeists'_** after the first successful attack on an Allied camp in France; the Nazis called them _'demon soldiers.'_

The idea was easy; electrocute a soldier and then moments after he's pronounced dead, inject him with a serum consisting of holy water, cyanide and another ingredients that were believed to have come from the devil himself. It would make the body super strong and super-fast, ultimately unstoppable. A 'super soldier' was able to attack Allied camps, killing forty to fifty people at a time until the life force that guided them depleted, which was about four hours later, then the 'super soldier would be killed instantaneously. Gravity would do the rest, making their lifeless bodies drop to the floor. Luckily for the Allieds, this only happened three times before the United States Government made a deal with the General. It all went according to plan, but then the unfortunate incident occurred.

It was a big mistake, a disaster waiting to happen.

Chapter 9

AT 17:49 THEY WILL FAIL

7 June 2009, 17:44, New York City

Five minutes before the '*New York City massacre*'

"Sir, the track is ready for diversion," said Special Agent Josh Williams of the Federal Bureau of Investigation, as he looked at his monitor which displayed the newly refurbished platform, about three hundred feet from the real 14th Street Union Square subway station. It took them three days to construct this exact replica of the station platform and luckily, there was an unused tunnel nearby.

They had planned this right down to the second. It was complicated, but still executable and it made the agents nervous. '*What if it failed?*' However, they had not failed so far. *But at 17:49, they would fail.*

They had been lucky so far and had managed to save seven bloodlines connected to the inferno in 1943.

In total, they had saved thirty two lives. These were people who were supposed to have died on the train over the past ten years, and if they included the bloodlines of the survivors like daughters, brothers, fathers and grandmothers, it would be seventy two in total who would never be haunted again. Some of them would never even know how close they had come to being trapped in insanity for eternity, concealed on a train like zombies, never able to disembark.

"Four minutes to contact," they heard over the radio.

"Lights up," another said from the control room. He pressed a couple of buttons that turned on the side track lights and then he dimmed them slightly.

He looked towards the light meter on the monitor, and then, deciding it was time, he turned on the thirty or so violet lights that were connected to the wall and the roof of the tunnel. This was the important part: they had to get the light exactly right; otherwise, *he* would see them.

Agent Josh Williams was pleased with the diagnostics check and he revealed that the tunnel was ready for the train. Then he turned off the lights, and surrendered the platform to total darkness. He then rebooted everything and activated the normal platform lights.

"Okay we're ready…"

With only three minutes on the clock until the train arrived, there was only one more thing to test. There was more than enough time and he started turning the violet lights on one by one again, while he kept a strong eye on the light meter until he saw the correct reading. He leant over to the left side of his table and pressed the access button on a second monitor. A red light turned to green at a secluded access door that led to the platform. Behind the door, five agents eagerly awaited the green light, and then they walked through the access door.

They walked on to the platform one by one, the hazardous material suits they wore made it difficult to manoeuvre through the narrow door, but eventually they got to the other side. Then all together they walked towards the edge of the platform, and stopped about five feet from the edge.

"We are ready." They awaited further instruction, as they turned towards the two-way mirror at the side of the waiting area.

Special Agent Josh Williams looked at them from his side of the two-way mirror and saw that everything was in place.

"Okay we are going blind in five seconds. Confirm…" he requested and received a collective confirmed response from all five crew members that were waiting on the platform.

The lights then started to dim, as it slowly darkened the pure white light with every second that passed. Then one of the special agents got the 'okay' from Agent Williams and activated the fog machine. The powerful machine started blowing a cool water haze into the tunnel, like a cloud forced over a mountain top, as it blew from one side of the platform to the other. By now, the white light had totally disappeared leaving them in darkness. Automatically a couple of fog lights switched on, and made them visible to each other, but only slightly.

Now they were ready for the final stage. This was what it was all about. If this didn't work the mission was finished; exactly like what had happened in London a couple of months prior.

He confirmed that everybody was ready and then cut the fog lights, leaving them in total darkness.

"Reaching electromagnetic spectrum in ten seconds," he said while they activated their transponders. This made them visible only to each other by a small emitting pulse light that could only be seen with their special glasses; without the glasses, they were walking blind.

"Franklin?"

"Yes…"

"Fix your transponder."

Franklin turned to his side and saw that his beacon wasn't working and he gave it a rightful smack.

"Good…" said Special Agent Josh Williams seeing that the agent's smack had worked. On his infrared cameras the agents were now as visible as daylight to the crew in the next room who were busy monitoring everything from heartbeats to visuals and oxygen levels.

"We have reached electromagnetic spectrum level two," Agent Williams confirmed.

"Level three," he paused for a few seconds, waiting for the monitor. It passed four.

Then, finally...

"We have reached electromagnetic spectrum level five."

The crew could feel the electro magnet working. It gave them headaches, which would be the worst that they would experience. It was normal and they would pass momentarily. There was no time to moan about the headaches; they knew what was to follow. The Bermuda Triangle could learn a thing or two from this.

"Activating nitrogen lasers...now," said the special agent as he filled the concealed platform with a purple blue light, making the five crew members invisible to the naked eye and it provided a visible blue glow. It was absolutely beautiful. The violet light lit up everything; even specks of dust particles were visible – all except for the five members of the team; they were completely invisible. It had worked. They had disappeared from normal visual range. However they could still be seen through the infrared cameras that were in the office. They were still standing in the same place, a couple of feet from the platform's edge. Everybody knew that a few lights and cameras didn't make people invisible; but still, there were many secrets around the Company's activities.

Agent Williams was pleased; everything was going according to plan. He saw the train on his monitor approaching fast. He held his finger above a bright red button in front of him, and then at the exact moment they would divert the train onto the opposite track, directing it straight into the concealed tunnel. At this point there was no turning back.

They had a job to do and the time was *now*.

The General appeared to notice something when the train changed tracks, but he ignored it and continued checking the tickets on the train, while some of the passengers complained about the old tickets. "Admit one…what does that mean?" they asked, but he paid no attention to them; he was making sure his victims were all on board, and as he checked the tickets, the faces of the Allied soldiers that were involved in his family's death on that train years ago, flashed before his eyes. It was his way of making sure they had the right people. He smiled.

Those who were not supposed to be there had gotten off at the previous station; forced off by him. Those who didn't want to get off were given a ticket, the last ticket they would ever get.

The General looked towards the door. For the moment he was happy as he saw his young daughter playing in the train, while some of the commuters were also amused by her, until they saw what she was playing with. They were surprised to see the girl playing with a doll that was over fifty years old. What worried them was that the doll was wearing a Nazi uniform, but it was the only toy she had.

After a while, the commuters began to make fun of the General in his conductor's uniform, but he just smiled and welcomed them as he always did. There was no need to get angry… well, not right now.

Ignoring them was easy, like ignoring a barking dog behind a fence; he just kept walking and continued to check the tickets while the train came to a stop at 14th Street and Union Square subway station *or so he thought*. He looked out of the window and was puzzled; he felt as if something was different; directly in front of him was one of the agents in his specialised suit ready to board the train.

The agent was shocked, how was this possible? He was not supposed to be able to see them, but the General was looking directly at one of the agents. The agent's heart rate increased rapidly, and the team sitting in the operating room saw this. Special Agent Josh Williams intervened; otherwise, he would blow the mission.

"He can't see you!" he shouted.

"Johnson…he can't see you," he shouted again as he tried to comfort the agent. It worked. The General turned towards the other side, and then he turned back around as if something was bothering him. Then one of the agents in the control room accidently pressed the monitor that opened the train door, which caused the General to grow even more suspicious.

Why did the train door open? The General couldn't see the icy fog flowing into the train carriage from the open door; it was below his vision of sight. The preparations were paying off and were doing their job; the General couldn't see it or feel it.

The General walked towards the door and stopped at the edge.

Just one more step he would be on the platform, but he decided against it. He had business on the train that he needed to attend to. The agent stood dead quiet in front of him, not moving a muscle.

The General was still curious about the open door; it wasn't supposed to have opened. His eyes scrolled the platform as he saw the sign that read, *Welcome to 14th Street and Union Square subway station.* He turned his head towards the exit sign on the far side of the station. Not a soul was in sight as he glared down the platform.

It seemed as if all was in order and he walked back into the carriage. The agents took the opportunity to walk into the carriage, one by one in their heavy gear, carefully regarded by Special Agent Josh Williams as he viewed them on his monitor.

It was a tense time; there was too much at stake and too much could go wrong. The other agents watched from a safely enclosed room a mere fifty yards away.

Everything was going to plan; the agents were on the train, had taken their places, and were ready to get the people off the train. They walked freely through the train, and opened doors like ghosts to get to adjacent carriages. But one thing bothered the new guy.

"Why can't the people on the train see our people?" he asked confused. This had bothered him since London. But this information was on a need-to-know basis and he wasn't qualified for the answer just yet.

He didn't see the Major walk up behind him, as he eavesdropped on his conversation. The Major felt obligated to answer him.

"It's a need-to-know situation. We had help from someone," he explained.

"Who?" he asked. His curiosity was killing him. He knew practically everything already, but why would they keep this from him? The truth was that they didn't really know who they had got the equipment from. The Major walked away; he was not in the mood for explanations, particularly during a mission.

The agent, still curious, looked towards one of the boxes with the insignia. He hadn't seen it before but it was distinctive and easily recognisable; a shield with a two-headed wolf. He didn't have a clue as to what it was, but the sign was commonly used by crusaders in the early centuries. Trying to find out precisely who the insignia belonged to, was a dead end in all directions. Even for an agency that didn't exist, it was impossible.

But there was one man who knew something; but he had decided to keep it a secret. He knew what had happened to the person who bought his missing ticket and not even he could hide from them. He knew they would find him, so he decided after the warning they had issued him to explain nothing.

"For your life..." they had warned him. He knew they would only give one warning; so Special Agent Martin Davis, in charge of the mission, would keep this secret until his death. That was his intention, anyway, but it wasn't going to happen like that.

History must not repeat itself. This was their duty. They were the protectors.

For now, his questions could wait until later...

Agent Josh Williams started giving his detailed report to Major Martin Davis; so far, all the equipment was functioning normally while General Ferdinand Schultz readied himself for his attack in the next carriage. Then he stopped again. He looked over towards the corner where one of the agents was erecting a prism mirror. They knew exactly how to get the people out and then they would activate the mirrors with a laser, and force him into the next life.

That was the easy part.

The problem was trying to lure him into the carriage where the mirrors were.

They all knew it hadn't worked in London, thanks to a group of people only dressed in black, called the Mondavians, who had sabotaged the mission. The Mondavians were a secret organisation that ruled Europe. In London, they had lost two agents, which included one of their British scientists. The British tabloids had reported that a person had tried to escape from the fire by jumping from the train; the truth was that he was swung from a moving train through a window, but not by the General. The people in black had been responsible.

They had moved so fast, almost as if they had super human strength.

The scientist had to be identified by dental records. The Company had been so close to sending the General to the next world, if only the Mondavians hadn't intervened. The Major said the Company didn't have permission to be in London, nor in most of Europe for that fact.

"It's time..." said Special Agent Martin Davis; he had instructed his team to proceed with getting the people off the train.

Agent Johnson had now erected the mirror and angled it directly at one of the other mirrors. Happy with how things were going, he bent down and opened his backpack. He turned around making sure the General was not in his range, as he spotted him walking into the next carriage. But the General every so often glared back towards to the carriage where Johnson was busy. Johnson was alone in the carriage with five people sitting on their seats without a care in the world, drinking their homemade brew. The more they drank the louder they got.

Johnson still stared down the carriage. He turned back towards his backpack and took out a large piece of cloth.

"I'm ready…" he said, as he waited for the control room to give him permission to continue.

"Standby," Agent Williams instructed, as he looked at his monitor to see what the General was doing.

"Okay… proceed. He is now two carriages away from you; it's a safe distance."

Johnson waited for Agent Franklin to enter the train from the open door that the General was still concerned about; 'Why had the door opened when nobody was waiting on the platform?' He didn't think much of it, as he knew that the doors sometimes opened when they stopped at a station, so he continued checking the tickets. But something was different about the fact that this door had opened. The agents were cautious of him; they instinctively knew that the General could feel something wasn't right while he was passed by the agents at the door carrying the equipment they needed. His body language changed, and it made Agent Johnson shiver, a chill crept up his spine as he walked to the next carriage.

But he started to calm himself, shaking it off. He knew the General was a couple carriages away from him now. Johnson thought he was being overly dramatic. The General couldn't see them, so why should he be worried? He was right; everything was still going to plan.

Agent Johnson was joined by Agent Franklin and both were now ready with the piece of silver fabric lined up like a screen. Agent Johnson stood still while Agent Franklin walked closer towards the first person they were attempting to save. They were lucky as he was already asleep. Agent Franklin turned around.

"He is already asleep...must I still spray him?"

"Affirmative...spray the whole carriage!" Special Agent Josh Williams said over the communication system. This was no time to question anything.

"Franklin, did you copy?"

"Copy that!"

They could not take the chance that he would wake up half way through the rescue. It would lead to anarchy in the compartment, and with the General looming only two carriages away from them, they couldn't take the chance. Agent Franklin took out a twirled piece of plastic pipe that was connected to a gas canister in his bag, he paused, and then he sprayed a light smoky substance from one side of the carriage to the other. He made sure everybody got enough gas. It worked almost instantaneously; the five commuters dropped to the floor, and fell fast asleep.

"Okay...move quickly now," Special Agent Martin Davis dictated, as he watched every move they made.

While they attempted to rescue the commuters, they forgot one small thing, a tiny thing. That tiny thing was he small girl who they didn't see coming into the carriage as she played with her doll. She wasn't interested in the five people in the carriage, but when they instantaneously dropped to the floor, she inspected the situation more closely. She now stood behind Agent Johnson. She couldn't see him; the electromagnetic spectrum and the nitrogen lasers were working wonders; in fact they were working so well that not even the people on the train were suspicious.

But every so often, the lasers could jump a frequency and the agents would be visible for a split second. But so far, this hadn't happened; yet.

The two agents covered the first commuter with the piece of silver blanket, and he disappeared from sight. The little girl watched.

She walked closer to the seat, wanting to touch it. She took her small hand and lightly touched the spot where the man had been sitting. Luckily, she wasn't alarmed, more disbelieving of what had just happened.

Agent Martin Davis opened the side door of the platform, a safe distance from the train, so that they could rescue commuters and take them to a safe place. Agent Davis could see on the monitor that the two agents had successfully rescued one commuter, and then followed behind them the other two agents also brought in a commuter from the side carriage. While they continued to rescue people, the Major kept a close eye on the General who had almost finished with his duties, checking that everyone had a ticket, remembering who their fathers and grandfathers were in the process. So far, the mission was going better than expected and they had already rescued twelve people. That left only seven to go. Agent Johnson and Agent Franklin only had two remaining in their carriage.

*"Remember the tickets..."*Agent Martin Davis said, as he of all people knew the importance of the tickets. They must always be left on the train...then burned.

"Blah, blah," Agent Johnson retorted, mocking Major Davis's remarks, but they knew what to do, as they searched one commuter for his ticket and then placed it in a small bag that had already been filled with the other tickets.

"Franklin?"

"Yes, yes, I know, get the tickets..."

"No, it's your transponder, it's dead again... we can't see you!" Special Agent Josh Williams said as he switched the camera mode to infrared so they would be visible at all times.

Franklin turned to his side and saw his beacon wasn't working again and he gave it another smack, but this time it didn't work. He walked towards Johnson who was already waiting on the train so they could rescue the final commuter on their carriage. Once this commuter was rescued, there would only be four left.

Johnson walked towards Franklin and waited for him at the train door. Agent Johnson knew what the problem was. He turned the transponder off and then on again, but still it didn't work.

Then a small spark came from the transponder, and even before Agent Franklin looked to his side, he felt that someone was standing next to him; someone small. It was the little girl in her school uniform. She stared directly at Agent Franklin. The spark had made his suit transponder malfunction and he visible, in plain sight. The alarms in the control room confirmed the problem; there was a breach in Agent Franklin's suit. The little girl looked straight at him. She knew he shouldn't have interfered, never ever.

"My daddy will not be happy... you are not on the list," and at that precise moment, her daddy became aware of him, the intruder on his train. They knew the rules; never cross the line if your name wasn't on the list.

"You are going to die now..." the little girl stated matter-of-factly to Agent Franklin, and then in front of his eyes her beautiful school dress transformed into a bloody red dress. There was no turning back now - it had begun.

Agent Franklin couldn't think of anything to say. He froze up and the control room witnessed the spike in his heart rate. It went off the charts.

He scanned the room, as he feared for his life.

"Is General Schultz coming...?" he asked her, hoping for some help.

She looked at him almost surprised. How could he know her father's name? But she answered him.

"No," she paused with a brief smile, "he is already here." In the control room, Agent Franklin's heart rate stopped instantaneously as his blood splattered all over the carriage floor, followed by his severed upper body. The bottom half of his body remained in the same spot.

Then a second later, gravity took over and the bottom half of his body fell forward like a sack of potatoes, spewing his guts from his body, the momentum making it slide a few feet; right in front of Agent Johnson.

Then the one word that had been drilled into their heads came...

"Mississippi..." Major Davis called over their radio; everybody knew what that meant.

The word everybody dreaded, the one word that couldn't be mistaken for anything else.

In layman's terms, **get out...get the hell out of there now!** Major Davis repeated it with alarm; **"Mississippi..."**

The Magnolia state had wonderful things to offer, but this was not one of them. With Agent Franklin lying half on one side and the rest of him splattered over the floor, Agent Johnson froze.

Major Davis took the hand mic from Agent Williams and gave him one last instruction; "Agent Johnson, don't move and you will live." He looked at the monitor which displayed the infrared image and he saw that the General was facing away from Johnson. He then turned towards the Agent. Johnson wasn't sure where he was looking; the

General's eyes darted from one side to the other. Something was attracting his attention. But they knew he couldn't see them; their suits were intact.

"He doesn't know you're there!" Major Davis reminded him, while he carefully watched the monitor.

Agent Johnson knew this, but he had a strange sensation that General Schultz had felt the radio signal. It could only be that. Every time he spoke over his communicator the General would stand dead still and scan the room.

Johnson was unsure, so to test his theory he switched his radio signal to an unused channel.

Agent Josh Williams saw that he'd changed his channel. He informed the Major about what he had done and they automatically changed the channel back to the right one.

The Major realised something, and then stopped Agent Williams before he communicated with Agent Johnson.

"Wait..." he shouted in an unsettling voice, as he pressed the mute button on the screen.

Agent Johnson was no fool; even if he was scared out of his mind he still kept calm. That was one of the reasons why the agency had selected him out of two hundred under-graduates. They didn't know what was going on, and he hadn't even applied for anything. All that they had to sign was a contract, normally for a period of twenty years, and then after that they could retire with a million Euros in the bank, and they could select any country in the world to live in. It was hard work though, with almost no time off. But then again, the money they offered made up for everything.

Agent Johnson was right; the General *could* hear the radio waves. In some way, it interfered with his 'poltergeist' senses. He couldn't hear what was said, but he could hear the static and the sound waves that echoed. Now Johnson understood - when the General looked straight at him, it wasn't because of him, but due to the chatter on the radio.

Johnson could see that the General was now walking straight towards him. This confused him, why was the General walking straight towards him? His heart rate soared. He knew the General could hear something; he was attuned like a submarine triangulating something, and he was looking for the origin of the beat.

"Clever…" Agent Davis said over the radio.

Major Davis, in the control room, looked at his monitor and saw the General's icon moving towards Johnson and he instinctively knew that Johnson would be the next one to die. There was nothing he could do about it.

Johnson thought the silence would help, but it did nothing to stop the General walking towards him. Then, with two feet remaining between the men, he thought of something.

"It should work…" Agent Johnson hoped optimistically to himself, and then he switched off his radio and all his equipment.

Then there was total silence. The General stopped in his tracks, as he struggled to hear the beat of a heart, including the vital sign monitor.

Everybody in the control room went into a panic, they thought Johnson had been killed; their heads drooped in disbelief. But all of a sudden they saw that the icon was still transmitting. "He is dead but his icon is still moving!" said Agent Martin Davis. They were confused, and they checked their systems again, and they found the problem; the manual override displayed the onscreen icon. Now they knew that he had unplugged his system.

Agent Johnson stared the beast in its pitch black eyes. He couldn't actually see any eyes, just darkness filled with pure evil, which reflected like a mirror.

Everything Agent Johnson had seen so far had been nothing compared to what he was about to see in twenty seconds; he'd been smart and it had saved him, but the other three remaining agents as well as the two people left would fill the train with their body parts.

General Ferdinand Schultz took two more steps then stopped, as he tried to listen for the heartbeat, but it had stopped the moment agent Johnson switched off his radio. General Schultz turned around, and looked at his daughter standing in her beautiful red dress watching every move she made, and then he focused his attention on something else that he heard; something thumped in his ear. It travelled on the radio waves from two carriages down; this time he knew exactly where it was coming from.

"Turn off your radios!" Major Davis shouted from the concealed control room. He could see the General was moving at an incredible speed from one side of the carriage towards the next, then through the door to the next one.

"Turn off your radios!" Major Davis shouted again, but his agents didn't hear him. They were trying to get off the train, dropping their gear, and running towards the open door.

Finally, they all heard his screaming, and from the control room he tried to switch off their radios. But he couldn't. Special Agent Josh Williams could only change the channel.

They needed to switch it off manually.

Then one of the agents bumped into a commuter on the train, making him fall a couple of feet. He slid against a seat while the other commuter just laughed; he was too high from the stash of marijuana he had in his pocket.

The General now moved faster than before, his anger turned him into a super being, his 'poltergeist' body passed through the separating doors like mist.

"Wow!" is all the druggie could mumble, as he saw the man dressed in a Nazi costume run through metal as if it was a hologram. He decided that it was probably a good time to stop laughing. The agent who had bumped into the commuter slowly struggled to get up from the floor, the size of his suit making it a difficult feat. He looked at the other two who were staring down the carriage, and he could feel the fear as it crept down his spine.

"He's here, isn't he?" he asked, his back turned towards the General. All of them had already switched off their radios. They heard the call for 'Mississippi', but it wasn't the fact that they moved too slowly, it was something else. They underestimated the speed at which the General could travel; and the fact that he could travel though the metal doors, was something that was entirely unanticipated.

"I have never seen anything like this before!" said Special Agent Martin Davis as he took the radio. He wanted to say something, but for the life of him, no words could make it out of his mouth as he knew his agents were on the verge of death.

"Major?" Special Agent Josh Williams asked confused. He knew that they had never seen anything like this before. After all, it was only their seventh mission together.

He looked towards the screen, noting that the General's icon had not moved in a while.

But Special Agent Davis had another secret. They had tried over forty five times in the past thirty years and he has lost twenty three agents while trying to save the bloodlines of those who were responsible.

"Forty five times..." the Major whispered, and by the looks of it he was tired of the secrets. He looked at the monitor and at the distance between the three men and the General. It seemed mission number forty six would claim three more agents and there was, yet again, nothing he could do about it. It was up to them now, with only a couple of feet between them and freedom. It seemed as if they were going to make it out the door; the two unlucky commuters who were left on the train would have to pay the price with their lives.

Or so they thought...

The General, however, had something else planned. The agents' radios had been switched off but not their transponders and while the General walked closer slowly, he saw only the two commuters and his daughter, still standing in the same place.

Again, he looked at the two staring back at him, but it wasn't them he was trying to find.

He kept hearing an annoying sound in his ears; it was faint and could easily be mistaken for a heartbeat, but it wasn't a heartbeat. He knew the difference. It was definitely not a heartbeat, definitely not a human sound. The sound almost lured him in and it made him curious. He focused all his attention on the sound, as he tried to amplify it. It worked, but it revealed three very odd sounds.

He could now pinpoint their exact location with the invisible lights faintly disrupting the atmosphere with small pulses, like a ripple in a pool of water. Then the General started to focus his full attention on the faint disruptions.

It worked. He could see their transparent figures in the carriageway, almost like ghosts. Now even being invisible wasn't going to help them. He could see them. They realised their visibility when the General smiled and his dead words would haunt them forever. He took a slow step forward. An ugly smile followed; as he released the words they feared the most.

"I see you…"

They tried to run towards the door. But the General stretched out his hand to the left side of the carriage, and then touched the wall of the carriage with his open hand, pressing his palm fully against the carriage wall.

And instantly all the train doors slammed shut with such brutal force that the agent who was halfway through the door was sliced in two; one piece of his body fell outside the train and the other part fell to the carriage floor, like a slice of meat from the butcher.

The General's power was immense; undeniably, it stemmed from pure evil. He had never done this before, but they were warned to never cross the line if their name wasn't on the list. His power increased each time they interfered and, coupled with his rage, he became unstoppable. He would do anything to take those responsible apart, even if he had to do it literally limb by limb.

The transponder linked to the control room died as the door collided with the agent's fragile body. He was only human, yet the agency had nothing in their armour to stop him; he had reached the peak of his wrath.

The two remaining agents and the two onlookers were at a dead end, they had nowhere to go and nowhere to hide; all the doors were jammed shut.

The lonely transponders still sent signals every two seconds, but the heart rate of the two agents was overwhelmingly strong; faster and faster they went as the blood throbbed through their bodies, as they knew that the end was a mere few seconds away. The two remaining commuters suddenly realised this wasn't a joke anymore. They tried to yank the train doors open. First, they tried the one, and then ran towards the next, but it was useless. The doors were jammed. The lights were still on, but they were flickering and that didn't help with the mood.

The General walked straight past the two commuters, not paying them any attention; they were not the threat. The two agents knew exactly where he was going.

He passed by the two commuters so closely that they could feel the sickness in him. They thought he had left them alone, but that wasn't the case. The little girl was by their side, and they somehow felt momentarily relieved.

But she knew they were on the list. "Don't worry... he will be back for you soon," she warned, almost as if they should be pleased that he had not forgotten them. They didn't like the idea and then they did something they should *never* have done.

They should have left the small girl alone; then they might have had a chance to escape. But the idiots that they were could never imagine that one of them would leave this world squished like a tomato, while the other commuter would land up with his heart outside of his body, as it ticked away in the hands of the General.

All she had to cry was "Daddy!"

It was a faint call, but he responded instantly and it was over in seconds. In a way he did humanity a favour; the world had no use for them. They had pulled a knife on the small girl and had made a slight scar against the girl's neck.

In a way, they got what they deserved.

This was all that the agents needed, the perfect distraction. When they saw Johnson trying to open the door from the outside, they were ecstatic. Major Davis shouted from the outside, "Don't open the door." They only had moments to get the door open with the help of Special Agent Josh Williams in the control room. They needed to cut the power to the train which would cause the doors to open, although it would leave them in total darkness, giving them just enough time to hustle out. They ran towards the door that led out of the platform with only the emergency light guiding the way, their suits made it difficult to move. Then dead silence - not a sound - it was if all sound had been cut from their ears.

The two made it. It could certainly be classified as the worst day of their lives…but they had survived to tell the story. Special Agent Martin Davis was also relieved. He checked the only monitor that wasn't affected by the power cut. "It's okay!" He couldn't see any paranormal activity. Then again, just to be certain, he checked all the sensors and performed all sorts of scans for visual confirmation.

He saw nothing of the General, the little girl or her mother. He rubbed his eyes; this was too close for comfort. Meanwhile, the lights started turning on one by one.

The monitor revealed nothing. The failure had cost them a great deal of money, but all he had to do was make a phone call and he would get all the money he ever needed.

The Major took out his phone and did what he always did after he'd completed a mission. Agent Josh Williams saw him making the call, and knew it was private.

The call wasn't for his ears, so he walked out, and hinted at the other two in the room to do the same. With no arguments they all left the room.

The Major waited for the three to leave, and then he dialled the number, reluctantly. He didn't want to, but it was the agreement he had with them. This would be the fourth time in a row that they had been unsuccessful, and he knew without a shadow of a doubt that they wouldn't be happy.

The phone rang and he waited for them to answer. They would answer. They always answered, no matter what time of day it was, they answered.

"Yes…" someone said.

"We failed…" the Major replied, but encouragingly he thought that at least they had saved some bloodlines from the General. "We did save twelve bloodlines." He tried to add some light to the dull situation, but they didn't care about the lives they had saved.

"Did you lose many men?" the voice asked calmly.

The Major could not answer, his cell phone lost signal and went dead, as did the lights on the platform and all the monitors except the infrared camera, the one thing they gave the General as a gift along with the monitor that wasn't affected by the power cut.

They could feel something wasn't right and they felt extremely uncomfortable. The three men were still waiting underneath the emergency light, as they saw all the lights go dead. They could feel something in the darkness.

Then they heard something. It broke the intense silence that loomed; an awful sound like someone was scratching their nails on a black board. The sound cut through their skin.

Major Martin Davis could see the three men on the infrared monitor still standing and waiting for someone to open the door so they could exit the platform, but from the control room it seemed everything was normal except for the power cut. The three agents still heard the awful sound, but it stopped just as the emergency door opened. Shock and fear almost killed them, but they were relieved; it was only Agent Williams opening the door from the other side. He gave them a fright when he burnt a flair when he opened the door.

They laughed at their own stupidity; they couldn't understand how they could be so stupid. Their relief was palpable as the lights went on.

"You see, I told you it was just a power cut," Johnson said laughing as the lights went on one by one.

"Come on... let's get out of here," Special Agent Josh Williams said, as he tried to encourage and calm them a bit, as they walked back through the door. Although he didn't really need to calm them, as they'd all been trained to accept death as if they were eating a slice of toast in the morning.

It wasn't brainwashing, but rather exceptionally disturbing training to which they had been subjected. The first weeks of training were the worst; they spent hours a day at a pig slaughterhouse on a secret farm in Virginia.

All of them started walking through the door one by one; this time they left their gear outside for the clean-up crew. It was over now.

"Agent Harvey, remember to shut the door behind you," Agent Williams reminded him, leading the rest of them into the corridor.

The major, still in the control room, saw something appear on the monitor. It was a normal heat signature but he knew it wasn't one of the agents, as he could see them walking through the door. At the same time Agent Harvey, the last to go through the door, got a feeling that someone was holding him by the shoulders.

At first he didn't think anything of it, but then the grip became tighter and tighter almost breaking his bones, and just before he let out a scream, he flew through air into the darkness of the train, disappearing forever.

It happened so fast that the others couldn't even see what happened - all they heard was Agent Harvey screaming as he was thrown through the air like a leaf picked up by a gust of wind. Then it was quiet again, only a burning ticket in the air. He had forgotten to leave the ticket on the train.

Only the Major really saw what happened. It was as clear as daylight for him as he saw everything on the monitor. The power of the beast had increased; it could be that they had provoked him.

Never cross if not invited, that was what the witch doctor had said. While he silently looked at the screen, his phone rang.

He knew who it was. This time they were phoning him. He pressed the answer key, but didn't say anything. The caller started to speak before he could talk.

"He is pleased for the people that you saved, but it has come to his attention that…" he stopped and thanked the person who was ringing him, the sound of Big Ben in the background, and then continued the telephone call with the Major Davis.

"…it has come to his attention that you did come close this time, but failed again. The organisation cannot keep on cleaning up your failures Major."

Special Agent Martin Davis, acknowledged every word the caller said. He knew it was true.

"We will send someone to observe the next time," he said and the General didn't like this idea one bit.

"You know we work alone," Major Davis protested at every word the caller spoke, but he knew there was nothing that he could do about it; even he had to report to someone.

"Don't worry Agent Davis…they will not interfere, you will not even know they're there." He understood, as he watched the clean-up crew work their wonders, making sure not a fingerprint was left on the train.

He stood quietly for a moment, and then sighed. He could hear someone speaking Italian on the other side, but he was used to them speaking Italian; that is where the Head of Operations was and where his missions were funded from. While he waited for them, he tried to remind himself how it was before he was contacted to run the mission, but he could no longer remember any good times; only this.

He could hear them speaking on the other side of the line again, but this time they were not speaking Italian. He tried to eavesdrop on what they were saying, but he could only hear the words, "Here Father..." He was given a letter with the easily recognisable insignia – the shield with the two-headed wolf inside, one looking up and the other down.

"Here Father...it's from them," the person said, as he waited for the Father to take the envelope.

"One moment," the Father said to Agent Davis, as he put down his tea cup and took the envelope, opening it while he still held the cell phone in his other hand. He thanked the delivery bearer and took a few seconds to read the message.

"Agent Davis, are you there...," he waited for Agent Davis to answer.

"Yes Father, I'm here."

"One moment..." the Father said, as he saw the porter walk back in the room with a second envelope, but this one wasn't white like the one he held in his hand. He took the second envelope, read it, sat silently for a few seconds, and then put the black envelope on the table. It seemed the porter was the bearer of bad news this time. The Father lifted the white envelope and brought the phone closer to his ear, then read the words written on the inside. Then he read the information on the white envelope, but that was good news.

"They will join you in the next mission; I have the letter confirming it."

He put down the phone. He was relieved the men could take a break before the next mission. They needed a holiday. The men would be ecstatic about the news. The Major walked out the room towards the other members to inform them of the good news.

Davis was, in a way, happy that they were joining the mission wherever it would be, he just wished they had been there on the New York mission.

Back in London, the priest walked out the door stopping before the one who gave him the black envelope.

"Why..." the priest asked in his best Italian, but without an answer, he walked out of the room.

He knew he was only one of the puppets; he, too, left the thinking to the puppet master.

They all knew that the black envelope was death and the person's name that was written within would have to die. The fifty-year-old ink spontaneously combusted and the name of Special Agent Martin Davis, in charge of this mission, burnt alongside his picture.

Chapter 10

AMERICANS AT THE NAMIBIAN BORDER

Johannes Roland was sitting silently in the police interrogation room. He wasn't feeling well; something was making his stomach turn and he didn't think it was the biscuits that the nice police lady gave him.

It was almost as if he was still under the spell of the train, but it wasn't that either. He kept on seeing the little girl everywhere and it was freaking him out.

Then there was a knock on the door; in walked Peter Richards with his release papers.

"Sign here, here and there…" Peter pointed out where he needed to sign, and then Peter's cell phone started to ring. He saw the call was from Charles le Roux and knew it was about the urine sample he'd given him to test, he decided not to answer the phone in front of Johannes; Johannes had enough on his mind. He turned the phone upside down so that it rang silently. But he was curious; so he decided to answer the call anyway.

"Hi Peter, it's Charles here," he greeted him and then went straight into giving Peter the results of the test. In a way, Peter already knew what the result would be as he'd seen the symptoms before.

"It's positive for Sodium Thiopental…" said Charles le Roux. He should know; he was the specialist. Even so, he wanted to be absolutely certain, so he'd tested it four times; and each time he got the same result.

"It's the same stuff," Charles said, then stopped. He knew where this conversation was headed and they'd promised that they would *never* speak of what had happened twenty years ago.

Never, ever again would they speak of it, but now it seemed as if their past had caught up with them. They were the only two left from the unit and Peter decided it was time.

"It's okay... I remember what we promised. I think it's time."

So Charles started to lay everything out.

Twenty years ago, they were young and stupid, but well-trained. They received information that there was an imminent attack looming on one of the South African Defence Force Camps, but they didn't know which one of the army camps would be attacked.

The information they had received came from the American observers at the border, and they knew the South African counter-insurgency team would be sent in.

They never questioned the information; the source was impeccable.

They never knew his name until they finally met him just four hours before the mission; that was where they had met Major Martin Davis for the first time.

The Major needed a distraction to carry out the task they needed to complete. The information that he'd received was correct; but then he gave them the serum. His intentions at the time were not entirely pure; after all, he'd been given a ticket earlier in the month and his life was hanging in the balance.

He gave them the location of the planned attack, which was only two miles over the border of Angola.

They planned the mission as they always did, by leaving them with a back door out of Angola if things went bad. After they'd used the truth serum things did in fact go bad; very bad, very quickly. They never meant to kill them; they only meant to get the information they needed.

For the Major, this was a clever plot to buy him some time to complete his own mission.

But then the Angolan Government forced the Americans out of the Company with a diplomacy regulation. The Major sent his team home and secretly stayed behind to do what he needed to do without the approval of the Company. He assumed they would not find out about it; what he didn't know was that he was continually watched by two mysterious men from afar; they watched every move he made. It was almost as if they were ghosts and the local tribes paid no attention to them. Only the small children noticed them walking through the village.

They had no names to give when a little boy asked them in his home language what their names were. They only replied that names were for followers and deeds meant more than a name, deeds suitable for a King. They did have names of course, but there was no need for them to divulge them.

In some way the young boy understood and the children left them alone after they caught a glimpse of the rings they wore on their fingers; it was a shield with an image of a wolf with two faces, one looking up and other looking down. It was a distinctive symbol, but only those who knew what it symbolised understood.

The two mysterious men knew what was going on. When Peter Richards, Charles le Roux and their team injected the serum into the hostiles, it was to extract information, that's all. What happened next was the work of Martin Davis.

When his team were about to be kicked out of Angola he needed a distraction, something to buy him time and as he was on the list, he needed to do something to save his own life, as he stood in the distance, holding the ticket in his hand.

Peter and Charles looked on while blood poured out of Angolan soldiers ears; the team knew something was wrong. They tried to help them by injecting a reversal serum, but it was too late. Their screaming could be heard in the village nearby. Moments later blood squirted out of their noses and their eyes dripped with blood.

It was nine minutes of pure and utter agony for the Angolan soldiers.

Charles le Roux, the chemistry specialist and medic of the team, stepped back. He knew there was nothing they could do to save them, as did the two mysterious men who looked towards a small village house in the middle of nowhere. They stared at the house and then turned towards each other; they knew who was responsible for the deaths of the two soldiers. It was not Peter Richards and his team. They made a decision and walked off into the darkness, disappearing out of sight.

Meanwhile Peter and his team frantically tried to reason about what had happened; they argued and almost killed each other over what went wrong and why. They reached a conclusion, and decided that the only feasible answer was that it was the serum that had done it. They knew it made absolutely no difference now about what they said; the simple fact of the matter was that they had killed the men in a horrendous manner. And as this wasn't an act of war, for them, it felt like it had been done in cold blood.

Then things got worse, way worse. His team accidently stumbled upon some schoolbooks that had fallen on the floor while they fought amongst each other. They realised that the people they had so brutally killed were not in fact soldiers. Richard crumbled the moment he saw the schoolbooks fall on the floor. Something was terribly, terribly wrong.

But why would they have weapons? Richard looked at the AKs leaning up against the wall. He stared at the two automatic weapons and then saw something else; he walked closer to the wall and carefully investigated. He realised that the weapons didn't reflect any light; it was only a faded reflection; he picked one of the weapons up and inspected it.

"Plastic!" he said angrily, as he snapped the firearm in two. He knew the

boys had only been playing, and now they had to explain what had happened. They left the small house one by one, the last to leave threw a burning lighter into the house; it was the only way. They walked away and looked back every so often as the house collapsed; the fire consumed everything, within a matter of seconds – it was gone.

Charles le Roux stopped and so did Peter Richards. They both had this strange sensation that this would haunt them forever, and they had made a pact to never talk of the incident, ever.

From afar, the Major was pleased; this was buying him loads of time as he watched the villagers running towards the burning house as they tried to stop the inferno. The crying of family members echoed into the African night and not far away Peter Richards stood, still agonised, feeling responsible, and hoping against all hope that they had destroyed all the evidence. And they did. But Major Davis needed more time, so he did the unthinkable. He put his hand into a small bag that he had been carrying with him and took out two items from deep within the bag; an army beret and an insignia patch from the South African Defence Force that he had stolen when he gave the truth serum to Charles le Roux. He dropped these near the burning house hoping someone would find them. Someone did.

The villagers went crazy. They attacked border patrols in the hundreds and while the fiasco occurred, the Angolan freedom fighters took the opportunity to board the train and rob passengers. That was a big mistake. Little did they know that there was something else on that train; that something else had a name, General Ferdinand Schultz.

The Major looked at the train from afar and took out his ticket, smelling the expensive perfume in his nostrils, a fresh summer fragrance with a hint of apple, and then he put it back in his pocket. One thing was certain; the tickets were not meant for them. In the last days of the war, the soldiers boarded the train and robbed and terrorised unarmed people. While doing this, they took what didn't belong to them, and in turn, they had taken the place of those who should have been slaughtered.

Then, when the little girl's dress bled red, it began.

He mumbled, but they couldn't understand him. He mumbled again, but still they couldn't understand him.

He still looked towards the floor; he wasn't worried about the four soldiers that pointed their automatic weapons at him. Then, he spoke again, this time in English, and they understood him very clearly; "They're not yours to take."

They laughed.

That was a mistake. The harder they laughed the angrier the General became.

The one who had the most to say when the little girl's father had mumbled the words, "They're not yours to take," exploded like a pimple against the wall, squirting and pasting the light green wallpaper with blood, while his hand stuck to the wall still gripping the AK-47, firing randomly, aiming at nowhere, until the last bullet ejected from the barrel. It was a reflex action as his body was no longer in control.

This confused the other two soldiers; they had never seen anything like it before. The man they had killed in the next room now stood and stared straight at them; without thinking they began to beg for their lives.

He stopped and looked at the two for a moment; this had never happened before. They tried to give back the tickets after they'd seen him collecting them from the two already dead soldiers. They thought that if they gave back the tickets he would spare their lives. But they were wrong, it hadn't even crossed his evil mind to save them; they had interfered in his business, and that was not allowed.

He reached behind his back, and held his hand behind him for a few seconds. First the barrel of a rifle appeared - it looked old, like an antique - but as soon as he pulled the trigger they fell to the floor; it was quick and clean. Even evil had a time limit, and the unexpected attacks by the soldiers had wasted time. The tickets were next to their bodies. The General's time had run out.

Ever since that day, Major Davis knew his own time would come. He stayed out of the train. If he entered, he would surely be killed like his father.

Chapter 11

IF THERE IS GOOD, THERE MUST BE EVIL

Peter Richards's forgot to ask Johannes one very important question; he stopped him as he walked out the police station's front door. Johannes didn't hear Peter calling him the first time and only on Peter's third attempt, he stopped. He was pleased to see his lawyer was escorting him out the door, but he probably couldn't be a lawyer anymore. Johannes remembered he had been barred from practicing any law because of associates that had implicated him in illegal activities; even if he was cleared of any crimes, his boss and the company he worked for wouldn't be.

With this little legal aspect tainting his career, he knew nobody would hire him. Peter stopped the chitchat and jumped straight to the point, "You never said how you got off the death train?" He was very curious. This was the last thing he needed to know and then he would be finished with the law, his wife and hopefully Africa.

He had done all that he could for his friend. He needed to go and find a new job.

Johannes stopped speaking and thought for a while; he struggled to remember how he got off the train. "What station did you get off?" Peter prompted, but Johannes was still thinking about it. He thought hard, moved towards the wall and rested lightly against it while a couple of police officers passed him. He got a killing stare from them and he knew why; the four cops were still missing.

"I honestly don't remember...the last station I remember was Klapmuts," Johannes said, as he clearly remembered the taxi driver hooting and waving him over.

"Ten bucks…"

"What?"

Johannes was also confused when he thought about it, but he had needed ten bucks for a taxi to take him to the Paarl train station, and then out of nowhere the ten rand note flew through the air and landed against the door frame. "I've got better things to do with the money," he remembered saying, and then he walked back into the carriage, and closed the door behind him. He remembered somebody being extremely sad; it was the little girl who gazed though the connecting door window; she looked very disappointed, and dropped her head downwards slightly. He was quite pleased with ten rand he'd scored, so he hadn't really taken any notice of her as he didn't have a care in the world. He'd already forgotten what he'd seen in the next door carriage.

"I woke up at Wellington station," he remembered. What happened before that was a mystery to him. The truth was known, but only to Special Agent Martin Davis, as well as his team. Davis gave the order and his team were required to comply. Even though it was against their will, they knew the risk if they faced if they didn't follow his orders.

The truth was that the little girl had helped him off the train. Nobody knew why she did it, but she pulled him by the arms out of the door at Paarl station and left him on the platform, unharmed after he'd collapsed on the train. His head had been knocked against the iron part of the seat. She was protecting those whose names weren't on the list. The special agents saw this as their team were already on the train. At the time, Johannes saw them, but it was only for a fleeting second. "Spacesuit…," he mumbled when he saw them.

He was sure he'd seen someone in a spacesuit, but it was difficult to tell through the fogged-up windows. He took his hand and wiped the window to see into the next carriage. He called the young girl. "Come see something funny," but the space man was already gone.

Agent Davis and his team had a loss of power for a moment and the violet light beams that were used to camouflage them from the dead, and to the human eye shutdown. Subsequently the nitrogen lasers and the electromagnetic spectrum system crashed, luckily only for two seconds, and then it was rebooted by a remote signal. They were saved from detection.

Johannes lay peacefully and safe on the platform at Paarl train station. Moments later, two black vehicles with tinted windows stopped outside the station and two of Agent Davis' team got out and ran toward Johannes. They picked him up and tossed him into the back of one of the vehicles, and sped away.

They needed to drive fast; they had to make it to Wellington train station before the train.

Again, this was at the instruction of Agent Davis who oddly enough had never been near the train himself. Some of the agents wondered why he was always gave instructions from afar. Of course Agent Davis knew why.

He knew they would find him, especially after the warning the priest had given him. He needed to stay under the radar to save his life.

"For your life..." they had warned him, and he knew they would only give one warning; so Special Agent Martin Davis, would keep this secret until his death. The rest of the team must <u>never</u> know.

He needed another distraction. This wasn't what they wanted. He was breaking procedure, and the Company with the insignia of a shield and the two-headed wolf, the one head looking up and the other down, noted his insubordination.

Now Johannes was safe and ready to leave the police station. He said his goodbyes and walked out of Cape Town Central Police Station. This would be the last time that Peter would see Johannes.

A few days later, Johannes was on his way to a friend staying in Langebaan, a beautiful small town on the west coast of South Africa, just an hour's drive out of Cape Town. It was still undetermined how his car had careened off the road and collided with a road-side tree.

He died instantly.

It was reported as an accident as he'd fallen asleep at the wheel; everybody believed it.

"It's done..." Agent Davis softly whispered to himself while he drove away from the accident scene; there was no one around to help Johannes this time. His lust to survive was taking control of Agent Davis.

Johannes had to die, as Agent Davis needed yet another distraction. He had to get rid of the only witness that could help the agency...or so he thought.

Peter heard the news on one of the local TV stations when he was back in his apartment. It was bad news; after all, Johannes was a friend. This thing with the missing police officers was really eating at him; it had been almost a week and still they hadn't found the missing cops.

He went through the old newspapers as he tried to solve the puzzle, but he gave up; he wasn't going to look for answers anymore. It was time to look for a new job. He threw all the old newspapers in the bin.

He picked up today's newspaper from his coffee table, and glanced at the front page.

"Lucky kid," he said, reading the front page headline about a young boy who had picked up a coin, a coin that some mysterious men had given him. It was auctioned for two hundred thousand United States Dollars; bought anonymously over the internet. It had helped him and his hard working family out of the slump they had endured for the past sixty years.

Peter didn't read the whole article. He peered at the picture of the coin, and then he noticed something. At first he wasn't certain, but he squinted through a magnifier and there it was! This would be the fourth time he'd seen the insignia of the shield and the two-headed wolf. He walked towards his safe, hidden away behind some old books, opened it and extracted something he'd stolen from the police station. If they caught him they would lock him up for sure.

"What the hell..." he said shocked, as he saw that the insignia on the ticket and the coin were exactly the same. He had solved it, well part of it, but he couldn't go to the police "What am I going to tell them?" he chuckled, "I'm sorry for stealing your ticket?"

There was a knock on the door. The only thing he could think was that it was the police. For a split second he thought of destroying the ticket, but he decided against it and put it back in his safe.

The knock came again, this time slightly louder. He made sure he was dressed properly and opened the door. Peter didn't recognise the person who held an envelope.

"Peter Richards?" the person queried and Peter acknowledged him. He could see it was a delivery. "From whom?" Nobody knew he was staying here and he'd only been in this apartment for three days.

He interrogated the deliveryman. "Who is this from?" But he was only the bearer of the parcel and he merely suggested checking the back of the letter. He slowly turned the letter around. It was as if the world had pulled him in; he was stunned, but curious. The deliveryman tried for the second time to get his attention, but Peter continued staring at the two-headed wolf insignia. He turned the envelope back around and saw it was from Italy. The stamp read 'Poste Vaticane'.

"Vatican City..."

"Sir, please sign!"

He signed for the envelope and stared at it for another couple of minutes, but still he resisted opening it; instead he placed it on the coffee table. He wanted to open it, but walked to the kitchen cabinet and poured himself a whisky. Then he walked back and sat on the chair directly in front of the envelope. It was definitely for him. He could see his name all over the letter.

The curiosity was killing him and after his final sip of the remaining whisky, he decided it was time to open it.

"Nothing..." he grumbled and threw his glass against the wall, as it shattered into a hundred pieces, as he wondered who in the world would send him *nothing.*

Then there was another knock on the door and in his angry state, he flung the door open. This time he recognised the two people.

"Peter Richards?" they asked, but they knew who he was. They just needed him to confirm.

"Yes." He remembered them clearly. They had stopped him on his way back from his friend Charles le Roux at the university. But that time they'd been dressed in police uniforms. He reminded them that he remembered them from the highway incident. They acknowledged it.

"There is something you need to know," the one said. Peter invited them inside and locked the door behind him. Even before he sat down, they started to pour out everything.

At first, he didn't believe them; how could something like this happen? The explanation was easy; *if there is good there must be evil.*

"Peter John Richards," they pronounced the full name. He knew exactly who they were talking about.

"What has my grandfather to do with all this?" he questioned.

"Everything."

So they began tell him the story...

Years ago, the Lieutenant who had tried to stop the attack on the wrong train was his grandfather. He was the only one who wouldn't receive a ticket. Peter didn't understand this. How could he, of all people, survive? It sounded like propaganda to him.

"It's all true," they insisted.

His grandfather, the Lieutenant, had asked why the train was shorter than what they had been told; it only had five wagons, and the train number was 104. "*They said nothing about a train number,*" his grandfather had explained, but they weren't convinced. He had tried.

"This is wrong..." the Lieutenant had said, not understanding why the troops had no weapons, not even pistols. But it was all part of the treaty; no weapons were allowed on the train.

While the Allieds walked from wagon to wagon, it became clear: something was wrong, very wrong.

Peter's grandfather could hear people in the next carriage screaming for them to stop, but the sounds of gunfire started all over again, blocking out the sounds of agony that the Nazi soldiers were experiencing. It went on like that for a couple of minutes - first the shouting, then the gunfire - followed by silence. The visibility in the carriages was atrocious, but when the moon appeared from behind the clouds, the newspapers, wine bottles and the documents that had been mistaken for firearms by the Allied soldiers became visible.

They never had a chance.

The darkness blinded them, and over-preparation was the main cause of the problem. It was impossible for them to see anything. All they saw were shadows and that was what they were prepared to shoot at.

The Lieutenant tried to stop the attack from the back carriage, but his screaming was drowned out by the gunfire. He had hurried through the door separating the carriages, hoping to be in time, but when he passed through the carriage, he knew he was too late.

Even in the dark, he could feel they had done something terrible. He couldn't see the bodies, but he knew they were there. While he walked forward his fears became reality. The train lights came on momentarily. He dropped his face in shame as he saw the blooded bodies on the stools, on the floor, while in the background the echo of gunfire filled the air.

It was a terrible miscalculation. Even now Peter felt the pain. He remembered that his departed friend Johannes had said that the little girl in the school uniform spoke to him. He remembered her name; Maria Schulz.

"Maria Schultz…" Peter repeated the name. "She is the one that keeps the General sane; he must just do what he is there for and nothing else," said one of the men. Peter laughed. He found the comment quite funny. "How can a person who had killed over thirty people be sane?" he asked them. It seemed they had an answer for everything.

Paranormal phone calls to unsuspecting people, inviting them to a function or similar; they used the free travel pass they'd been given on the train and if they had forgotten their ticket, one would be issued to them at the nearby ticket office by the General's wife, who was also called Maria Schultz. She had to comply even if she didn't want to; Ferdinand Schultz had forced her in his supernatural state. She always complied in the hope of returning to the next world; but for now, she and the others were trapped in a spiral.

It still didn't explain how they knew of the attack. But then he finally got the answer he was looking for - technology, satellite technology. Even their satellites bore the symbols of the shield and the two-headed wolf. They used satellites to pinpoint where their next attacks would be. A ripple would appear days, weeks and sometimes months before the time, easily visible by the technology incorporated in the satellites, like a light being switched on in darkness.

Peter still wasn't comfortable with the two men in his apartment. He stood up and walked towards the kitchen, returning with three glasses and an unopened bottle of whisky. Without asking, he poured whisky into each glass. They looked at him and he answered before they could say anything. "The taps are broken... this is all I have to drink." They weren't interested in the whisky and while Peter took his first sip, they started to explain the 'loop' or a cloud if one was in possession of specialised sunglasses.

It was easy to explain, but the only reason they didn't want him to know was to protect him. If he had the specialised sunglasses, he would know where the General was. This would affect him.

"Evil deeds are guided by evil himself," the one said, assuming Peter would understand, but Peter was cautious; he needed to see for himself if he was receiving information from a reliable source. And these two mysterious men that sat in front of him, who refused even a sip of expensive whisky, were not reliable in Peter's mind yet. He decided to test them. If they were fools, they would leave him alone, but if they could answer his questions, well then he'd be even more confused.

Before he could formulate his questions, they said something shocking, and he felt his whole world falling apart.

He was only one of five people that knew the secret. He got up from his chair and walked towards the fridge, opened it and threw two ice cubes into his whisky.

"Sodium Thiopental," they said again, just in case Peter hadn't heard properly the first time, but he had heard them. There was certainly nothing wrong with his hearing. But his conscience stabbed him in his back. He thought nobody knew and for a moment he relived the pain and disappointment in himself that had consumed him since that night twenty years ago. They had murdered two innocent people that night, and what made things worse was the school uniform and books lying on the table. It had belonged to them.

Peter turned around and looked at the two men, who still stoody by the table. He gulped down the rest of the whisky, and then walked back and saw the two items that had been recovered from the burnt house almost twenty years ago - the beret and the patch with the insignia from the South African Defence Force. Yes, it did belong to his team. Mistakes happened. It was referred to as South Africa's Vietnam.

He concluded that they were here to arrest him for war crimes and he gave himself over to them.

He had lost everything - his job, his house and then his wife - so there was nothing to fight for anymore. He was ready to do his time. He sat down on the chair and he looked as if all his energy had been drained out of his body.

The two men looked at each other, wondering whether they should tell him the truth - that Special Agent Martin Davis was actually responsible. They knew this as they had been there; they had been watching Agent Davis for years and years. He was on the list; they had to watch his every move. They also knew that people who wanted to save their own lives did stupid things. They decided against telling him the truth, it could wait until later.

If he survived, he would be rewarded. *If he survived*. The odds were stacked against him, but it was worth the risk. They gave Peter a choice; if he helped them, the charges would be dropped. There weren't actually any charges; but they knew that this was the only way he could be coerced into helping them. They needed him badly...

The problem was that he still didn't believe a word they'd said about the General. In order to persuade him, they offered him twenty thousand American Dollars. This was more than enough for a man who had lost everything.

He agreed even though he knew he could be killed in the process.

"I'll help you catch your killer...where must I sign," Peter capitulated. All he could think about was getting out of the slump he was in, and quickly. They handed him the letter that had come and placed it in front of him.

"There is nothing on it..." he said, as he looked at them and then at the letter again. Weirdly, there was now writing on it.

He took it and quickly flipped through the pages and then stopped. He couldn't read it.

"It's in Latin." He was a lawyer so he had studied in Latin, but it had been years since he'd used it. Now he could only make out a couple of words he still knew; "liability", "binding until death" and "prosecution." In his mind he quickly compared what he had lost to what he could gain from this job. This is exactly what this was to him, a job, and an opportunity to get out of the mess he was in.

He signed it.

He gave it back to them and they handed him another envelope, thicker than the previous one. He opened it. Inside he found three thousand Dollars, a plane ticket to New York with his name on it and a long letter of instructions which was dated 10th February.

"First class!"

"You will get the rest of the money once the job is done," they said and walked towards the door.

"Wait...how am I going to get through customs? And my passport expires in March 2011." It would be impossible for him to enter the Unites States without a visa.

"Passport?" the one with a German accent asked. Peter walked to the cupboard, removed his passport, and gave it to them. One of the men flipped through it and saw it was empty; Peter, sadly, had never travelled anywhere.

"I never had the time..." he tried to explain himself.

He scrolled to the right page on the passport, pasted a visa on the page, and stamped it. It was as easy as that.

"You guys come prepared."

They had talked a lot, but Peter still didn't know who they were and who they worked for. This bugged him.

"Who do you work for?" Peter asked, but they paid no attention to his question, and walked out of his flat, leaving him, finally, with a modicum of ambition. He was looking forward to the trip to New York. All there was to do now was wait.

Chapter 12

BUILDING NUMBER EIGHT

The next couple months went by quickly for Peter. Now he was on the plane to New York, and best of all, it was first class all the way, with expensive whisky and sparkling wine from France lining his tray! This was all new to Peter, but he certainly wasn't going to protest. It was paid for by 'them'. The more he dwelled on it, the more it puzzled him; there was one question that still bugged him and that was how they knew so much about him?

They were not like the people in the black suits who took the urine sample from him, no, they were different. He decided to read the letter they had given him, but there wasn't much information about what he actually had to do. While reading it, he was interrupted by a flight attendant.

"Sir…" she got his attention, she was holding something large in her hand; he turned slightly to the side to get a closer look. *"What now!"* he thought and then he adjusted his view and saw she had a suit cover in her hands. Obviously, then, there was a suit inside. She gave him a card that she was holding in her other hand. He immediately recognised the markings - it was from 'them' - the shield and wolf bolting out on the front of the card. He also saw his name on the side. The card said he needed to wear it; as someone would be picking him up on arrival.

He took out some money from his jacket pocket to pay for the suit.

"It's paid for," she stated. He didn't complain. If they had paid for it, fine, it certainly looked sharper than the jeans and t-shirt he was wearing. She showed him where she would keep it for him.

There was no need to put on the suit right now as there were still five hours before arrival in New York, plenty of time to get some sleep. He turned around, rested his head on the pillow, and fell asleep, and soon after he started dreaming. At first, it was a pleasant dream of how things were before cops raided his work place.

"A good investment," his boss had remarked; but little did he know that his money would be used in a crime syndicate. The day the 'Hawks', the specialised crime unit, raided the Company was still very much fresh in his mind. It was terrible not knowing what was going on, but when he caught his boss shredding some file; it became very clear to him that something was not right. His boss confessed to the deeds for a lesser sentence, but Peter was left with nothing. He was forced to sell his house, and shortly after that his wife left him. But his wife leaving him was the only good part of the whole thing and he had decided that his son would be better off with her.

Then his dream turned into something out of the ordinary. He didn't recognise the surroundings; it was dark and he could hear a scuffling in the woods just off the clearing.

The dream felt so real he could even smell the pine trees and the crisp wind that was forcing him slightly sideways. Then he saw something coming into the clearing – it wasn't an animal - then there were two, then three. Soldiers!

He could see them clearly now, as the full moon appeared from behind some clouds. They walked straight towards him. He wanted to run, but he couldn't move. There were at least thirty of them.

Peter looked at their firearms; they were old, maybe fifty years old, at least. Then one of the soldiers marched past him. He glanced at the name. *"No way!"* He had to be sure, and now his ability to walk was back, and he ran around the soldier. He needed a second look. There it was. "Richards!" he yelled, as he stopped in his tracks, while the other solders walked by him as if he wasn't there.

Then in his dream he remembered the story the two men had narrated to him weeks earlier.

However, his mind refused to accept what he saw and while he lay in the first class seat, in an almost horizontal position, he twitched and turned in silence. Nobody paid any attention. They were all sleeping. Not even the flight attendant that walked down the passageway switching off the reading lights noticed him.

He tried hard to find the balance between reality and where he was at the moment; it was a powerful dream that gripped him. He was unable to wake up, so he gave up fighting and drifted off further into the dream. He was startled by a train passing him that came to a halt, soldiers lining the sides of it.

It felt different now. The initially pleasant breeze that had drifted through the woods had disappeared and the initial silence was now filled with the clattering of bullets against the wall of the train, followed by screaming. It was not a man screaming, though, but a little girl.

He walked around one of the carriages and climbed on the train from the back; he walked through each train carriage one by one. He knew what was going to happen - the two men had told him - so he walked towards the carriage where the General was sitting on the floor with his daughter in his hands. He knew she had died moments earlier and he had found her resting place in a pool of blood.

"The box..." he said, seeing the box. It all seemed so real. He bent forward and tried to touch it, but his hand passed straight through the metallic container. The General turned it over and he saw something that felt like a ten-tonne train hitting him; he knew instantly that the two mysterious men were part of this and he also knew how he fitted in to all of this. The symbol was different, but somehow the same; the two-headed wolf was antique, but unmistakable.

Then, seconds later, he found himself outside the train, as he watched it burning like an inferno. He turned his head to the side and saw the General and his family. They weren't burning, and it was just as they said. Peter turned towards the right and saw his grandfather looking back, with the General and his family looking straight at him and the other soldiers. They could see, unmistakably, that the General was not happy. The anger felt as hot as the burning train.

Then he saw the two mysterious men standing at the side of the forest as they looked towards the train and he walked towards them. He was angry. They hadn't told him everything and he needed answers to his questions. He tried to shout at them but no sound escaped his lips, only silence. He took a step forward and then another, but when he attempted the third step he stopped - it felt as if he was walking into an invisible wall.

He tried again, but his body refused to move. He felt like a statue frozen in time. And then total darkness covered him.

"Sir…" he heard in the darkness, a familiar voice. Then it sounded again: "Sir, wake up. The plane will be landing in one hour." He woke up from his deep sleep, and for a moment he was disoriented, not sure where he was. The smell of breakfast loomed in the air. He felt like he could eat a cow and jumped in straightaway. After finishing his breakfast the stewardess reminded him that she was keeping the suit for him. He hadn't forgotten about the suit, he was excited to get rid of his jeans and t-shirt. He got dressed into the expensive suit in a private compartment. He felt the imported material and the double stitched linings; it felt good and he certainly wouldn't mind living like this. But even so, he knew what he was going to do with the suit after the mission; he was going to sell it. The extra five hundred dollars would help him find his bearings.

In a way, he felt happy that his wife had left him for someone with money; he found comfort in knowing that his son would be looked after. His daydream was interrupted by the seatbelt sign being switched on. It was time.

He exited the room and walked over towards his seat; he had a distinct feeling that he was being watched. He turned around, but found himself staring down an empty compartment. All of a sudden he saw a man in a black leather jacket standing at the back of the first class compartment. This time he wasn't dreaming. Peter didn't know it, but this was the very same man who had been standing on the side of the road when the two mysterious men had pulled him over on the highway. The man in the black leather jacket turned abruptly, walked towards the business class compartment, and disappeared behind the curtains.

Peter sat down and looked out the window; the concrete jungle welcomed him with only twenty minutes to landing. He felt excited, but cautious at the same time. He reminded himself why he was on this plane.

They had killed two innocent people in Angola. This would clear his name. It had to.

The landing was normal, not that he would know as it was the first time he'd flown in such a big plane. The last time he flew was twenty years ago in an army helicopter, but hopefully after this he could forget about his past.

"Passport please!" the controller demanded, and Peter didn't hesitate to extend it.

"Peter Richards?" the passport controller read. There appeared to be a problem. Peter Richards had been flagged by the computer. Everybody knew what was going to happen next.

First, the customs officer double-checked the picture and the passport. When he confirmed the unverified documentation, step two was the supervisor. Peter knew these people were too good to be true, and blamed himself for the mistake.

"I should have known…"

"What's that?" the customs officer enquired.

Peter couldn't think of a single excuse and with the stuffy mood in the air he knew it was all over. The officer moved towards the phone. He could feel the handcuffs clamped on his wrists already. Then the customs officer was startled; only seconds away from picking up the phone and dialling security, his booth phone rang. He slowly picked it up and listened. The conversation was brisk and the officer nodded, as he acknowledged what the caller had said. Without saying a word he put the phone down.

"Welcome to the United States…" he announced, and allowed Peter to pass. Only the sound of the stamp in his passport broke the silence. Peter knew it was them, those mysterious men who followed him around. He remembered they had mentioned that they had people everywhere, even high up in some governments. He realised he'd wanted proof that their claims was true, and now he had it. So it was still possible to clear his name from the horrific events that had happened twenty years ago.

"Money can buy anything," he mumbled, as he walked towards the exit, passing people who had not been as lucky as he had been; the only thing left in their bags was the material that they were made from, with the rest of their stuff laying on the floor, as the customs officers worked their wonders. This was the first time he'd been in the United States and it felt inviting, almost as if everybody was happy that he was there. It was probably more due to the fact that he enjoyed the change in surroundings. The truth is that nobody knew him here – and that was the way he preferred it.

He strode towards a few taxis that stood on the side of the road, and carefully followed the instructions that were given to him when he'd received the expensive designer suit.

He waited for the car to pick him up where the taxis parked, but it had already been twenty minutes and no one had arrived to get him. Then, from the distance, a black vehicle drove slowly towards the taxi parking area; the car appeared to be gliding towards him.

The way it stood out amongst the other cars made him feel like the hunted with the intimidating black vehicle as the predator that drove straight at him. The black vehicle stopped right in front of him. But then nothing. It stood and idled.

Then the back door opened slowly and he recognised the man sitting in the back seat.

"Charles?" he questioned, as he saw his old friend. He was surprised but in a way not. He knew they were both involved twenty years ago.

"Hi Peter…" Charles greeted him casually. He for one was not surprised to see Peter as he knew the truth serum had something to do with everything. Peter climbed into the powerful black vehicle and they drove away towards Manhattan. But something bothered Peter while he spoke to Charles.

"Why both of us?" he asked Charles, while looking at the giant skyscrapers that filled the sidewalks. Charles couldn't answer as he didn't know.

"They said they would inform us soon," Charles reassured him, as he turned away from Peter. He took out a picture of his wife and children and stared at it for a few seconds while Peter turned back towards him and looked at the picture as well. His mood dipped to sadness. He had accepted the outcome of this mission. Even if he helped stop these killings by this unknown man and cleared his name he could never return to his family.

"Kicked out like a dog!" Peter mumbled.

Charles heard what he'd said and knew what he was talking about; it had been blasted all over the newspapers regarding the trial of his boss.

"I knew you weren't involved in the scandal." Charles assured him of his friendship and Peter appreciated this as he'd been feeling very depressed. Peter smiled and returned to looking at the skyscrapers that never seemed to end.

"We're here!" the driver announced, and halted the intimidating black vehicle in front of a tall glass building. Peter got out, looked up at the skyscraper, turned around and looked at the other buildings. He noticed something.

"They all have names!" Peter exclaimed, as he looked back at the giant glass building staring him in the face.

"What?" Charles asked, standing next to him and he also looked at the giant glass building. Charles asked again, but Peter didn't hear as he was still amazed by the size of this giant.

"The buildings all have names..." Peter stated again.

"Yes I can see that...what are you on about?" Charles replied, not really understanding what Peter was trying to say.

"Look...this one has only a number, number eight," Peter tried to explain what he saw, but by the time Peter tried to show him, Charles had already figured out what he was trying to show him.

"You're right, Building Eight."

They stood still for a while. It seemed so suspicious. All the buildings had large names printed on the walls of the skyscrapers; all except one - Building Eight.

The tall, dark tinted windows of the building revealed nothing except for a giant door that opened cavernously the moment they arrived. They were escorted by the driver of the black vehicle, but he stopped exactly seven feet into the building.

"Wait!" he called abruptly, "you need to be cleared. It will only take a few seconds, maybe minutes, sometimes a day or two," the driver explained.

They could see the person behind the front desk was busy with something, clicking away on the monitor in front of him. After a few seconds, he nodded.

"That was quick," the protector said, as he turned towards the few people standing next to the waiting area drinking coffee.

"You see them," he said again.

"They have been here for a week, and they are CIA."

While Peter and Charles walked towards the lift, they scoped out the two men standing on the side of the wall that led up to the lifts. They didn't notice it at first, but then they saw the automatic weapons sticking out from underneath their jackets.

"Guns and sunglasses..." Peter said with a grin, seeing the powerful weapon that almost bolted out from underneath the jacket. Charles turned his head towards Peter.

"What?" he asked while he tracked the lift coming down; only five floors remained before it reached the ground floor.

Peter also watched the lift, but he still didn't answer Charles. Then they saw four more men walking down the staircase in the far corner, walking towards them, but they weren't here for Peter and Charles. They walked straight past them towards an office in the corner. Peter glimpsed at the heavy weaponry they were carrying around with them.

"What are they hiding here...the President or something?"

Then for the first time, the driver said something, both disturbing and confusing at the same time. "You could say that Mr. Richards. They're all here for you and someone else you'll be meeting soon."

"Who?" Peter enquired. His curious nature meant he just had to ask.

"We call him 'the watcher,'" he said, as he opened the lift. They all got in. When the door closed, one of the men who had been standing in the lift when it arrived pressed his thumb against the panel of floor indicators.

He thought he needed to explain to Peter and his friend what was going on in this building, but he didn't; instead, he called out the floors as they passed. He started slowly,

'1..., 2..., 3..., 4..., 5..., 6th floor the FBI...7th floor CIA, and then they passed the Secret Service at floor number 8. Nobody ever goes past floor 8, they know the rules." This would be this first and only time they would be allowed to explain the rules to Peter; next time if they were invited back they would travel alone to the top floor.

"Never pass floor 8, never." At floor 9 the lift stopped just as it always did and issued a warning to the person inside to press the ground floor button now if they had made a mistake. After a few seconds the lift continued and stopped at floor number 10, and issued the same warning. Then a dark blue fluorescent light moved from side to side, scanning Peter along with all the other occupants in the lift.

"Scanning for weapons?" Charles asked, but that couldn't be the reason; they were the only ones not carrying any. The fact that they had been searched twice already suggested it could be for something else. Charles decided not to ask again; it seemed as if they weren't going to get an answer anyway.

"It's for something else," one of them said quickly, as he turned his head forward again.

"Who?" Peter asked, but there was no answer. They blatantly ignored him.

It didn't take long for the lift to arrive at its destination, as it passed all the floors and came to a halt at the last floor. The lights turned 'normal' and the lift door opened moments later.

The two friends peeked out of the lift and saw a large pentagon-shaped room with only a reception desk a few feet from the lift opening, situated in the middle of the room.

Peter walked out of the lift, followed by Charles a few steps behind him. The two stopped and looked back at the other three in the lift who they'd presumed would follow them, but they weren't moving, but just stared at Peter and Charles.

"We're not coming," the one said and he quickly added that they weren't allowed there; it was only for those who were invited.

The lift door closed with them still standing halfway between the lift door and the reception desk, not knowing what to do, they were perplexed and confused. The woman at the reception called them forward.

She opened a door at the side of one of the pentagon walls, and without hesitation, the two walked in.

Chapter 13

WE SEE WHAT WE NEED TO SEE

So here they were. They looked around, nearly blinded by a light shining from the corner of the room. Someone appeared as a silhouette from behind the blinding light. And then a voice called for them.

"Come closer..."

As the light dimmed, a white table with two chairs were revealed which they hadn't been able to see previously. The man that had called them sat down on a pure white leather chair and was joined by Peter and Charles, neither of whom knew what to expect.

It all started off fairly well and was friendly enough.

"Coffee?" he offered, and before they could answer the reception woman set down a tray with coffee and three cups. The man was the first to take a cup, pour coffee, and sip it.

"I just love coffee..." he said after a long sip. At first this strange man that was sitting at the white table appeared as if he'd lost a few marbles. Peter and Charles looked towards each other and smiled. They had expected a tight cold welcome, but instead they got a warm and kind of funny welcome. It made them feel at home, as they saw this man with his open face, who seemed fairly easy to communicate with.

"You must be Peter Richards," he commented and Peter nodded, but he wasn't finished, "I'm sorry to hear about your friend, Johannes Roland." He then turned his attention towards Charles le Roux.

"Do you know why we elected you to come here?" he asked. Charles paused and reflected on the odd way he had asked the question, almost as if he wasn't supposed to be there.

"Anyway, in the end, you are both important to us." He walked towards a window at the side of the room that overlooked Central Park, turned around again and walked back towards Peter and Charles, who were still enjoying the good coffee. He sat down. Someone walked in from a side door carrying a large black book, and placed it on the table.

The book looked old, really old, as if it was from the sixteenth century. Peter noticed the insignia engraved on the front of the book. He had seen it before and he bent forward to get a closer look. There it was, just as he remembered it, the two-headed wolf. Charles, on the other hand, hadn't seen it before; in fact, he was wondering why a modern office like this would have such old books that were practically falling apart.

"It looks almost two hundred years old..." remarked Charles.

"Nine hundred..."

"What?"

"It's nine hundred years old," the man stated matter-of-factly.

They stared at the book, amazed and curious at the same time. Where would they get a nine hundred year old book, this odd dark looking book? Somehow the symbols had a meaning. It could only mean that the lone wolf was always aware.

He made them sit down. Peter and Charles didn't know it yet, but the time had come for them to swear an oath.

"I never introduced myself..." said the man, and he was right. From the moment they arrived downstairs there had been secrecy surrounding them. They had been told half of the story, and nothing else. VERITAS they called him, but that wasn't a name, it was just something they called him, a nickname.

"I'm..."

The suspense was killing them; the more time passed the more they wanted to know.

"Carl..." he announced, which didn't sound as spectacular as they'd imagined. In fact, the name sounded normal, like a next-door neighbour.

Carl was just an abbreviation, however. His name was actually Carlito Mario Columbus.

Many had wondered how the book had made it to America.

"Here, look. I'll show you where my great uncle signed...then I'll explain why you must also sign this book," Carl explained, as he paged through the book to October 12, 1492.

"Columbus Day!" Charles said.

Charles wasn't just a lab rat; he was a history buff as well. He knew many things that most people didn't care about at all.

"Yes..." Carl said and they looked towards the signature. It was unmistakable. Then again something bothered Charles - why would he sign the book twice? And who had given the book to Columbus?

"Henry VII of England?"

"Yes, he gave the book to Columbus."

Everything was just unbelievable. Carl continued, "If you receive the book, you sign it, and the warden of the book will receive a sign so that he knows when it's time to sign it off to someone else." So the custodians were Columbus and King Henry VII and there was another signature they'd seen before. This troubled Peter Richards. The two men he'd met in South Africa had explained to him what had happened to his grandfather. So why would Adolf Hitler sign the book twice?

"That means he was the custodian," Charles admitted impulsively.

Carl turned towards the two, and for a moment wanted to tell them everything, but he decided against it. They wouldn't believe him anyway.

"All in good time," said Carl. He turned away and picked up a pen, placing it in front of them. They weren't all that comfortable with signing it, but then again seeing the names that had already signed it, kind of made them feel honoured to have their signatures in a nine hundred year old book. Peter picked up the pen and examined it.

"A hundred years old?" he questioned, as he looked at the pen. Carl grinned, and then laughed faintly to himself.

"No, 99 cents...bought it at the corner shop," Carl chuckled. Somehow they didn't believe him, but they'd made up their minds and they were going to willingly sign the book.

"It's done," said Carl. Two men strode into the penthouse office and then towards the table where the book was lying open upon it. Wearing almost pure white gloves, they closed the book. One took the pen and placed it into a glass box container, and sealed it in front of them. Peter looked at the odd way they were handling the pen and smiled. He could sense that Carl certainly had a sense of humour.

"Now I really know that pen is not from the corner shop. May I ask where it's going?"

"The book stays in my vault..." Carl replied and winked towards a giant door that opened on the side of the wall. Hidden behind it was the safe Carl has spoken about. He turned back towards Peter and glanced at the pen neatly placed in a briefcase.

"...but the pen will be transported to Fort Knox." He didn't smile and they could see he was serious. "Fort Knox?" Peter asked. He didn't receive an answer. The time for chitchat had passed, and it was now time for action.

Carl explained to them the terrible ordeal they would have to endure; at the end, they would walk out with a hefty sum of money. And even though Carl explained the job at hand, they were more interested in the pen being whisked away out of the office.

What Peter and Charles didn't know was that each pen was kept secure and safe in Fort Knox. Each time someone signed the book, the pen was then secured back in a safe place, and that place was Fort Knox. At Fort Knox the pens were neatly stacked in an enclosed room, alongside other gold coloured pens, some dated from 2004, 2000, 1923 and even all the way back to the year 0962. Alongside the pens was an opened box with an engraving on it, a two-headed wolf. If you looked over the rim of the box there were twenty golden rings that stared back at you, and unmistakably they belonged in the box with the insignia of the wolf on it, locked up safely in the most secure vault in the world, protected by its own army. The rings were a symbol of the power of the Company; one had to earn it to receive one, just like Carl and a few other lucky men.

"Do you believe in God?" Carl asked unexpectedly, and for a moment, total silence descended upon the room. Peter and Charles stared at each other. What had instigated Carl to ask such a question? It was a very important question that he had to ask; after all, they knew the stories of the evil General and in his footsteps, the devil that followed. The problem was, they had heard the stories and seen pictures of the aftermath, but they hadn't yet looked evil in the eye, those dark black eyes. Peter turned towards a painting against the wall; it's odd, he thought, that he didn't notice it when they walked in, only now he saw the shield with the two-headed wolf on it. He was reminded of what he had wanted to ask Carl the moment they met.

"What is this Company all about?"

Carl paused mid-sentence and looked towards Peter, who by now felt rather uncomfortable. Peter apologised for asking the question while Carl continued, explaining something else. But Peter decided that he had nothing to fear and he needed an answer; he asked again. He knew that there was some sort of explanation for all the paranormal activity, the book and the pens, and what about the names in the book like Columbus, Hitler, former presidents and moments earlier, his name and his friend Charles?

Peter asked the question in such a direct and forceful manner that Carl couldn't ignore it this time. He stepped closer to Peter, and for a few seconds he looked him straight in the eye and nodded a few times. He decided that they actually did have the right to know. Carl knew they wouldn't understand, but soon they would have to face the evil riding the trains, that was killing innocent people. But were they really so innocent. Are we all really innocent?

Carl turned towards the penthouse window, put on sunglasses; not to block out the sun however, but rather to see something else. The sunglasses revealed negative energy and the presence of evil that the General brought to the city. There was a luminescent light that almost blinded Carl. After a few seconds his eyes adjusted and revealed the forces building and moulding into shape through the sky scrapers like snakes twisting towards unsuspecting prey.

"Enough, the clouds are building over the city..." said Carl, but of course he was the only one who saw the clouds snaking through the skyscrapers, doubling in size every few minutes. Peter and Charles looked at each other and then turned towards the window again. Of course, they didn't have glasses to see the clouds forming along the skyline. They knew what he was talking about, but just hadn't seen it yet. The only thing they could see was the sun shining as it did on a hot summer's day.

Carl, still stared at the self-propelled clouds and pressed a little red button on the side of the window. A darkened screen slowly dropped from the top of the window.

He needed them to see; it was the only way they would truly believe.

When the screen lowered towards the bottom of the window, there it was, as clear as daylight - the clouds grinding, moulding like energy, building up ready to release.

There was that one thing Carl had wanted to tell them earlier and in a way, they deserved to know. But not now. First they had to successfully complete their mission and only then would they be able to see the truth, the reality that we lived with every day. For some of us, it was a good thing that we couldn't see.

Only society knew the truth, and Carl Mario, one of the masters, held the key.

Chapter 14

HE'S ALREADY HERE

They left the building silently, followed closely by Carl. They didn't say a word to each other; there was way too much confusion. Carl opened the car door for them and they got in. They thanked him for the hospitality. Carl closed the door, and looked at them through the open window. This bothered them. He seemed incredibly eager about the trip, and by the way he spoke in the building, they assumed he was going to join them in the vehicle, but this wasn't the case. Carl leaned against the door slightly, still staring at them through the open window; he seemed as if he wanted to say something. Perhaps he was about to give them an excuse for not coming with them, but they both knew it was something else. He was an important man so it seemed logical that he wouldn't be part of the mission and so far, he'd handled the whole ordeal in a warm and friendly way. So maybe his last words would be inspiring. Then they got the shock of their lives.

"Don't come back here again, if you do...I will kill you myself," Carl said with no visible emotion on his face. They kept very quiet as they knew that this was not something to be taken lightly.

Carl closed the door of the black monster while Peter and Charles sat motionless in the back seat. They were stunned. The driver of the black monster looked in his rear view mirror and turned to face them.

"Only with an invitation!" the driver said and they knew that what he said was true. Never visit building number eight without an invitation! This was the one rule that should never be broken. There were way too many secrets in that building - especially on the top floor.

They drove off into the busy New York City streets with only one day left until they would come face to face with the real reason they were here; Ferdinand Schultz.

Meanwhile the preparations were going according to plan; the rotten apple in the team, the one who had been with the Company the longest, Special Agent Martin Davis, also readied himself for the task ahead. He knew that soon he would get his invitation; it didn't matter where he was or even if he tried to hide; the invitation would reach him in the form of 'the ticket'.

Special Agent Josh Williams, who part of the joint task team, seemed relaxed; he was just back from his holiday but he could sense that something was wrong with Agent Martin Davis. The Major wasn't himself as he scratched around in boxes, looking for something he'd misplaced and not being able to find it was driving him insane. In frustration he tossed the boxes all over the back of the truck. Agent Josh Williams decided to confront him. Although he would be out of place, it was necessary. His attitude was making the new recruits worry, and at a time like this, it was critical that everything worked precisely according to plan. For them, worried agents meant mistakes *would* happen.

The new recruits hadn't found out about the other dead agents yet, they were here only for the money. In his haste to find the item he'd misplaced, Agent Martin Davis bumped the crime scene photos from New York City in 2009 over. Even as they picked up the photos, they still couldn't come to a conclusion about the events that had unfolded. When a new recruit recognised one of the names on the dossier, Agent Franklin, that would be when trouble came.

Special Agent Josh Williams started reading the short report, while the Major still tried to locate the item he'd been looking for. The recruit took the DVD and placed it in the player. He started to watch what had gone wrong in 2009. He had heard about the 'New York massacre' but had never seen any evidence. It was hidden away and labelled 'TOP SECRET'.

They started to watch.

"My daddy will not be happy... you are not on the list," and at that precise moment, her daddy became aware of him, the intruder on his train. They knew the rules; never cross the line if your name wasn't on the list.

"You are going to die now..." the little girl stated matter-of-factly to Agent Franklin, and then in front of his eyes her beautiful school dress transformed into a bloody red dress. There was no turning back now - it had begun.

Agent Franklin couldn't think of anything to say. He froze up and the control room witnessed a spike in his heart rate. It almost jumped through the roof.

He had to ask her something while he scanned the room, as he feared for his life.

"Is General Schultz coming...?" he asked her, hoping for some help.

She looked at him almost surprised. How could he know her father's name? But she answered him.

"No," she paused with a brief smile, *"he is already here."* In the control room, Agent Franklin's heart rate stopped instantaneously with his blood splattering all over the carriage floor, followed by his severed upper body. The bottom half of his body remained in the same spot.

Then a second later, gravity took over and the bottom half of his body fell forward like a sack of potatoes, spewing his guts from his body, the momentum making it slide a few feet to right in front of Agent Johnson.

The images on the DVD were horrifying; the two new recruits knew nothing about this. Again, it was Special Agent Martin Davis who'd decided to keep it to himself, and he believed that keeping this a secret would give him the upper hand.

Major Davis stopped, as he realised that he'd given his own game away. At the very same moment, he found what he had been looking for, as he held the item up to the light.

At first, they couldn't see what he was holding up, but when the back light dimmed slightly, they saw it; the ticket he'd kept from the Cape Town mission.

They were stunned. It was the first time they'd seen a ticket in real life; the previous time had been in a picture. But they still didn't know who the ticket belonged to, and their interest shifted from the crime scene pictures to the train ticket.

"You talk, or we walk!" one of the new recruits stated emphatically, as he placed the crime scene pictures neatly on the table. This was bad news for the Major; if they walked, the other four new recruits would also walk. If they resigned, he would be left with nothing.

He had to do something. Without them, the mission would be dead and he knew that shortly after that, he would be too. "Wait..." he faltered reluctantly. He knew he had to tell the truth. His life depended on it.

He sighed and then turned towards them, pulled out a chair from underneath the desk and sat down with the ticket in this hand.

There was no getting out of this; the only thing that would keep them there was the truth.

He put the ticket down on the table, picked up a black light and called them over. He switched the black light on.

For the first few seconds their eyes adjusted to the violet light. And then a picture became clear. It was a picture they'd seen many times before, but this one had the text printed underneath, the two headed wolf was secretly hidden away from visible sight. But they knew that. It was the other thing on the ticket that shocked them - the bar code.

"Scan it..." one said. One of the new agents grabbed the scanner, but the Major stopped him, as the agent had grabbed the wrong scanner.

"Use the one with the wolf!" barked Major Davis. The agent followed his instructions and picked up the correct scanner.

"Then turn up the volume."

They were stunned. This was all new to them.

This was the sound of evil that the Company had hidden away for years. It was frightening. There were a thousand voices speaking at once, but in Latin; they couldn't understand a thing.

Then Agent Williams offered to help with the translation. He'd been with the Company for ten years, and even he hadn't heard it before.

"Help us!" Agent Williams translated, and the words replayed themselves over and over again, "Help us!"

They were all the trapped souls, Agent Davis explained to them; he knew this as his father had been one of them.

Then, it became blatantly obvious that the Company was responsible to a certain degree. Agent Davis turned the ticket over so that the new recruits and Agent Williams could see it clearly. Agent Davis mumbled something, which nobody heard the first time. Then he said it again, and this time they all heard it.

"They could have stopped it all along..." he lied. He was such a good liar that they all believed him, except for one. Agent Williams, who was standing close to Agent Davis, didn't believe a word of it.

Agent Williams walked closer and inspected the ticket himself. He took the light out of the Major's hand, seeing the 'Admit One'. He shone the light over the ticket, and then again, the bar code appeared. He did this a few more times, and wondered how it was even possible; they'd never seen it before and yet they'd tested it with all sorts of lights, including black lights.

He turned the light over and it all became clear as he saw the two headed wolf insignia on the side of the flashlight.

"Their technology..." the Major said as he reminded himself of the chance he'd taken. This was only one of the many secrets that he'd been keeping for so long.

Agent Williams took a step back and placed the ticket and the light on the table. He had gone from conservativeness to curiosity in seconds.

"Where did you get the light?" he enquired.

"Building eight. I was invited nine years ago."

It was obvious the company had given him the black light. He knew that it was something he would need in the future. When he tested the light he had made the discovery, and it made him angry.

Then again, he knew the insignia of the Company; if you didn't need to know, you didn't need to know. But they still didn't know that the ticket belonged to him.

Not far from them someone listened in to every word they were saying; Carlito Mario, the master of building eight. He looked at the monitor and watched the four in the truck; but he sat very quietly. In his head he was deciding what to do with Agent Davis who had broken so many of their rules, especially the first rule; 'Conceal forever, never reveal'.

Carl picked up his phone; it was time to make the call.

He hadn't dialled the number in a while. In fact, it had been nine years ago. The last time he'd dialled the number, it had been about the very same person that we was calling about today; Agent Martin Davis.

The phone rang on a different continent. Even though it was long distance it didn't matter what time of day it was, someone always answered.

An old black wooden phone started to ring in an even older stone room. A man walked closer to the phone and a second person with a white coat walked into the room and answered in his purest Italian, asking who it was. He received an answer quickly.

"New York..." Carl answered.

"Yes."

"It's me," Carl said, but they already knew.

Carl himself had only been invited to the Vatican City once, thirty years ago. The same rules applied to him - never return if you are not invited –they were so covert that not even the Pope knew what was going on.

Carl explained why he was phoning, but there was no need for explanations; they already knew what had happened; their video feeds ran right around the world.

They agreed that Agent Davis was no longer an asset, but rather a nuisance.

It had gone on for too long, the man in the white coat turned to his left and nodded to his assistant, who left the room without any questions, as he closed the door behind him.

Now, alone in the room, he sighed and said decisively, "It's in your hands now." Then he turned around and walked past the two mysterious men who'd been with Peter right from the start. The two men nodded to the man in the white coat and opened the door for him to exit. It was a rather mysterious room; not a picture on the wall, not a plant in the corner, just the table with the phone standing on it like a pedestal.

Only the light on the wall revealed that there was life in the room. Slowly the door closed and the two mysterious men disappeared, just like the telephone cable that led to an unplugged wall socket.

Chapter 15

CLOUD OF EVIL

Peter looked out his hotel window. It was a beautiful sight. He was reminded once again of what his life was like before his boss and the company he worked for had folded, and before Johannes and this case. He tried to place his options on the table, but he was still left with nothing. At least there was one thing he could rely on; the fact that his wife had married a rich man and he knew that his son would be looked after.

The only thing he hoped was that his son never found out about the two children they'd killed in Angola.

That was the way he'd made the deal - do this job and the slate would be wiped clean. By the looks of it this highly secretive Company had people all over the world. He wondered what Carl meant when he said, "Things people don't need to see." Perhaps he meant the fact that people turned a blind eye when somebody did something wrong? Peter was daydreaming when Charles walked up behind him.

So far, everything had been amazing; they had travelled to the city that never sleeps, and to top it all off, they had a room with a view over Central Park.

"I could buy a car with the rates they charge here."

"It's free..." someone said from behind them; it was room service. At first they wondered how he had got in. The remark 'it's free' enticed them to question him. This hotel was so exclusive that people had to be placed on a waiting list for months for a room. They didn't understand how it could be free, what with it being one of the top hotels in the city.

"This floor belongs to your Company," and he walked towards the door. As he looked around the door he saw three armed guards walking the hallway, and then said to them, "You two must be important!"

They laughed; but they were uncertain as to what he meant. They asked him about his comment and his explanation is short and to the point. The rooms were always full for months, but two days ago, everybody had just left.

"...and I mean everybody, two senators and get this..." he bent slightly forward as he had to make sure nobody was listening in, and then he continued, "...even the VP left here as if the building was on fire."

"VP?" Peter asked.

He was the one who was laughing now and explained, "They received one phone call and the Vice President of the United States was out of here in less than half an hour!"

Peter laughed. "That doesn't make us important!" But he had to admit that having the whole floor to themselves was fairly impressive.

"You're not alone!" the bellhop interjected. Now they were confused, as a few moments ago he'd said they were alone on the floor.

"I said you were the only guests here in the hotel," he said. He could see Peter and Charles were confused, so he decided that he was going to show them what he was talking about and he led them out the door.

He was right. There they were, two lining the hallway and one at the lift. Then they turned their attention towards the room across the way. They couldn't get a clear view so they took another step forward. In the room they saw computers, televisions, security screens, and about five heavily armed men in black suits sitting, watching, ready to protect them.

"Wow..." Peter mumbled. Just as a picture says a thousand words, this time a word explained a thousand pictures.

Then the phone rang in Peter's room.

Peter and Charles walked back into their room. The room service guy felt like he'd overstayed his welcome and left, as he closed the door behind him.

Charles answered the phone this time.

"Yes..." he said, as he stood still for a moment to listen to everything the person on the other side had to say.

"What glasses?" Charles asked, as he looked around towards the table to which the person on the other side had directed him. He was sure there had been nothing on the table moments ago.

"Okay...," he said, as he put down the phone on the side table. Peter also saw the sunglasses lying on the table.

"He wants us to put the glasses on and look towards the park," Charles said, as he walked toward the table, opened a glass box and removed the glasses.

Peter laughed when he saw the logo on the side of the sunglasses.

"At least they're stylish."

Charles shook his head, put on the sunglasses and picked up the phone before he turned towards the window facing the park.

They both wondered what could be so important that they'd got a special delivery and phone call from Carl. Then, moments later, their question was answered.

But the moment Charles looked up the smile dropped from his face just like the phone that bounced a couple of times before coming to rest against the wall cabinet. Charles had wanted to say more, but what he saw had made him drop the phone. Peter knew something was wrong and quickly put on the sunglasses that Charles had handed him.

"What does this mean?" Peter wondered, as he saw the clouds fumbling and rolling forward, snaking down towards the building, the cloud screamed in a thousand Latin voices - "Help us!" By the looks of it, it was heading straight towards their room!

Peter then picked up the phone and without pretence insisted, "What does this mean?" Carl heard him clearly but didn't give an explanation.

"You two are invited back to building eight," he stated calmly.

There was silence, as Peter and Charles, and the rest of the people on the hotel floor looked on as the giant snake cloud headed right in the direction of their hotel room.

"The invitation is immediate...and I suggest you hurry, they are coming for you..."

"They...who are they?" Peter asked. He looked at Charles.

But his question was answered with silence and a dead tone in his ear.

Carlito Mario had already put the phone down and was busy looking at the two mysterious men who had made the deal with Peter and Charles.

"Will they make it?" Carl glanced at them, hoping for a 'yes' answer. He knew it was far more serious than Peter and Charles could ever have imagined.

"It's not up to us..." the one said and the other one nodded at his remark.

He sighed, and then turned towards them.

"Can't you intervene?" Carl asked, but the two men had already left the room.

Back at the hotel, Peter and Charles were getting ready to leave, but they had absolutely no idea what was about to happen to them in two minutes time. There was a knock on the door and one of the security guards from the hallway walked in carrying something they hadn't worn in years; two top-of-the-range bulletproof vests.

"Really? For a cloud?" Charles said, finding this rather funny. However, the security guard was not amused.

"The cloud is a guide; it's what you can't see..." he was interrupted by gunfire streaming down the hallway.

"They are here and they are after you!" He still held the bulletproof vest up for them.

"We will protect you!" He then forced the vests against their bodies while the sound of gunfire rambled on not far away from them.

This time they didn't argue and put the vests on quickly.

"I don't understand!" Charles said while Peter helped him put the vest on.

But there was no time for an explanation; well, not now, with two guards already dead.

They opened the hotel room door and were 'welcomed' by ten heavily armed guards.

The moment they stepped into the hallway the guards flanked them like a cocoon, and offered safe, total protection – at least for the time being. The gunfight hadn't reached them yet, but they could feel the tension in the air.

The group walked forward about twenty paces and then stopped, not by their own accord, but by the person who sat in the control room monitoring the cameras on every floor. Peter and Charles were crammed together like an over-filled jar, but they recognised what their protectors were doing. They themselves had the same counter-insurgence training; even though it was years ago, they still remembered it.

Then there was dead silence, not a shot was fired.

It could be over; whoever it was had failed in less than five minutes and for now they stood quietly. It was so quiet that you could hear the chronograph watches ticking away the seconds, then screams echoed down the hallway followed by two gunshots; the screaming stopped, and still they had no idea what was going on.

The dark truth was that the evil was roaming the building, like a virus attacking the body; its target was the two unlikely heroes trapped between ten heavily armed men that were there to protect them, no matter what.

The room service guy had said they were very important, but this was ridiculous!

"Pawns…" one of the protectors remarked.

Peter looked towards him unsure as to what he was suggesting. He opened his pocket and gave him a hand radio communicator.

This was a good idea. Now at least they would know what was going on.

"Chess," the protector followed up on his first remark.

Then Peter and Charles understood, but it worried them; if the pawns could kill these highly trained protectors…

"What will happen if the knights arrive or the bishops?" Peter asked, but the problem was not miscommunication, or clever synonyms.

The pawns were the followers of the darkening, those that worshipped the evil one, some in secret. This was the way they preferred it.

They would hide away until they were needed, hiding in plain sight such as hotdog vendors, executives and even law enforcement.

The General's evil deeds had awoken these normal loving family men and women and so far, the protectors had managed to stop twenty from breaking down the doors on the ninth floor. This was the floor that Peter and Charles were on, at the moment huddled together like a flock of sheep forced into a barn.

The problem was that this was not a farm and they were not sheep; they were men.

Then the radio blared; two dead on the first floor, and another on the fifth floor.

"The knights are coming..." the operator at the monitors said. He could see them clearly driving up to the building in their possessed vehicles. After the monitor operator announced it over the radio, Peter turned his head towards a clicking sound at his side; one of the protectors had started shaking the moment he heard that the knights were coming! The sight of the protector shaking made him worried, very worried.

The knights, they were few, but they were effective *and* deadly.

"Knights?" Charles asked.

"Demons that are living on earth...we need to be quiet now!" the protector answered quickly.

'People see what they need to see,' that was what Carl had said.

People always thought the game of 'Chess' had been made up by someone a few decades ago.

The truth was it was based on fact; good versus evil. Like a door, it swung both ways. The followers were the pawns. The knights were those destined for a calling; they went where they were needed.

Then there were the bishops, who monitored activities around the world.

"Like Carlito Mario?" Peter asked the protector.

"Yes...a bishop," he whispered his answer.

The gunfire started again, interrupting the conversation. They moved forward towards the corner of the hallway, following the instructions of the man behind the monitor.

They looked left and then right, but saw nothing. So far, they had been guided to perfection by the man behind the monitor. They had two options, left or right; one that went down the fire escape and the other that went down the lift.

"Fire escape is a go!" they heard, and then they moved towards the fire escape quickly, that was just thirty feet away from them.

The knights were still outside; it was almost as if they were waiting for something. There were five of them in total; they all looked up at the building and then towards each other. They didn't seem to like each other; maybe the promise of immortality to the one that accomplished the job lingered in their demon minds.

Between them and the front door, the world went on; nobody even lifted an eyebrow towards them.

People see what they need to see, that is what Carl said.

Chapter 16

THE FIGHT BEGINS

Everybody carried on with their business, buying, walking, and talking on cell phones, oblivious to what was happening right in front of them, unaware of the five knights that were still waiting outside the hotel, standing tall and strong and waiting to enter. They hadn't been cleared for entry yet. They were waiting. They also had to follow the rules. If they entered before the time was right, they would disintegrate from the paranormal force field around the hotel, designed specifically to stop only them.

Now there were only four; there was one who couldn't restrain his eagerness and he disintegrated in less than a second. This time a few people saw the dust cloud, but were completely oblivious to what had happened.

The knights looked on and were pleased at the destruction of one of their own. While they waited, the followers still streamed into the building, one by one as they tried to prove their loyalty. After a few minutes all of the so-called followers had made it to the ground floor of the hotel; they, on the other hand, weren't affected by the invisible supernatural force field.

The remaining four knights became aware of something and turned towards the side street.

Something disturbed them, but they couldn't see anything, it was a feeling. All they could see was an empty street; but then from afar, a car approached. As soon as the sun reflected on it, it seemed to disappear.

The four remaining knights, who hadn't shown any interest up until now, were nervous and kept their eyes on the approaching vehicle. They were uncomfortable with the uninvited guests, showing their dissatisfaction by hissing and growling like angry cats at each other, clearly afraid of something in the vehicle.

The vehicle stopped about twenty feet from the entrance of the hotel, but nobody got out. Whoever was inside was clearly disturbing the four onlookers.

All of a sudden they turned towards the entrance. They could feel it was time to go inside, and as one, they walked forward and disappeared inside the main door.

Back on the ninth floor, Charles was getting restless; they had been in the same place now for almost five minutes. Both Peter and Charles were listening to the radio communications. So far the news was good. Well, that was what the radio communicator said, so who were they to disagree with him?

Unfortunately, he was wrong; he could only see half of what was going on.

Twenty seconds earlier, before the four darkened knights had entered the building, the ground floor cameras switched off for a millisecond, changing the picture feed. The picture was restored, and showed the ground floor clearly. The operator noticed something odd. Charles felt restless. He'd been in the same position now for almost five minutes, down on one knee, and his legs were beginning to feel the strain...

The camera that had switched off for that millisecond was certainly no accident. The order came from one of the darkened ones. And he had help, though not from one of his own. It was from someone else, and that someone else was someone on the inside.

"Team four, ground floor. Breach in five seconds..." instructed the team leader of group four, who reported to the monitor operator. Five seconds later the locked ground floor door blasted into pieces.

"Door breached…" the team leader reported again. His five man team quickly secured the hallway. The malfunction with the monitors worried the controller and he checked his system for a possible problem, but he couldn't find anything wrong with it. He looked at the monitor displaying the time ticking away as normal - not even a second out. He then shook off the feeling and continued with monitoring; they needed him as he was their eyes and ears.

"Team four, code three…" the controller asked for their location. He was certain they'd said ground floor, but he couldn't see a thing on the monitor, and from his side everything looked clear.

"Team four respond!"

"Ground floor, hallway delta is secure!"

The monitor operator double checked the hallway delta, but still no team four and no busted open door. On his monitor, he still saw the locked door. Then it went from bad to worse for the camera operator.

First it had been the cameras. Then someone cut the radio communication. "Team four respond!" the operator called frantically; he was now absolutely sure that something was wrong. Without communication, they were sitting ducks. However, the team leader of group four had already ascertained that there was a problem.

"Our communication has been sabotaged," the team leader reported. He turned towards his men, took off his headgear and shortly thereafter, they followed his actions.

They knew they couldn't go back; the hotel was sound-proof which didn't make things any easier. Screaming for help wouldn't help them as outside the hotel it was 'business as usual'. Everybody on the outside world was completely oblivious to the gunfire and the odd explosions that were happening inside the hotel. That was how it should be and how things would be; *they must never know.*

One by one their headgear dropped to the floor; they knew someone was responsible for their soon to be dead bodies that would be lying on the floor. By the time their heads would hit the ceramic floor, nobody would ever know.

For now they were still alive and eager to stay that way. They smiled away their fear and readied their firearms for the last fight. They could run away but they knew their duties. Unlike the rest of the world, they could see what was going on in the world around them and the four knights that awaited them on the ground floor.

The team leader turned around and tried to encourage them, but he could only think of one thing to say; "Even if we are mopped from the floor, they will know what we did."

Outside, the vehicle that was parked a few feet from the entrance to the hotel still remained stationary, doors shut, with the darkened windows obstructing what lay dormant inside. It was only the idling engine that suggested there was someone inside.

Team four started moving down, dead quiet in their tactical formation, not even a hint of a footstep, but they knew their death was imminent, just around any corner. The only thing they knew for sure was that there were four evil knights - that was the last true message they'd received. With every second that passed the sound of their breathing intensified. Adrenaline rushed through their systems, which made them sharp, alert and ready.

"Keep the faith!" the group leader encouraged. He of all people knew that bullets were only half the fight. Just around the corner there was someone waiting for them, as if they knew they were coming. He had help; they didn't have the ability to know. The only thing they could feel was fear. But in this building, it meant nothing; their abilities were clouded by faith.

Then the fight began...

The first two hundred or so bullets flew down the hallway, entering one of the knight's bodies with absolute precision, but still he stood his ground, staring straight at them. The protectors then began to doubt themselves. Again the group leader shouted, "Keep the faith!" Seeing them brittle, he had to say something; a human against this half-life, dropping the odd stun and grenade alongside the evil onlooker. This had an effect, and his half-human body started to show signs of fractures, his arm ripped into pieces by the throw of the grenade.

Whatever they were doing seemed to work. Every foot they won made the protectors more dangerous and more accurate. They were getting the sense of victory in the air, while the evil knight walked back, trying to cover himself from the onslaught of bullets with his only remaining arm. The group passed a hallway that was linked to the main hallway, and there, looking at them while they shot their way through was another one, just looking. He knew the other knight was competition; he would only intervene once the other evil knight was shredded and unable to continue.

However, after a few seconds, he reconsidered. He knew they could over-power them; they could fight it out later.

He started walking casually towards the protectors from behind. They didn't see him approaching.

The last protector didn't feel a thing; it was over in one movement. They weren't kidding about the mopping up of pieces. The blood splatter on the hallway wall reflected the brute force that was used against the defenceless protector. By the time they realised that he was pasted against the wall, it was too late. The knight that had done the deed was already gone. They were way too fast. Normally they were almost invisible, but with the teams' specialised glasses they could see them. But even so, if they approached from the back, the glasses couldn't help them.

The team knew the knights were capable of this; their evil made them powerful and fast, but even so, they weren't unstoppable. A well-placed bullet or grenade would bring them to their knees.

The evil knights had a powerful ability. The one thing they needed the most - although worthless in this hotel - was the ability to sense fear. The hotel jammed this ability. If you looked carefully at the hotel helicopter landing zone on the top of the building, and then looked beyond the large 'H', you could see the lone wolf with two heads, one looking up and the other downwards. It was the hotel's insignia.

It was a sad moment for team four. But while they had lost a good team member, they had succeeded in their attempt to stop one of the evil visitors in his tracks.

They walked away from their friend and colleague, as he was now in a better place. It was better to leave him in peace.

Then their attention turned to the half-dead, half-human, and all the evil on the floor.

They knew they couldn't kill him, only subdue him, but he couldn't harm them now; without a body he was powerless.

The team leader turned towards the lifeless demon on the floor; only the eyes remained aware.

"Bad luck..." the team leader mocked, but then he noticed something; a small device on the ear of the severed head.

He had seen this device before; it was a communication device belonging to the Company. It wasn't possible, he thought to himself. He slowly bent over the head and picked up the device, he saw that it was still working as a small blue light shone on the side of the earpiece.

"It's ours..." he showed the rest of the team.

"Sir, are you sure?"

He didn't say anything and turned the device sideways so that they could see the insignia on the side - the two headed wolf was clear. It was unmistakable. While they stood in silence he could hear a sound permeating from the device; he brought it closer to his ear and listened. He took a few seconds to take it all in; he listened to the instructions that were given by someone, but by whom? He didn't recognise the voice.

It was time to intervene.

"Who are you?" he interrupted the voice on the other side. Silence followed. After a few seconds the voice on the other side replied, "You are all going to die."

The team leader thought for a moment, and then smiled.

"So be it..." he said, then disconnected. They were here for a reason and following orders was a priority. For now the orders were to protect Peter and Charles, at all costs, and with only four men left they needed a strategy. They had no communication, no back up, and no idea where the dark ones were.

Outside, the vehicle that had pulled up earlier was still parked in the same place with the engine still idling. Whoever they were had angered the evil knights, but they were more afraid than anything else.

Meanwhile Peter and Charles were still concealed in the cocoon of bodyguards, still waiting for an 'okay' from the radio operator. But the radio was dead quiet.

The team was concerned; it had been ten minutes without a single word from the radio.

Then the team leader called the controller. Nothing.

In the radio control room, the radio operator lay dead. He'd been assassinated from behind with a single shot to the head. On his seat sat someone else. This someone else was definitely not one of the protectors and was definitely not supposed to be there.

This traitor was listening to every word the teams were saying. They were all calling for the controller, but none of them were able to communicate with the other teams patrolling the hotel.

He decided he had amused them long enough and switched off all communication, jamming the signals. They now knew with absolute certainty that there had been a breach in the hotel.

The traitor decided it was time to go and walked out the control room. He turned around and quoted something, but no sound left his mouth.

There was something the traitor had forgotten, and from a couple of thousand miles away, someone was watching the images that were streaming to him. The surroundings were old, yet familiar, and between the fortified thick walls he saw exactly what the traitor was doing. He looked at the monitor for a few seconds. He put his tea down on the table next to him and then got up and walked towards the corner of the room, followed by two heavily armed protectors. Their weapons weren't visible, but they were there.

He opened a door leading to the hallway and walked on a bit further to a door he had visited before. The protector opened it, waited for him to enter, and then closed the door behind him, guarding the door from outside. This was a mysterious room; not a picture on the wall nor a plant in the corner, just the table with the phone on it like a pedestal in the middle of the old stone room. Then the old black wooden phone rang in an old fashioned ring tone. The sound didn't leave the room as it was embedded deep underneath the Vatican City. Silence filled the hallway corridor, the two protectors stood like two statues alongside the door.

It was time for him to answer the call. He knew who the traitor was and it was time to inform the rest of them. "For mankind" he said and picked up the phone.

Chapter 17

SECRETS IN THE VATICAN CITY

It had been decided. The man in the white coat picked up the phone and said only two things. The one wasn't particularly important; the message was, 'Please return after the mission'. They needed to discuss something. "It's important, but not now." And then there was the second thing. This was the important one; the traitor was Special Agent Martin Davis who had run this mission and many others. He was the one responsible for loads of deaths in the hotel, but it was expected, they had to protect them.

"Take him out," the man in the white coat said and dropped his head slightly. He felt ashamed.

This wasn't what he wanted, but it was necessary.

Then the voice on the other side replied; "Do they know?" Carl asked, meaning the two mysterious men who were always everywhere.

"They do now."

"He betrayed us again," he put down the phone. It was real; he knew that; otherwise the call wouldn't have come to his phone. He put down the receiver and it looked exactly the same as the one in the bunker room, deep underneath the Vatican City.

There were five of these old telephones.

One was in Carl's office, safely stored in his safe; one in the Vatican City in a bunker deep beneath the city; the third one sat on a table in the White House, although someone thought it would be a good idea to paint it red and until today it still remained there. Luckily, that one hadn't rung in a while. The fourth was miles above the earth in a space station that had 'apparently' been placed there to explore earth, but this was only a smoke screen. It was through this space station that they could see everything that was happening. The fifth one had been missing since the Second World War; it had belonged to Adolf Hitler, but it had been stolen from him years before and with it, all the records of the phone had vanished.

Carl quickly walked out of the room, leaving only his footprints behind, but soon they also disappeared from the granite floor. He was disappointed; he didn't think this day would come. This man, this traitor, had been in his office and the idea made him sick.

Back in the hotel, team four were still on the ground floor. There was only one of the four darkened knights left on the ground floor. The other two evil knights had made it to the third floor without any hassle, as they easily moved between floors using the unguarded lift.

Team four prepared themselves for an attack. So far they'd only had to deal with the small fry - pawns attacking the protectors - but they were no match for the highly trained commandos. It was like a story book; each time the team confronted the evil followers, the team were given the option to give up, walk away, and live, but each time there was the same reply. That reply meant that they would die a few minutes later.

They had been so engulfed in evil deeds that they were totally blinded from any good. They lived a lie and today that lie would creep up on them.

"No...kill them...kill them all!" the evil followers screamed, their words echoing down the hallway.

This was what the team had expected. The killing was quick. There was no need for them to suffer. Finally there was no one left on the ground floor, only themselves and the other evil one roaming the corridors. They could feel his presence in the hallways, imagining him around every corner, but they searched the corridors twice now, and there was still no sign of the darkened knight.

They knew he was there, but where was the beast hiding?

The engine of the vehicle parked outside had now been turned off. Signs of life begun to show; the back door opened and the three remaining beasts stopped simultaneously and looked in the direction of the parked vehicle. They knew their days were numbered, or in this case, minutes, and whatever the beasts were looking for, they had to double-time it.

Back on the ground floor, hidden in the darkness, one of the dark souls appeared; his mission was to kill anyone and anything that got in his way and for now those were the four protectors that were left on the ground floor covering the hallway. The protectors knew that if they had to do something, they needed to do it now. In one way or another, the dark soul needed to get past the protectors, as behind him was the exit leading out to the main street. He certainly wasn't going that way as that's where the vehicle they all feared was parked.

Then a foot appeared from the parked vehicle. Someone was getting out of the vehicle and the evil one on the ground floor knew it; it made him nervous. The team could sense his nervousness, but they had no idea why.

"Just walk away…" the team leader coerced. He knew that even if they shot him to pieces his soul would still remain evil and he would return in one form or another. *The evil would remain.*

The beastly man was restless and jumpy, and he made absolutely no effort to hide it.

While the team gazed at him, he changed his stance and ran towards them. The half-man half-demon looked unstoppable. With each step closer, they could feel his eyes burning on them. However, they weren't meant to be victims of an attack, he was merely running from the main entrance where the parked vehicle stood.

The man appeared from within the parked vehicle, and the beast that was running towards the four-man team felt his presence outside the entrance. He was ready to walk into the building.

However, as the darkened evil half-human moved forward with immense force, the team happened to be in his way which was unfortunately for them.

The first casualty was the protector closest to him. But he died a quick and painless death; a blow to his head ended his life as he fell against the wall. Shortly after he was joined by the second protector; the bullets seemed to do nothing to stop this thing, his sheer strength cutting the third one into two pieces.

There was only the team leader left, and for a moment, he was sad that he was going to die, as he shed a tear, but kept up the barrage of bullets flying towards the evil one.

Then, there was utter silence.

It was unclear at first whether the team leader had been successful or not. He hadn't. He looked down at his hands and saw his own blood dripping from them. He looked up and saw the face of the evil one who had done this to him. But he didn't fear him. He closed his eyes, and waited for the final blow that would leave him dead and forgotten. He knew that in a few short hours, this place would be wiped clean, with not a hint of the blood splatters to be seen.

He readied himself, but the final blow didn't come. Instead, a blinding light burnt the corridor walls straight towards him, and the evil one was standing right in front of him.

Then in an instant, it was over. The protector opened his eyes and saw that the killer had gone; he had been burned to the ground the instant the light had touched him. From behind the light, two figures emerged. His eyes shot open wide and in shock; he never thought the day would come when he would see *them* again.

For him it had been fifteen years, the day he'd received his gift to see what others couldn't see, and should never see. The gift was rare but every so often, someone received a gift from them.

It was the same two men who had been looking out for Peter and Charles, only now their true identity was revealed.

They were white night angels, here to keep the darkness under control.

He got up slowly, almost falling from his wounds, but there was not a burn on his body. He could only see the blood dripping from his hands.

"I have wished for this day..." he said, as he collapsed to the floor.

"We will save you!" they said and the one put out his hand and said a prayer for him. The protector grabbed his hand and said, "No don't!" They respected his wish just as his dead hand dropped to the floor.

It was time. A simple nod between the two of them confirmed their agreement. The millions that the Company had spent on the hotel would be put to good use now.

Outside, simpletons walked past the hotel, oblivious to the horror that had been happening within. Meanwhile on the ninth floor, the safety of the cocoon that Peter and Charles had found themselves in was beginning to fracture. The attack on the team had commenced and there was no way out. They were blocked by someone dressed in a fancy black suit. They weren't sure who it was and they had to look twice to see if he was one of the darkened knights. At first he tried to play the 'trapped human' on the fifth floor, and were it not for the accidental discharge of a grenade by one of his own pawns hiding in the open lift, they would have been overwhelmed by his power. The grenade exploded a few feet from him but when the smoke cleared he was still standing with only an arm missing and a slight burn to his human body. At that moment, the millions the Company had spent on the hotel came to use.

First, the windows of the hotel locked automatically, and then moments later a solid steel plate covered the windows. The only thing left open was the entrance door to the hotel. This hadn't happened by accident, as running from one of the rooms was Special Agent Martin Davis who'd been in charge of all the missions; well, not all of them and certainly not this mission. He wasn't even supposed to be here. How he had got in was a mystery....and he knew what they were planning.

This was the Company's contingency plan; when there was a breach, lockdown.

"Nobody in, nobody out," said the protector, standing alongside Peter, as he kept a watchful eye on the demon that was missing an arm. The demon was certainly not amused about losing an arm and showed his dissatisfaction toward his accomplices by ripping the arm off the one who had dropped the grenade.

The protectors pointed their guns toward the lift where the ruthless thing was standing. It was like they said; he only cared for the immortality that they promised.

"Why did the doors and windows lock?" Charles asked.

"Wait...it's not finished," he said, and then moments later he gave the instruction for them to put on their scope lights.

Peter and Charles were confused; why did they need to put the lights on when there was ample lighting in the corridor? "They've lost it," mumbled Charles. Before he could say anything else, like clockwork, the lights turned off, one by one, while the traitor Special Agent Martin Davis disappeared into the street. He had managed to keep the doors open. He looked back and saw the doors shut behind him, leaving everybody in darkness, everybody except the team on the fifth floor that was still missing.

There hadn't been a single word from them; at least not since all communications had been shut down by Agent Davis. The possibility existed that they were all dead, as one of the demon-humans was still roaming around in the hotel.

But there was good news; the missing team was still alive, trapped on the fourth floor, only five floors below Peter and his protectors.

Then from outside the hotel someone came running towards the main door. He could see the door was closed and he knew it was made of solid steel, but even so, he increased his speed at the last second and then connected with the six inch solid steel door, denting it and making it move slightly off its rails. He fell back a few feet. It was the same person who had been following Peter around Cape Town as well as on the airplane to New York. For the first time he showed his face as he took off his hoody. He was in his mid-forties, super fit and by the looks of the dented door, strong as well. He realised he was too late. It was as they said; nobody in, nobody out. Out of anger, he punched the solid door while a young boy watched. The boy was astounded as he saw the damage that was done to the door; he stared on in amazement and dropped his ice cream. The hooded man knew that he could carry on hitting the door all day but he would never get past it. He rubbed his left shoulder. The impact had injured him, but only slightly and he wasn't in the least bothered about it; he knew it would heal in a day or two.

 Back inside, all the protector teams had their backs to the wall. Their ammunition was nearly depleted; the fight had gone on for too long. They had very little chance of surviving when almost thirty demon followers pounded at them. Only the team's flashlights on their gun barrels shone forward. The demon follower's attacks suddenly stopped. The human followers were cautious; as the lights had died they had no idea what was going on. Then the followers of the dark ones started to show their fear; surprisingly they were afraid of the dark.

They paused for a moment and they ran out of the stairway door, as if death was brushing against their hair. As they came closer to the main entrance door, it slowly swung open and the building released them to live another day. They were not the problem however, they were only human. The remaining two dark ones that were roaming around the hotel were the problem.

Just like on the trains, nitrogen lasers and violet lights started shining down the hallways. This was good news for the protectors who had only two teams remaining, the one team was with Peter and Charles and the second team was still on the fourth floor with only one of the half-human evil things staring them in the face.

Then they gave him an ultimatum; the team leader of group two stepped forward, and issued him with a final warning.

"This fight is not for you!" he yelled, as he loaded his last ammunition clip into his automatic rifle, arming it so that the demon human could hear it. He hoped his ultimatum would work; they were only three of them left and if he attacked them now, there was no way they would survive.

The demon laughed and considered his options. For him to get to the ninth floor he had to pass the three protectors who shone their lights in his face from not too far away. He replied with force, *"This is not your decision, human!"*

The team knew their time was limited, but the demon gave them hope. Who would have thought a demon could give a human true hope with just a few uttered words? *"Not even your two friends downstairs can help you now!"*

The team leader looked up; now he was confused. What did the demon mean about the friends downstairs? It could be one of the protector teams downstairs, but the way he said it was almost as if he was afraid of the 'friends' downstairs.

Then he realised it could only be 'them'.

"It's them! We are saved!" he called to the remaining two on his team. Their mood shifted quickly from fear to pure and utter relief! The team leader dropped his weapons on the floor and shortly after, his two colleagues did the same. Everything that had the ability to kill had been dropped onto the floor.

"Fools…like sheep you have faith," the human demon whispered, and slowly walked towards them with the violet lights shining across his face. A smile crossed his face. He knew the protectors were no threat to him now so he increased his speed, and ran towards them like the wind, passing corridors and rooms along the way and in his wake papers from tables and floors flew through the air.

The protectors didn't flinch one bit; they had made their peace. The group leader then said, "We know where we are going when we die, do you?"

When the demon was just two feet away from the protector team, his human face started to show strain; it was almost as if he was feeling pain. His eyes started to twitch, not fast, but he was aware of something.

But by the time he figured out what was going on, he was already part of the paint that covered the corridor.

It was such a severe force that the team fell backwards on the floor. It felt like a bomb had exploded; but it wasn't a bomb.

"It's them…" the group leader said, as he staggered to get up. He picked up his automatic rifle and pointed the light that was still shining brightly towards the wall where the darkened soul had ended up, but there was nothing left of him. Only the stench of evil lined the wall.

The team leader looked down the corridors trying to find the two beings, but he couldn't see them; they had made themselves invisible. Even with the specialised glasses he couldn't see them. Disappointed, he turned around and walked towards his two teammates that were resting against the wall. As he walked back, he mumbled something.

"Just once," said the team leader. They heard him; they nodded to each other and touched him on his shoulder.

"Raymond..." the one said.

He stopped. He knew it was them. He slowly turned around. His teammates couldn't see him turn around, but they weren't so lucky to see them; they were still young and wouldn't appreciate meeting them.

"Thank you...you saved us!" he said, crying gratefully as he fell to his knees.

They didn't look too pleased with him for dropping to his knees.

"No you saved yourselves... faith is the key!"

"Raymond, please get up," they instructed him gently and explained why.

"We only bow down for Him...and so should you," the one said, as he disappeared into the violet light. He tried to stop them, just to ask them one thing, but they were already out of sight. He shouted, "How are they?" hoping they'd heard, and they did. He was talking about his wife and child he'd lost five years ago. He believed, but like all people, he had doubt in his heart.

Then he heard one of them speak tenderly, "They are fine. They are waiting for you."

"Thank you!" he yelled and dropped to the floor again, his emotions getting the better of him. His two friends helped him up. He explained what had happened, but they thought he was mad. He glanced to the left and suggested they went a particular way. He knew where this idea came from and chuckled silently while he walked them to the safety of a secret staircase hidden alongside the lifts.

While they walked down the stairs, they felt safe. And so they should, as nobody could find them in these walls.

Then there was nowhere to go. After walking down three levels of stairs, they came to a dead end; but only for a moment. According to their calculations, they should be on the ground floor. A door opened on the side of the wall. The door itself looked heavy; almost a two-tonne door that was six inches thick. They looked around the corner, which revealed the outside of the hotel. They walked out and the door closed behind them, spilling them onto a side street across from the hotel.

"How is this possible?"

"'Impossibility' is only a word for them," Raymond said and looked up at the skyscraper as he saw a few birds flying about. They walked into the busy sidewalk and disappeared amongst people lining the streets. They looked as if they'd just come from a war zone, but nobody paid them any notice, even though they were dressed in their body armour.

Back on the ninth floor, however, it was a completely different story; a killer-demon was on the loose followed by ten of his followers, all wanting to kill the two unlikely heroes, Peter and Charles.

So far, they were still protected by their body armour, as they moved from corridor to corridor, losing a few men with each contact. But whatever the protectors were doing, it was working as they finished off a few followers every couple of minutes.

They took a rest for a few seconds; the strain was getting to them. They looked tired and weak, and wondered when it would end.

"Soon..." Peter heard a voice.

He looked to one side, and then to the other trying to figure out who had spoken.

He looked to the protector on his left side, "What did you say?" but there was no response from him, so he grabbed the protector's hand. "What did you say?" he prodded again. The protector looked towards the arm Peter was pulling on and signalled for him to be quiet, as he slowly pointed towards the end of the hallway.

Peter looked, but saw nothing. The violet light wasn't helping. Now Charles pulled on his arm.

"I'm not well," said Charles as he collapsed on the floor.

Peter quickly helped him up, but he could only lift him up halfway as he was too heavy.

"He's been shot!" shouted one of the protectors. Peter lifted up his hand and looked closer, seeing a liquid substance. In the light, he couldn't see what it was and only when one of the protectors shone his barrel light on Charles' hand could he see the red dripping from his hand.

"Why do you think they call it bulletproof?" Charles said, looking shocked at the hole the bullet had made in the vest.

"Take care of my family." Those were Charles' final words.

One level down, the two mysterious men looked up. They knew what had happened to Charles.

"Must we help...he should live," said the one and turned towards his mysterious friend who was still looking up towards the ninth floor. "He should live..." he said again in his German accent, but there was no reply from his friend. Then he dropped his head.

"No...it was his destiny."

Then after a five second pause he said, "Coffee then?"

"No...first we need to go visit someone," the one suggested, showing no remorse and no guilt. They walked into the linked corridor and disappeared.

At the moment the two angels left, the half-human demon smiled. He was pleased they were gone; they were the only thing that stood between him and the only prize left; Peter Richards. He was now halfway to glory.

Peter laid Charles' head gently on the floor, and rose, tightening his vest. "His family will be looked after," the team leader offered as a comfort.

Suddenly they saw a dark shadow that reflected against the wall.

"It's him...he is coming for you!"

There were only four men left in the group, each of them left with only one ammunition clip; they paused and considered what might happen.

"Sir?" the team leader asked. He had to confess. They had tried so hard to keep everyone safe but it looked like they weren't going to make it out of this one alive.

And they were right.

"We will try and keep you alive," he promised as they readied their firearms waiting for the imminent attack.

A dark voice called to them from behind the visible corridor. Then the shadow moved closer until they could see him.

He set the ultimatum, "Give me Peter Richards and the rest of you will live."

Peter looked at them and saw that they were considering the proposal.

"Really...you have got to be kidding me!" Peter protested adamantly.

The team leader smiled. It was only a joke, but by the time Peter smiled from relief the demon was already halfway down the corridor to kill them all.

"It was nice knowing you!" the team leader said and Peter knew it was all over, the fear on their faces showed their disappointment.

Outside, the two angels had made it to the sidewalk; then one stopped.

"I forgot something..." the one said and turned back toward the hotel, as he started towards the ninth floor where Peter and his protectors had begun the fight.

"Not today!" the angel said and in that instant the half-human evil-bodied person exploded into a blob of liquid flesh, his leftovers dripping from the corridor roof and splashing the team in foul liquid.

"Not for 'you' to take," the angel smiled and walked away from the busy sidewalk into a deserted street.

"Coffee?" the other angel asked.

"No, later. What's up with you and coffee anyway?"

He didn't answer, and they disappeared into nowhere.

Chapter 18

INVITATION BACK TO BUILDING EIGHT

Peter got up from the floor; the force of the power that had blown the demon apart was tremendous. He was confused.

"What just happened?" he asked, baffled, wiping the leftover flesh off his jacket.

For the team, this wasn't unusual. Although it had never actually happened to them, they knew what was going on as it had been part of their training.

They tried to explain it to Peter, but his attention was centred more on Charles' dead body that wasn't even ten feet away from them. He bent over the body and covered his face. He was sad that he'd lost a friend, but it always seemed worse for the people who were left behind. That would be Charles' wife and child; they were still under the impression that he was on a business trip to Namibia for the university.

The lights returned to normal and the windows opened, blowing a gust of fresh air into the corridor. The team leader pulled Peter up and explained to him that they needed to go before the clean-up team arrived.

"What about him?"

"They will take care of him...trust me."

Peter was alive and this was what persuaded him to leave with the team. He turned back and took one more look at Charles' lifeless body lying on the floor.

They exited the hotel and Peter saw someone familiar; Special Agent

Josh Williams of the Federal Bureau of Investigation.

"Hey I know that guy…" but the protector didn't give him time to talk, as he rapidly pulled him into a concealed van.

"Who are those guys?" the protectors looked at each other, yet none of them were willing to answer. However they realised that Peter deserved to hear the truth. He had seen way more than he was supposed to, especially for someone who hadn't undergone training.

Not the physical part, no…it wasn't that; he had been part of a counter-insurgence team back in Angola, so he knew what it was like.

It was the mental side he lacked.

Could his brain handle it all? The team leader was convinced he was going to collapse when the demon exploded in front of his eyes.

"How are you feeling?" the team leader asked Peter as he noticed his eyes turning red and then he collapsed.

They quickly strapped an oxygen mask on his face and lay him down to rest on the seat.

"Let's take him home."

Peter awoke full of energy and the familiar surroundings confused him. He was, in fact, in his bed, in his apartment in Cape Town. He got up and saw the half-full bottle of whisky on the table. Just the way he had left it…

"This is wrong!"

He walked towards the window. There was one way to clear things up, the view. He had an almost perfect view of Table Mountain from his apartment. But when he opened the door, he saw Central Park. In a way, he was relieved. It would be comforting to be home, but there was nothing there for him.

Here he could start anew. With this thought in mind, he smiled. All of a sudden he was startled by a voice behind him, "Did it help?"

This was what they had meant by taking him home; the intense stress of Charles dying in his arms. It was too much for one man to handle and stress had been responsible for his collapse in the van.

Waking up in familiar surroundings was a good way to reboot the brain. Peter had to admit he felt refreshed and awake. It felt like he'd been asleep for a whole day.

"Two days!" the protector corrected him.

"Two days?" Peter couldn't believe it, but he felt better about it when he considered the circumstances.

The protector switched on the TV and searched for one of the South African channels. There was something he needed to show Peter. When he saw it, he would be at peace with the death of his friend Charles.

And there it was. The news had reported everything; Charles le Roux had been killed in a plane crash just outside the Namibian capital, Windhoek.

"Is that the best you can do for him?" Peters spluttered angrily.

He wasn't happy about the news report, but the protector indicated that he needed to watch more.

The news that followed *was* somewhat comforting; Charles le Roux had been nominated for an award for his work in Namibia, and prize money had been awarded to his family.

"How much?"

"In dollars...one million!" announced the protector.

Peter was happy; in his death, Charles' family would live a carefree life from now on. And they needed it. While they didn't live in the slums, they were living 'on the bread line' as the locals called it. They were behind on school fees, rent and everything else.

The protector rudely cut their conversation short.

"VERITAS wants to see you!"

Peter was only the third person who had ever been invited back to building number eight. The last time they had visited building number eight he could clearly remember Carl's warning.

"Don't come back here again. If you do...I will kill you myself" Carl had said.

The building was impressive and he wouldn't mind going back, but the words that the friendly Carlito Mario had spoken to him put the thought out of his mind, permanently.

"Now!" the protector ordered and it was only then that Peter recognised him; it was the team leader who had escorted him out of the hotel. Peter could see he wasn't in a good mood. Peter had lost Charles but this man had lost four of his men.

He was upset; this wasn't how it was supposed to go; and all because of a traitor that lived amongst them.

"I'm sorry about your team."

"Friends...they were my friends," he corrected Peter. Peter put on his jacket, and then turned around and asked the protector if they'd caught the traitor. The protector dropped his head slightly and shook his head; the truth of the matter was that they didn't have a clue as to who the traitor was. Then his mind took him back to the last thing he could remember seeing as he left the hotel with the protectors; the people he knew from back in Cape Town.

"I know them..." the protector answered.

The protectors have nothing to do with the agents, but occasionally they bumped into each other.

"We have the same boss, VERITAS!"

Carl forbade them to communicate with each other. The less they knew about each other the better, but they all knew the agent in charge.

"Special Agent Martin Davis…"

"Who?" Peter asked, as he'd never heard the name before, but the description the protector offered fit the description of one of the people he'd seen. "He is a good man…" the protector added.

Clearly he didn't know that he was a bad man with a darkened heart. He also didn't know that the man he held the upmost respect for was the one responsible for the deaths of almost forty people in the hotel, both good and bad. There were only four people who knew; Carl, the man at the Vatican City, and the two mysterious men. They had decided that everything would happen in good time.

By the time they'd discussed the men he'd seen outside the hotel, they were already down the stairs on their way to the car.

"You guys sure like your black vehicles," Peter joked, but the protector didn't think it was funny. All of a sudden Peter had a flashback about one of the men he'd seen a few minutes before he collapsed in the van.

But Peter didn't know who the man was; he'd never seen him in his life before.

It was remarkable that the man who'd been standing next to Agent Martin Davis fit the description Peter's friend had given him.

He was talking about Special Agent Josh Williams, the one who'd pretended to be a lawyer from Florida. Peter tried to think of his name again and then he remembered, but of course it was only an alias.

"David Thomas!" Peter shouted out, and the protector looked at him. He'd heard that name before.

"How do you know that name?" Now Peter was the surprised one.

The protector turned around and this time asked in a more appealing way, though still somewhat aggressively, "How do you know that name?"

The driver of the vehicle also glimpsed towards Peter; he, too, had also heard the name and was very curious.

"It's a code..." is all he would say.

The name David Thomas was a code word for something else. Only if you knew the code would you understand the meaning.

The name struck fear in the hearts of some, and normally, the name would not be spoken aloud.

Peter explained how he'd heard the name David Thomas. His mind flicked back to his friend Johannes Roland, who'd died in an accident near Langebaan, a beautiful holiday town on the west coast of South Africa. The thought of Johannes made him feel sad. The accident was still a mystery, and no one knew how his car had left the road and collided with a tree. He had died instantly.

It had been stated that the accident happened as Johannes had fallen asleep at the wheel, and everybody believed it. So had Peter.

And why not, he thought. Anyway, there was no evidence to believe otherwise.

But in the background 'a good man' lingered according to the protector, *if they only knew.*

"It's done..." said Agent Davis softly to himself as he drove away from the accident scene. There was no one around to help Johannes. He had

been acting alone again. His lust to survive had taken control of him. Johannes had died as he'd needed another distraction and getting rid of the only witness helped his agency, or so he thought. His lust to succeed in his endeavours gave him a dark heart.

Peter continued explaining how he knew the name, telling them the whole story of the killing on train 3535, to the detention by the police. No evidence had been found against him, and the police had eventually released him. The odd thing about the killings was that they'd never found the four police officers. "Seven dead, four cops missing and one survivor."

"...anyway," he got back to the name David Thomas and told them it was the name the lawyer had given to his friend. This part sounded familiar to the two protectors and the driver glanced at Peter again in his rear view mirror.

The driver turned towards Peter and readied himself to ask something that would make Peter's stomach turn upside down.

"Your friend Johannes...is he alive?" they looked at each as they waited for an answer.

Now Peter knew something was going on, the way the questions were asked made him uncomfortable.

He struggled to get the words out of his mouth, not because Johannes had died, but because a second friend of his had died within a short couple of months.

"He died in a car accident..."

The two protectors looked at each other. They wanted to say something to Peter, but Peter turned towards the windows and looked out while the car glided down the street.

After a block or two, they decided to tell him what they knew about the name David Thomas.

At first, Peter didn't believe a word they said. It was absurd! How could a name be a code for a hit?

But Peter misunderstood the first explanation.

"No, not a hit, a possible threat," the protector corrected him just as they stopped in front of building number eight.

The protectors spoke amongst themselves for a bit. It didn't make sense; if Johannes Roland was a threat he would've been eliminated before he got off the train.

Peter stayed seated in the car. He sat quietly, listening to the conversation they were having amongst themselves.

This was extraordinary for Peter; it was the first time they'd spoken of anything since he'd gotten to know them. The problem was that Peter was feeling threatened; first Johannes and then Charles. In an instant they stopped talking as if someone had ripped out their voices.

"You need to go...you were cleared!"

Peter was filled with doubt; the death of Johannes, and then the link between Peter and Charles, and then the truth serum. Something stank. It smelt of a cover-up, he thought as he got out the car and closed the door behind him. Just as he started walking away, the passenger side window opened and one of the protectors said something to him, closed the window, and the black vehicle drove away.

The protector had to tell him that he was probably going to lose his job, and Peter had to know what to say.

Now that he knew what to say he walked into building number eight with an eager foot.

On his blind side, someone bumped him hard. The man apologised, and hid his face away; but the bump was so hard that Peter's neck was instantly in pain. He rubbed it until the pain subsided slightly. He wanted to shout at the person; but the pain was like a bee stinging him in the neck. Peter picked up his small bag and continued walking in the direction of building number eight.

This time the lift door was open, waiting for him, and as he walked by he saw other people milling around in the lobby. They all turned their heads as they saw him.

Not far from the lift entrance there was a reception area and one of the people was waiting for the 'okay' to go up to the private floor. The man turned to the person sitting at his side. He didn't know him, but figured it was a good idea to ask him something about Peter.

But he wasn't the only one; almost all the people waiting on the ground floor wanted to know who this person was. They knew that no one walked in off the street and just went up to the lift, while everyone else had to wait for clearance inside the reception area.

"What floor is he going to?" the one asked the reception manager while they watched the floors jump on the monitor on top of the lift, counting each floor it reached. It started slowly; 1... 2... 3... 4... 5 - and then the 6th floor, the FBI, 7th floor, CIA and then it passed the Secret Service at floor 8. Nobody ever went above the 8th floor; they knew the rules.

At the 9th floor the lift stopped like it always did and gave a warning to the person inside to press the ground floor button if they'd made a mistake. Then after a few seconds the lift continued, stopping at the 10th floor, issuing the same warning. But Peter had seen this before. It had been scary the first time, but not now.

He was far too angry now, he was seething.

They were keeping something from him and he didn't like it; he had lost two friends and his life was on the line.

Now came the interesting part, and he couldn't hide the fact that he was curious about the blue lights that were emitted and scanning the entire lift. He still wanted to know what the one protector had been talking about the first time they had visited.

He could still remember the words; "It's for something else."

Finally, after more scanning and a couple more floors, the lift moved upwards until he was at the right floor. Then the blinding light came on again, but his time nobody called him, there was nobody to meet him.

This was certainly not the reception he'd expected. Only an empty room welcomed him.

He heard people talking in one of the side rooms. It was Carl and somebody else, an unfamiliar voice. He walked closer, and the closer he got to the room, the more Carl's voice seemed to elevate. He didn't sound happy, but it seemed to be a one-way conversation. The other person didn't seem to agree with Carl.

"He will be here any minute...you tell him!" Carl's shouts continued.

It sounded as if they were talking about him. Then he heard a third voice in the room; Peter recognised the German accent. Then there was silence. They knew he was there and they opened the door. Peter saw all three standing in the room and Carl waved him over.

The mood was sour. Carl turned away and walked towards the corner window. He apologised to Peter for the loss of his friend. Carl knew it wasn't part of the deal; Charles le Roux was not supposed to die. Peter greeted the other two men and looked towards Carl.

"Coffee?" Carl asked Peter. One of the mysterious men looked over to the coffee maker while the other one shook his head.

"What? It's Columbian coffee," he explained, but he didn't walk over to the coffee maker. Peter didn't hear what the two were saying about the coffee. He was here on a mission; there was a question that he was determined to ask Carl.

They sat down at the table while the other two stood alongside. Peter turned toward them wondering why they weren't sitting; they never sat, not even in his room in Cape Town. *"Weirdo's..."* he thought.

"We're leaving..." the one said and walked towards the door. But Carl called to them; "Are you going to ask him?"

"Ask me what?" Peter interrupted.

They turned around, walked back, and finally sat down. Carl was surprised. They never sat down. They got right to the point, and explained to him that it was all about his grandfather. Peter knew the story; they'd told him before.

But there *was* something they hadn't told Peter.

It hadn't been important until now. They didn't waste time. They got straight to the point.

"Your grandfather was one of us. Bring the book," Carl ordered and after a moment a man wearing white gloves appeared.

But Peter had already seen the book and he hadn't seen his grandfather's name inside.

Carl paged through the almost thousand year old book, and stopped at the page dated 1942. He scrolled down the names listed.

"Here!" He pointed to a name in the book. Peter couldn't see clearly and turned the book sideways.

He saw the name, got up from his chair, and walked towards the window.

Carl was surprised at Peter's reaction; it was almost as if he knew the name.

And he did...   *'David Thomas...'*

Chapter 19

LIES AND COVER-UPS

Peter walked alongside the window while being regarded by Carl and the other two. Carl finally thought it was time to explain. Peter needed to know the truth.

Carl admitted that they should have removed the name out of the book a long time ago.

The dream he'd had on the plane was the truth; just as he'd seen it. So it had happened. He couldn't explain how he'd dreamt it; however the two men sitting at the table knew how it was possible; they'd had something to do with it; they were angels after all.

'Divine intervention' they'd called it, and bending a few rules was often necessary.

Then he remembered the name 'Richards'; the name he'd seen in his dream; however he was blinded by his own name. He then saw the name 'Richards' disappear and the surname 'Thomas' appeared on his grandfather's uniform.

"What happened?" Peter said as he sat down at the table.

He was tired and wasn't feeling particularly well, which he thought was a bit odd; he'd been feeling on top of the world an hour ago. He rubbed his neck slightly. There was still some pain where the man on the sidewalk had bumped him.

"You don't look well..." noticed Carl. He was right; Peter looked a little pale. Carl offered him a drink and continued with his story.

A year after the incident on the train, his grandfather had started behaving erratically. At first the Company took no real notice with regards to what was going on until the day he had been invited back to *Building Eight.*

Carl remembered that day as if it was yesterday. The truth was, Peter's grandfather didn't die of old age, or as they'd proclaimed, *'Peacefully moved on'.*

"He died horribly…" said Carl.

There was a small amount of truth in what he already knew; they'd told him that he died in France.

That was only half the truth. They had looked for his body for over seven years, but it had never been found.

Carl looked sincere whilst he told the story, almost if Peter's grandfather's death meant something to him. It had been sad for the Company and Carl had made a promise to David Thomas on the day they'd found his body in France.

Before Carl continued, he had to ask Peter a question. He wasted no time. "What do you believe in?"

This was an odd question and caught Peter off guard. He mumbled something indistinct and then answered predictably, "I go to church…sometimes."

But this is not what Carl had asked and it wasn't the answer he wanted, but then again, it was a start.

Peter now knew of good, evil, and the paranormal.

If this is what Carl wanted to hear, he had to ask directly. Peter was confused, and realised that the other two men in the room were staring straight at him. They were also keen to hear his answer. Peter turned towards them and tried to recall their names, but in fact they'd never given up their names. All he knew was that they worked for the

Company, but he never asked what they actually did for the Company.

But that wasn't important now. First he needed to know what the promise was that Carl made to his grandfather.

This confused him even more; it was almost as if they were testing him.

"How could you make a promise to a dead body?" Peter asked incredulously. But Carl wouldn't continue until such time as Peter had answered the question he'd been asked.

"What do you believe in?" Carl reiterated. This reminded Peter of everything he'd seen in this past few months; secret organisations, conspiracies, cover-ups and manipulation. But then there was also the paranormal part; the demon-bodied humans. That for him was the scary part.

"What else could there be?"

"Lots more!" Carl said as he looked at the other who still sat at the table. Then he said it again. This was the rule humanity needed to live by.

"People see what they need to see," said one of the two mysterious men. The way he said it, made Peter feel assured that he knew what he was talking about.

Carl had been saying this since the day they met, always the same thing, but he never once told Peter what he was actually talking about. The longer the conversation carried on, the angrier Peter got. Come to think of it, he'd been angry when he got there!

"Enough!" Peter yelled, as he stood and pushed his chair back. With a determined face, he insisted, "You tell me everything, now!"

But there was no response from any of the three; all they did was look at each other.

Peter nodded a few times; he had had enough, so he laid it on the table.

He started and gave them no time to answer. He had made up his mind.

He didn't care if he was responsible for the death of those two school children in Angola. It was sad, but it was time for him to wake up.

"You were not responsible!" said Carl sternly, as he looked straight at Peter. Peter wasn't listening.

"I don't care..." Peter shouted, as he stormed out the door while the three still sat quietly waiting for him to return.

They didn't have to wait long; the moment Peter pressed the lift button he realised what Carl had said. He stood dead quiet for a moment, as he watched the lift door open and shut again. Then after some thought, he walked back into the room where the other three still sat in silence.

Now it was time for Carl to lay it on the table; the Company, the tickets, the lies and the traitors involved, starting with the death of the two school boys in Angola, and continuing to the truth serum.

It took Carl almost an hour to explain everything, and he'd only got half way. Peter's grandfather still hadn't been mentioned; the mysterious David Thomas that everybody seemed to know, everybody except Peter.

Carl stopped talking. Peter had still not answered Carl's question. .

"What do you believe in?" Carl asked again.

Carl thought for a moment, and realised that the way he had asked the question was confusing Peter. He asked again.

"What do you think lives among us?"

This question scared Peter immensely.

It was the 'what' that worried him. He understood the question and he also understood that the only way he was going to get the full story out of Carl was to answer the question.

He thought long and hard about what to say, but the only thing that came to his mind was what his father had told him about his grandfather; "He saw angels..." Peter mumbled, just loud enough for the three to hear him. Carl rose half way up from his chair. Peter laughed as he thought about what a crazy old man his grandfather had been for believing that angels had spoken to him.

He was totally mad so Peter asked Carl a question, "Angels...you haven't seen one lately?" Peter laughed.

Carl looked towards the other two sitting at the table, but they just smiled and shook their heads out of Peter's sight. This was certainly not the time to tell Peter about angels, so Carl said 'No' in response.

Carl knew who the two mysterious men were; this was the one secret he couldn't tell anyone, ever. But if Peter was destined to know, they would eventually show him.

Like his grandfather, they had appeared on the day of the accidental attack on the train back in Germany.

But Peter wasn't finished.

"There was this book my father gave me before he died," said Peter.

The book had belonged to Peter's grandfather and when he got the book as a gift from his father he wondered why the name has been rubbed out from the diary. The book that he was talking about had mysteriously disappeared twenty-five years ago. While Peter was talking, Carl grew increasingly uncomfortable every time he mentioned the book. He knew of the book; not because he had heard of it, no not that...it was because his team had been responsible for the book disappearing.

Peter remembered the front cover of the book clearly; the cover was red and the name had been rubbed out by a thick dark marker. Written on top of the rubbed out words was his grandfather's new name, Peter John Richards, written in bright red.

Carl was curious too; curious about what Peter remembered about what he'd read in the book. He looked towards his safe.

Carl knew exactly where the book was, neatly stacked alongside the missing scrolls of Egypt that contained the secret to how the pyramids were constructed, and the top secret world map which was dated ten years from now.

These secrets must never get out and they never would.

"He said angels told him his family will never be harmed."

And that was the promise Carl had to break...

Peter was the key to stopping the evil that was killing the bloodlines of all the people who were on the train on that awful night. It was Carl who suggested the idea that Peter could hold the key, but if he left now, they would never stop the evil until everyone who was on that train was dead.

Carl knew that Peter would never get a ticket, all thanks to his grandfather. He was the one who realised the wrong, but couldn't do anything to stop it.

Some could ask how it was possible that only one was exempt from the killing, but it was thanks to Maria Schultz, the General's daughter. She was the missing link. When she crossed over, she'd seen that he'd tried to stop the train, she had compassion.

Now Peter understood...

He was the only one who could help and they were the ones who needed him.

They had no more leverage on him; he now knew that he wasn't responsible for the deaths of the two boys.

But he still couldn't tell him who was responsible; it had to be someone within the Company.

Who else could have moved freely in and out of Angola?

"Give me a second."

There was something Peter needed to think about. He was still a good man.

For years he'd looked around for someone who knew the secret, a secret that was not their fault.

"I've wasted twenty years blaming myself!"

He asked for a piece of paper and made it clear to them that he was going to write down ten questions of which they *had to* answer eight or he was back on a plane to Africa.

After fourteen seconds of discussion, which felt like ages, they agreed that they would answer five questions only.

"What if he asks something about his grandfather?" Carl whispered to his colleagues.

"You must lie to him then...or make sure it is one of the two questions we don't have to answer," they cautioned.

Peter strode to a side table, sat and wrote down his questions. It didn't take long for him to finish the first question; he already knew what he wanted to ask. There was only one question on his mind, but they were giving him five. So he was going to put the other four to good use.

Once he'd finished, he walked over to them and sat down like he owned the place, as he put his feet on the table. Carl glared at him and he quickly dropped his feet to the floor.

Then he started...

Peter looked over to the two men he'd met in Cape Town and asked his first question while they waited in anticipation.

The first question was something they had not anticipated.

"Who the heck are you two?"

It was a valid question; they had never told him their names. This was an easy question to answer.

The one spoke, as he pointed towards his German friend.

"His name is Frederick...and I'm Jones."

"Nice to finally meet you," Peter said smiling.

Then he moved on to the next question; only four to go. Peter checked his list to see what question he wanted to ask next.

Carl glanced at his watch. This was taking far too long. He had an important meeting in ten minutes with the most important man on the planet - well, at the moment the second most important man - the President of the Unites States of America.

"Can we hurry this up?" he asked dryly, but was interrupted by the other two; Carl had already forgotten how important this man was to the success of the mission. He heard a whisper in his ear.

"Do you want another Chernobyl disaster?"

But Peter heard him. Instantly the phone in Carl's office started to ring.

He answered the phone, "Not now, I'll let you know when I'm ready."

Meanwhile the President was in the lobby just about to get in the lift, when it closed moments before he could step in. He was quickly blocked by two of the protectors. There were only seconds left to try and stop a gunfight as the Secret Service pulled out their weapons, and then shortly after, the protectors, about twenty of them, armed with their weapons.

They were serious, and the President knew it. He himself had made an oath, he had signed the book, and he also had one of the antique phones in the oval office.

His Secret Service agents had no idea what was going on; it wasn't their job to know. The President was the only one in the group who understood.

He stopped his men quickly, before they did anything stupid. The reception manager moved towards the President from behind the desk.

"Sir, he can't see you now."

The President turned around, followed by his men, ready to leave the building, but the reception manager stopped him.

"Sir, he didn't say you can go!" The manager cautioned, looking only at the President, showing no emotion whatsoever.

The Secret Service was confused; this was a serious case of insubordination. But it was quickly laid to rest when the President replied calmly, "I'll wait."

"Chernobyl?" Peter said, shocked.

Carl was upset; Peter should never have heard that.

But what Carl didn't know was that this was intentionally mentioned by the mysterious man called Jones.

Everybody knows what happened at Chernobyl: the disaster occurred on

26 April 1986, 01:23, at reactor number four at the Chernobyl plant. A sudden power surge took place, and when an attempt was made at an emergency shutdown there was a jump in power output. The rupture of a reactor was the source of the first explosion, and then after that a series of explosions followed exposing a graphite moderator component to air and then causing it to ignite; the resulting fire sent a cloud of radioactive fallout into the atmosphere over a wide area, forcing thousands to flee the area.

People hear what they need to hear...the truth was not for everyone.

Carl called it, *"The billion dollar cover-up."*

His friend Frederick was pleased with the way the conversation was going.

Carl rubbed his eyes. He felt tired. This 48 hour day was starting to get to him.

"Is that one of the five questions?" Carl asked, getting clever with Peter.

Jones quickly nodded to Peter, the moment their eyes were out of Carl's line of sight. Peter was baffled. Why would this Jones man help him with the questions?

Then after a while...

"Yes!" Peter declared. Deep inside he knew he'd made the right decision.

"The billion dollar cover-up," repeated Carl.

Then from the side of the table, Frederick leaned forward.

"Only tell him about his grandfather's part in it...*not about them*!"

He thought Peter wasn't ready for 'them'.

"You once asked me about the lights in the lift...scanning lights, you called them."

Charles was right; Peter thought to himself, they had scanned for weapons.

"No...not weapons, something else," Carl interrupted.

By now Peter realised that his grandfather had something to do with all of this, and he was right. But their timeline was all wrong and certainly not in chronological order. According to them he had died horribly in France twenty odd years ago.

"We lied...sorry."

Peter flung his chair across the room and walked towards the door. Again, he'd made up his mind.

The lies, the deception...he had had enough and was only too pleased to walk out the door!

"He died at *Chernobyl*" admitted Carl, breaking the tense mood, and just like that, all lies ceased.

Peter stopped. He thought about what Carl had just said, but it was impossible; his father had been at the funeral.

The Company had many means to cover stuff up, and if this was true, where had he been for forty years?

"We have been hunting him ever since..." Carl stopped talking and dropped his head forward slightly. This was the promise he had broken.

Carl had promised *never* to contact his family, *never* to involve them in any Company business.

The hunt that Carl was speaking of came to an end at Chernobyl, Russia, when a missile hit the power plant dead on. It took ten seconds to kill about a hundred of them. It was so easy. They had all gathered on the day which they called 'the day of the sun'.

"Radiation, it's the only way to kill them."

This was what Carl was afraid of, 'them'. All these precautions, safety measures and extra protectors were not against any normal attack...it was all for 'them'. The blue light that greeted people beyond the sixth floor was an energy burst of pure radiation, safe for humans, but lethal to any of 'them'.

Carl had said a lot and Peter was happy with the truth so far, but he still had not said anything about his grandfather and why he'd made the promise.

"Why do you want to kill them?"

"We don't ...they want something we have and will stop at nothing to get it."

"What?"

"Do you really want to know?"

Peter nodded.

"It's none of your business!" Carl burst forth, and by the sound of it he wasn't going to budge on this.

Peter agreed, it was none of his business, but then Carl, unexpectedly, said; "Thanks to your grandfather, we have two things they want."

That was the promise; he would give them what the Company wanted, as it was needed to keep peace amongst humans and 'them'.

The deal was to bring what they needed and the family would never know the name 'David Thomas' and would never get involved with the Company.

"Destiny!" Carl exclaimed.

"No... Special Agent Martin Davis!" said Jones and he was right. If it were not for him, the secret would have been kept. Then Carl realised that Jones had just surreptitiously given him the name of the traitor, but it was no accident.

"And..."

Peter needed to know as very soon they would meet each other and he would find out that the agent in charge was responsible for the death of his friends Johannes Roland and Charles le Roux.

So Jones told him, and his pleasant and friendly manner stopped dead in its tracks.

There was one thing he couldn't understand and it was not a difficult question.

"Why has the Company not done anything about him?"

Carl glanced over to the black phone which stood on the table that overlooked the city; Carl was not the one calling the shots. He also had a boss to whom he reported.

"I'm in, under one condition," said Peter. They already knew what the condition was going to be; it had to do with payback.

Peter was going to kill him, the man called Martin Davis. He didn't say it out loud, but they all knew it.

Then the black antique phone rang and both Jones and Frederick felt something different in the air around them.

"The General is leaving the city!" Frederick said as he looked towards his friend Jones. Almost as if they were one, they jumped up from their chairs and walked out the room while Carl lifted the phone.

They were right, the call was from Italy. The months of planning for New York had been wasted now; he had gone somewhere else. The bleeping sound of the Company satellite revealed where he would go next. As soon as the General had decided to leave, the tickets started to appear in the mailboxes of the targets.

Carl waited for a second and requested confirmation from the satellite feed while he switched on his TV which had a direct feed from the satellite control room. He put down the phone and walked over to Peter.

"How is your French?"

Chapter 20

WHO'S IN THE COFFIN?

They left New York City two days after the phone call from Italy. With military precision they all boarded a private plane to Paris. The only excited person was Peter; he'd never been to Paris or any European country for that matter. He was excited about the visit but also excited about the fact that it was where his grandfather had worked under the name David Thomas. Carl had promised him that when they landed he would show him where his grandfather had stayed for fifteen years, after the first attack on the Ferdinand Schultz train. According to Carl, it was almost at the foot of the sea in the south of France.

They had a few days to relax before the death train departed. That's what Peter called it - the death train.

But so far Carl had not spoken of it and Peter wasn't prepared to ask as everybody on the plane seemed happy, without a care in the world.

Peter looked towards the back of the plane and saw something that didn't quite fit with the upbeat mood on the plane.

It was a solid locked door, guarded by two protectors and after a few minutes of fighting with the idea of whether he should ask Carl about it, he eventually did.

"What's at the back?"

Carl thought '*What the heck!*'

"Remember that thing your grandfather captured for us?"

Peter leaned forward; now Carl was making it sound like an animal!

"Well, we are returning it in good faith to them...their turf, their rules."

It was easy; they were going to return what David Thomas had stolen. This would give them protection against an attack by 'them', but that didn't include Peter. Carl told him that the exchange would be made on the airport runway. That was the easy part. "They will know who you are the moment you step off the plane...let's hope they don't kill you on the spot!" Carl said while laughing, but Peter certainly didn't find this comment funny.

Peter was distracted by the door at the back of the plane as he saw the door open. He could quite easily see inside the room now. He saw two more protectors flanking the sides of something. Peter had a good view; to him it looked like a giant box. But before he had any time to absorb more details the door was abruptly closed.

"Get some rest. We will be landing in three hours."

Peter was quite tired, but before he rested he needed to ask one more thing. "Where are Jones and Frederick?"

"The a..." Carl stopped. He had wanted to say angels, but it was inappropriate. They needed to tell him themselves.

"They are in Italy visiting a friend."

Peter nodded. They sure moved fast he thought and then said, "They must be very important."

Carl nodded.

"You won't believe how important they are," he said, as he lowered his seat and turned to the side. He also needed some rest. Peter instinctively knew that this was the end of their conversation, so he lowered his seat as well and dozed off.

Peter fell into a deep sleep quite quickly and again found himself dreaming about events from nearly 65 years earlier.

He was on the old train again, but no one was around. There was only the faint sound of a little girl crying.

It flowed through the carriage like a summer breeze. Slowly they all put their firearms down on the floor, and felt the sorrow through the stench of the burnt gunpowder. He knew what was about to happen as the soldiers walked out of the train into the forest. Everything was exactly the same as he'd seen in his previous dream; exactly the same as he'd remembered it.

But not quite, there was one thing different. Peter heard a movement in the bushes on the far side of the train. It was different to the previous time.

Is this what Carl had meant when he said that he could see things that others couldn't? He had mentioned that it would start with dreams. He walked closer, but saw nothing and heard nothing. Only silence followed the little girl's screaming.

He knew someone was watching him, but as it was only a dream he knew that everything would be fine.

But he was getting an eerie feeling that someone was standing behind him. He didn't want to turn around, but the eerie sensation that was creeping up his spine scared him. Even the sweat on his forehead felt real; as did the realistic breeze that was blowing. The moon was bright and he could vaguely see what was going on around him; it was forcing him to turn around.

'Nothing...' Just as he'd thought. He turned around again, looked at the forest, and tried to see what had made the sound he'd heard earlier.

If only he'd looked down; he would have seen the footprints in the sand. The more he looked towards the forest the more he thought he saw something moving towards him.

"Hello!" called Peter. He thought that the person walking towards him would reply. Even though it was a dream, Peter really believed the person would say something; but before he could see the face, the person stopped dead in their tracks.

"Who are you...?" he asked, feeling humiliated as it was just a dream. Who did he think he was talking to? He turned around just as he thought it was time to wake up and didn't see the twenty odd pairs of red eyes hidden in the forest staring at him before they all disappeared.

"We're here!" said Carl as he woke Peter up while the flight attendant set a plate of breakfast in front of him; the best English breakfast money could buy.

"Eat something. We will be landing in thirty minutes," Carl suggested. Carl then looked at him and asked about the redness on his neck where the person had almost knocked him down on the pavement in New York. He rubbed his neck in an effort to get rid of the red and wasted no time at all in starting his breakfast. He felt as if he could eat a horse the way he was feeling, but he was distracted by planes flying all around them. In total he counted almost twenty five planes just circling the Paris air space!

"What's going on?" Peter asked.

"We can't wait..."

"Aircraft Authority of France?" Peter asked.

"What about them...we own them all. All over the world" he stated matter-of-factly, as he sat back in his chair readying himself for the landing. He was informed that the meeting was ready to take place, for the trade at the airport. At the exact time that their plane approached all the signs in the airport changed from 'on time' to 'delayed'.

"Trade?" Peter asked.

It was just as Carl had explained to him; they would return the stolen item and in return, they wouldn't harm Peter; that was the deal.

"On screen," Carl said and a satellite image of the Paris airport appeared in front of them. Peter looked at the image displayed on the screen and saw a red detailed area of all the runways. Carl could see that Peter wanted to ask something and he knew exactly what.

"We are not allowed to cross the red area before the exchange...if we do the mission is over!"

The plane landed on the runway that had been allocated for the exchange; there wasn't a soul in sight.

The plane stopped and the doors opened, but still nobody was around.

"Do you think they forgot?" Peter joked.

"No, they know we are here...look!" Carl pointed towards the roof of one of the buildings a couple of feet away from the plane. Peter squinted but couldn't see anything out of the ordinary.

"Look closer..." Carl instructed, as he showed him a second and then a third building, and then Peter saw what he had been showing him. Hidden away between the satellite dishes were a few mini-guns and cannons.

"All remotely operated...," said Carl.

Carl knew this as it wasn't the first time they'd met; the previous time was 26 April 1986 at a place called *Chernobyl*.

The place where David Thomas had finally died.

"If we go back on the deal, we'll be dead in less than a minute."

Peter looked towards Carl. "Luckily we're *not* going back on the deal, are we?"

"No, not this time..." he laughed.

They saw five vehicles approaching the runway from the eastern side of the airport. Carl checked his cell phone with the satellite feed. By the time they looked up from the monitor the five vehicles were already surrounding the plane. Two very large men got out from one of the vehicles.

"Russians?" Peter asked.

"No, something worse...remember, don't open your mouth."

Then the strangest thing happened; the two big men erected a table with two chairs and put a small vase with a red rose on the table for decoration and alongside it two glasses.

When they were finished, seven men got out of the other four vehicles forming a semi-circle around the table. They were all heavily armed with odd, powerful looking weapons.

Peter couldn't help but look up again at the almost thirty planes now circling the airport.

Then Carl walked closer to the table. As he did so, he could see a red dot on his jacket. He knew exactly what it was and so did all the protectors around him, all of them tensed up their hands against their weapons. If something happened they were ready to react. By now Carl had almost fifty laser scope dots on his body and one of the dots was from a mounted mini-gun on one of the vehicles.

Carl smiled and pointed towards the side of the plane. A door opened and when they saw what was being brought out, the red dots started disappearing one by one. Now they could see that he was true to his word; well, true to his word *this* time.

And for the first time, Peter was able to see what they had been transporting.

"A coffin?" Peter accidently let slip, his words slowly gliding in all directions as they were being taken by the soft breeze that was blowing from behind.

And then the very thing that Carl had been worried about, happened.

The spotlights, followed by the spinning mini-guns and almost a hundred red scope dots pointed straight at him and he could hear a rumbling of voices. He could only make out two words; "David Thomas."

Peter put up his hands and stood dead still, just as Carl had instructed him to do, while a man approached him from behind.

Peter could now feel the man standing behind him, his presence was overwhelming.

He sniffed at Peter and then the strange man broke the silence. There was something different about Peter and he looked at the redness on his neck.

"I've not smelt that in a while," the strange man said.

"If the case is empty you will die first, and then your helper." The way the strange man said it was as if he knew they were the real deal.

He walked over towards the coffin and slowly opened it. He looked at what was inside and without emotion, he nodded.

He was pleased, very pleased, and without a single word, the almost hundred dots that had been aimed at Peter disappeared completely.

The man walked away from Peter. He went and sat down at the table which had been set out by the two large men, and Carl joined him. The man called Peter over, and asked him to join them at the table. Another chair was placed down.

Peter wasn't sure whether he should join or not, but the strange, cynical man insisted and poured all three of them a glass of red wine.

Immediately the strange man jumped into conversation and got straight to the point. It made Peter uncomfortable. The main subject matter was Peter's relationship to David Thomas.

He knew they were family, but he had no idea how far the family tree went. Then the conversation quickly moved towards the killing of almost fifty of his associates at *Chernobyl*.

He looked at Peter again, and he could see the resemblance. He never thought he'd see a Thomas again in France.

"Richards…"

"What?"

"My name is Peter John Richards," Peter said, as he looked up again at the planes circling airport, waiting for the green light to land.

Then he nodded, not in agreement, but in fact in disagreement with the statement that Peter had just made. The strange man thought it was a good time to introduce himself, but before he did, he sniffed in Peter's direction, "You still smell like a Thomas, anyway…" But before he gave his name, his bodyguard whispered in his ear that they were ready to leave.

He took something out of his jacket pocket and gave them an ultimatum.

Peter leaned forward and saw it was a timer with days, hours, minutes and seconds.

"If the clock runs out and you are still in Mondavia…you all die."

And with that he pressed the button which started the countdown.

"Five days…," he said.

"Plenty of time…," Carl replied.

Then the strange man took a sip of his wine and got up. He and his associates drove away.

Peter was confused; he'd never heard of a town called Mondavia.

"Their country!" Carl said, 'That's why the Company failed in London, all because of them. Our time ran out...."

Peter wasn't interested in the long or the short story, but he knew they had to give them something for the privilege of staying there. Carl took a long time to answer. First he waited for them to be alone, and then at the table in the middle of the runway he said just two words.

Peter got up and took a quick sip of the red wine and immediately spat it out. He dropped the glass on the table, and spilt red wine all over the white table cloth. Its redness was unusual and was really thick.

"The French should really stop making wine...that was awful," he complained while a couple of protectors laughed at his assumption. They knew the truth.

Chapter 21

THE VISIT

All the planes started to land as soon as they'd received the green light. Peter took a moment to glance around. He couldn't believe he was in France! It was dark but he could feel the allure and ambience of the city. He closed his eyes and took in the warm summer breeze blowing gently over the runway.

Then a bright light shone directly on him from the sky. "It's a helicopter," Carl said, as he snuck up behind Peter and startled him.

It was so bright that Peter couldn't look at it. They both stood aside and waited for the helicopter to land.

"It's for us…" said Carl.

In some cases, Carl could be a real dictator, and then there were other times…

Like now…he'd made Peter a promise. "I'll show you where your grandfather stayed." And they went.

The flight was amazing. Peter had thought the smell of the air breeze at the airport was nice, but the view from the Paris night sky was overwhelming. Even so, an hour into the flight he fell asleep.

This time he didn't dream, and by the time he woke up the helicopter pilot had radioed in their approach to the house Peter's grandfather had allegedly stayed in. He couldn't make out which house was which, as there were too many lights and it was still too dark outside.

"The one on the left," Carl pointed out.

But still, Peter couldn't make out much; the border of the house was obscured, so he waited until they'd landed to have a closer look. He couldn't really see where they'd landed, but he didn't care. Besides a slightly nervous feeling, Peter was also excited to find out where his grandfather had hid away for almost twenty years.

After a few minutes of walking Carl stopped; so far they'd passed a lot of beautiful houses, and Peter thought each one of them was his grandfather's. "Here we are," stated Carl.

The house they were looking at didn't look spectacular at all; it was old and hadn't had a paint job for over half a decade.

Peter was disappointed.

"Do you want to go inside?" Carl asked, but the posters and the sign said it was too dangerous to enter.

"No, I've seen enough," Peter replied, taking out his cell phone. But then, oddly, he realised that the cell reception was off. "That's impossible," Peter said, as he saw there was no signal, but seconds ago there had been. He took a step back and the signal returned. He did this twice, and each time he saw the signal disappear as he stepped forward, closer to the house.

Then he heard Carl speaking, he was saying something about a satellite phone. That was what his grandfather had been like; secretive and prepared.

"Are you stupid or something?"

'That's it', Peter thought, Carl had been asking for a punch in the face for a long time; he treated him like a child sometimes.

"Peter!" Carl said, raising his voice slightly. Peter whipped around with all sorts of emotions flooding through him, he practically screamed,

"What?"

"Why are you looking at the outhouse?"

"Outhouse?"

Peter slowly turned back around and saw all the others looking in one direction - not the direction he had been looking in. He felt exactly like Carl had said; stupid!

But the mansion that greeted him, made up for all of it; it was beautiful and stylish.

It was nothing like his grandfather.

"Who owns it?"

"You do, and we will be staying the night!"

After dinner, Peter wanted to take a walk through the ten-bedroom house; after all, Carl had said it belonged to him. This shadow that hung over his head was a curse, but now, for the first time in his life, he owned a house!

There was only one problem; according to his watch, they had less than five days to get out of France and England and who knew where the borders of this Mondavia lay.

Nevertheless, he decided to enjoy the view. He walked over to a cabinet. It somehow just didn't fit in with the room; he tried to open it, but was unsuccessful.

He pulled and pulled, but it was stuck firmly in place. Then something caught his eye; he turned and saw a picture. He was dumbstruck.

"It's me!"

He knew the picture as it had been hung up in his father's house and had mysteriously disappeared fifteen years ago.

He realised that his grandfather *did* actually care and the thought made him smile, even if he had been responsible for the deaths of a hundred people at *Chernobyl*.

But in a way, his grandfather wasn't directly responsible, Peter mused. He didn't kill them, the bomb did. He wasn't the one who had strapped a missile to his back and walked into the power plant in Russia.

It was a missile that had killed them. *"But why, and who are they really?"*

Peter looked at the picture and thought back to his life before all this had happened; a change was good for him.

Then he saw a reflection in the glass of the picture. At first he stood dead still, but he wasn't afraid. He was trying to see who it was. It was now the third time that he'd had the feeling that someone was watching him. The first time was when Jones and Frederick stopped him, dressed as South African police officers; the second was before he entered building number eight in New York for the first time; and the third time, now.

But this time it was too close for comfort.

He spun around quickly as he tried to see who it was, but as with all badly thought out plans, there was nothing.

This time he thought he was losing his mind, but he wasn't. Standing behind him was the person, who'd been following him for the past couple of months, and then...

"Don't turn around!" the voice commanded.

Peter wanted to, but the steel object that was pushed against his head persuaded him not to. The voice was strong and very persuasive.

"Okay...I won't turn around, and you don't shoot."

"Deal..."

There he stood, his face towards the wall, as he waited to hear the reason for this man being in his new house. He thought that it could only be that guy at the airport. Like them, this assassin in his house also reeked of expensive leather, as he held a gun to his head, and he was mere moments away from being shot.

But this assassin wasn't there to kill him; he was there to warn him.

"Be careful...they wouldn't mind if you didn't make it out alive."

Then the metal piece that had been forced against his head subsided.

"What do you mean?" Peter asked, but there was no answer and when he turned around, the leathered assassin was gone. He looked at the table and let out a laugh.

On the table was the 'gun' that a moment earlier been forced against his head; and in fact it wasn't a gun, just a cleverly held bottle opener!

This was good news for Peter, not the fact that the assassin hadn't blown his head off, but the fact that there was someone who knew more than Peter did.

Carl walked in on him while he still held the picture in his hand and immediately felt the mood was different. Peter thought hard about whether he should tell Carl about the intruder or not; he decided against it. The peculiar way in which Peter greeted Carl, made the Company boss suspicious.

"I heard voices..." said Carl

The only excuse Peter could think of was that it was a TV, but unfortunately there wasn't one in the room. Then Carl gave him a light blue envelope. Peter looked at it. There was no name on the envelope.

"Open it!"

He opened it and saw a money transfer receipt in the name of his son. The words that the visitor had said to him seemed to be coming true already; *they wouldn't mind if you didn't make it out alive.*

Carl had made it out in a trust for Peter's son; when he turned eighteen he would receive everything.

"It's a lot of money," Peter said, and he was right; $10 000 for a study fund would certainly come in handy. But for the Company, it was nothing. "Pocket money," Carl mumbled.

The Company's net worth had just been checked ten minutes earlier when Carl had transferred the money to Peter's son's account - and it was $550,000,000. Peter was supposed to get one million; that was the deal that Jones and Frederick had made with Carl regarding Peter, but while doing the banking, he deleted a couple of zeroes.

"They are ready for us!" Carl said and Peter nodded. He knew what Carl was talking about; the train was nearly ready for them. Carl suggested that Peter should get some rest, but Peter was too amazed by the surroundings. He felt like a king.

He went back to his previous struggle with the cabinet door, and he tried to open it again. It wouldn't budge, but he kept on at it...after ten minutes of struggling, it finally gave way and he managed to open it. There seemed to have quite a few of surprises inside, but one thing in particular caught his eye which he was sure would come in handy.

The morning came quickly, and what a beautiful morning it was! Now he could see everything around him, including the large number of expensive boats docked in the waterfront. "One of them is yours," said Carl

Peter couldn't see which boat belonged to him, but it didn't matter. All of them were awesome. That was where he stopped. He was *not* going to die for a ghost; he wanted to come back to the place his grandfather had left him. But that left him with another problem; if he made it, he would have to leave the country. That was the deal Carl had made at the Paris airport.

"Pity...I would have loved to bring my son here one day."

"What about your wife?" one of the protectors asked him. Peter had forgotten they were only human behind the riot gear and protective clothing they wore - human.

"She left me for a rich guy..."

The protector laughed although Peter didn't think it was amusing at all. He asked him why he was laughing. But when he gave his explanation Peter had to laugh too.

"You are richer that most people now," the protector chuckled, as he looked at the mansion that towered behind them.

That was true. If he survived he would be a very wealthy man. *IF he survived of course.* They set off to Paris.

The trip back to Paris was exciting and uncomplicated, until they landed somewhere that was almost on top of the Eiffel Tower! Peter was beginning to think that Carl was losing his mind, and he wasn't the only one. Some of Carl's colleagues were beginning to feel the same way. The 'normal' angry outbursts were becoming all too frequent. His lust for power fogged his mind and every so often he took pills to calm his nerves.

Across from where they had landed, two vehicles waited for them. Before they got in Peter saw someone staring at them, but not at 'them'; he was only looking at Peter. Peter stopped and looked directly back at the person that was staring straight at him.

He wasn't afraid; in fact he felt protected.

He knew it was the 'assassin' who had warned him about the Company. Then, just like that, the person disappeared between the crisscrossing pedestrians.

Now that they were all in the vehicles, Carl made a call, the same one he made before every mission. This was not a social call; he needed to get permission to continue.

A few thousand miles away a phone rang in a secluded room; a man in his white coat walked into the room, closed the door, and made certain he was alone before he answered.

He said only a few words, "You have permission", and then put the phone down. But this time he added something different; "Finish it this time."

They had decided that after this mission, the Company would be disbanded and Carl knew it.

The man in his white coat turned around and behind him stood Jones and Frederick. The man in the white coat had to be sure, so he asked them again, "Are you sure?"

"We have spoken to HIM; it will be so," Frederick answered.

"It's a go," Carl said and then also called for the satellite feed, and announced the countdown to the interception. They didn't have long; only four hours and twenty minutes.

Chapter 22

CARL IS LOSING HIS MIND

They arrived at the train station in a matter of minutes with the police escorts that Carl had organised for them. This made the others unhappy; they were in fact furious. Carl had always spoken about keeping a low profile, but this was absurd.

The protectors led the way towards the departure area and they arrived at the international train. Carl stood and looked at the train for a few seconds.

"This is not going to be easy," he noted.

He was right. If they reached the tunnel at the English Channel and they still hadn't completed the mission, it wasn't going to end well.

"Why?" Peter asked. The answer was easy; the Company relied heavily on satellites, but if they went underground they would be useless to them.

That left yet another problem, so they had to hope that the teams had done what they were supposed to do.

If they made a mistake on this one, it would be disastrous, and would cost another billion dollars, again.

Before they boarded, as always, there was a debriefing. According to the satellite feed, the General would board at the next station so this would give them enough time to become invisible.

But first the passengers would need to board; this time there were over a hundred and they all checked out as they showed their tickets at the entrance.

The lady in the ticket box was happy; if this was over she too could rest, as they would cross over.

She was none other than the General's wife, Maria Schultz Senior. This was her duty; she needed to check that each of them had a ticket; the rest was up to General Ferdinand Schultz.

Now it was up to the engineers and the one man Peter really wanted to meet, Special Agent Martin Davis, the man in charge.

Peter couldn't wait; he looked around but saw nothing. Then someone bumped into him.

It was a little girl dressed in her school uniform.

"Sorry, little girl…" he apologised. It wasn't his fault but he was so much bigger than she was and she could have been hurt.

She stopped, and she looked at him, but differently, not like she looked at the other commuters. She was under the impression she had met him before.

She stood as still as a statue.

Peter picked up her doll. What a strange looking doll for a young girl! At that moment he didn't remember what his friend Johannes had told him.

She was still spellbound and gazed at Peter. While she didn't recognise him, there was something familiar about him. She walked away and in the hustle, she dropped the doll. Peter picked it up for her, but when he looked up she had disappeared.

He didn't think much of the doll, but placed it in his pocket, and didn't really look at it.

"Peter," Carl beckoned; they were waiting for him.

It was time to start up the train. The cameras recorded all the passengers on the train, and they counted 112, one hundred passengers and 12 of them.

Then a whistle sounded; the train was ready to depart.

For this to work, they needed part of the train to be invisible. And that's exactly what they did.

"Welcome to the ghost train..." one of the engineers said, and he explained while the protectors left the station, that their job was over. The covered part of the train was revealed; they had heard of stealth planes, stealth boats; but here was a part of the stealth train.

The part was solid, almost like an armoured vehicle - no windows, no external lights - just a solid shell. Carl pressed a button on his monitor and a few feet from them a door opened and the engineers walked in. So far Peter hadn't seen the team with Special Agent Martin Davis.

Peter grabbed Carl's hand. "Where is Davis?"

"They board at the next station with the General." That's all he said and he got on the train. Now with everybody strapped in, the train slowly chugged out of the station. Inside was very impressive, almost like a space shuttle launch control room with cameras in each compartment, ten monitors and a red button covered by plastic.

"Systems report..." Carl hollered.

"We are a go on all...the hub will be invisible in ten seconds."

Carl was pleased and lit up a cigarette. They only had two minutes until they got to the next station, *the unscheduled stop*.

The camera located at the back of the normal train exposed no extra carriage. It had been successful; the train was only invisible on the light spectrum of the crossed over.

This was all done in good time, and then the train started to slow down.

Inside the control hub an alarm sounded....the General had taken control of the train.

"How's the driver..." Carl asked, clearly not too concerned. They would've taken care of him if there was a problem.

"He's out cold sir..." the one operator said, as he looked at the monitor as he'd seen the train driver collapse on the floor only moments before. It happened the moment the General took control of the train; he took the driver and his co-driver out. They were not on the list, so there was no need to kill them.

The team checked the satellite feed. All was in order. The beacons on the waiting team were blinking every few seconds and on the monitor the names were displayed. Peter could see Special Agent Martin Davis was among them. He nodded and walked back to the main screen which revealed the picture of the front view of the train.

But there was a problem; they had no visual of the General.

"Find him now!" Carl shouted.

The team that were waiting on the platform could see the approaching train decreasing speed even more; it stopped at the station and all the doors opened, whilst inside the hub the team were frantically searching for the General.

"Still nothing sir..." they reported.

Then silence fell on the hub, only the bleeping sounds of the beacons of the team waiting on the platform could be heard.

They couldn't board until they saw the General.

"There!" one of the controllers said.

He could see the scanners were going off the charts; a signal was coming from behind the resting area and was moving towards Special

Agent Josh Williams.

"Agent Williams, whatever you do don't move..."

Agent Williams' heart rate monitor jumped a couple of beats. The General was so close to him now, the Agent could almost touch his arm, but he passed him with no incident.

So far, so good. The General walked towards the end of the train, like he always did. The people on the train, like the idiots they were, started to complain.

Then an announcement came on the intercom, first in French and then in English, "The train will depart shortly, please remain seated."

In the hub there was confusion; they didn't send the message!

"It was him!" hissed Carl.

This was the first time he had used the intercom system and Carl was worried. He looked towards the red button on the panels on the side wall, and Peter saw him staring. He knew that the red button was going to be trouble.

'But at least it's got a key to open it,' Peter thought. He didn't have to guess who had the key, as he saw Carl spin it around his finger.

Now the General was moments away from stepping on the train, but he stopped and looked towards the back of the train. A normal human could see the hub easily, for them it just looked like a boarded up train. But with all the equipment and measures they'd taken, it was impossible to see the hub.

The hub crew checked the video monitor; everything looked okay.

According to the visual spectrum, the train was invisible to the General and any other lost soul out there.

"Then what is he looking at," they wondered.

The General sniffed and glared further down the platform.

Then he sniffed again. Then Peter smelt it too; it was Carl's cigarette that was polluting the air with a foul odour.

Carl put it out quickly. There was definitely something different about the General this time. It was almost if he'd gotten stronger since they last saw him, but that was impossible.

Thankfully, it didn't take long for the General to lose interest in the cigarette smell and get on the train.

"It has begun!" Carl murmured.

The remainder of the team that were waiting on the platform had to hurry. This was their only way in; the doors were closing fast and again they had miscalculated the entry point...so Carl had to intervene by ensuring the doors opened for longer than needed, as he caused a power surge.

This had an effect on the General; it was almost as if the surge had made him weaker for a second. This was unexpected and left them with the conclusion that this could count in their favour. The General needed the power from the train to survive on a dimensional platform!

By now Special Agent Martin Davis and his team had made it into the train and were invisible to the General. The cold air that was needed to help hide the Agents had already permeated throughout the whole train, which had now reached containment. As it departed the station, the only things that were left behind were the two train drivers that were dragged to safety by Special Agent Josh Williams. He thought it was necessary to remove them, even though by doing that he had disobeyed a direct order from Agent Martin Davis.

"We will settle this after the mission..." Agent Davis warned.

He didn't want to discuss it now, but the others could see it had upset him. Agent Williams couldn't understand why the Major was so upset;

they were supposed to save as many lives as possible. But for some reason this had made him furious. They tried to calm him down, but their efforts were unsuccessful. Carl quickly intervened into the conversation, and he alone was the only person who could calm him down.

Carl only had to say: "For your life…" The others had no idea what they were talking about, but Davis knew.

Earlier, back in Paris, Agent Martin Davis had secretly placed his ticket in the pocket of one of the drivers. The train driver was supposed to take his place in the killing spree; however the unselfish acts of Agent Josh Williams had foiled his plan!

Agent Davis had planned this for months; he had kept his ticket hidden from them for a long time, and was leading his team on lies that he had told to protect himself, as he hid his true colours from them.

On the monitor Agent Davis' heart rate was still off the charts; he could hide his emotions, but not his heart. Then Davis increased the oxygen in his tank to try and help with his impulse behaviour, and it worked, not because of the oxygen, but because of the little extra illegal substance he himself had added.

After a few moments, he calmed down, as did his heart rate.

"Good to have you back Major…" one of the members in the hub acknowledged.

By the time they had double checked everything, from the violet lights to the air pressure in the compartments, the General had already started checking the tickets of the passengers, with only one agent there to keep an eye on him. The agent stayed as far back as possible from him.

"Reaching electromagnetic spectrum in ten seconds," blared over their radios, which gave them the much needed feedback from the hub. As they were already invisible to the General, it would make it easier to move around him without raising his suspicions.

In the hub, Peter kept a close eye on everything - the passengers and the agents - and his mind wandered back to what had happened in Cape Town.

"What ever happened to the four police officers?"

It was a valid question. There were no bodies and nobody had a clue as to what had actually happened. Those men had been missing for over a year. Then Peter's mind wandered back to the coffin; he couldn't help but wonder what was inside.

He stared at the toy doll the little girl had dropped earlier. He only realised then what he was holding after his short, but distracting daydream. It was the doll Johannes had told him about, the tell-tale Nazi uniform was unmistakable.

"She's here..."

"Who?" one of the agents in the hub asked.

After his explanation with the doll as some proof, they began checking all the sensors, as they tried to locate the little girl, but to no avail. She was nowhere to be found.

"She was supposed to surface already!" growled Carl.

Now they went into overdrive as they tried to find her, but above all they had to continue to keep an eye on the General. So far so good; he was still in his conductor uniform.

"Time?" Carl shouted.

Unlike the previous missions they needed to be wary of the time. They needed to finish before they reached the tunnel entrance. Carl looked towards the red button again, that was beckoning him to press it.

Time was still on their side.

"We found her...here look."

The team switched over the main screen to the infrared monitor and alongside it, they had the normal view. It checked out, she was on the second to last compartment from the front, but she was alone.

Not a soul or un-dead was near her. But something was wrong with her; she didn't look like her normal friendly self.

Then a problem arose; the temperature started to increase in that compartment.

"Decrease it..."

The room started to fill with freezing air, yet the temperature wasn't going down.

They scanned the room with every available instrument they had, as they tried to determine the problem.

But nothing worked, and they were left with only one remaining choice. They needed to send the team in to check it out personally.

Special Agent Martin Davis smiled; he knew the perfect candidate for the job.

"Agent Williams...you know what to do!"

Williams, unsuspecting, entered the compartment. He spotted the girl, and he knew that she couldn't see him. They had done this before, and as long as no part of the body was revealed, nothing could happen. As he entered, he could feel something was very different.

The girl wasn't moving an inch. The air had gotten so cold that his suit began to freeze so much that he couldn't see through his protecting visor.

"It's extremely cold in here" he said.

But the temperature on the monitor was increasing. All of them checked his instrument gauges and read the temperature. The gauges *must* be incorrect.

"Forty degrees!" the agent in the hub alerted, but Agent Williams continued to maintain that he was freezing.

He gave them urgent instructions to increase the temperature, which they did. Special Agent Josh Williams thanked them and walked forward towards the girl.

He then heard a beep coming from his suit and looked towards the windows of the compartment which were slowly freezing up. He looked at his suit gauge again.

"Forty-five degrees!"

Whatever they were doing, it wasn't working! The temperature was still increasing, but the agent was freezing in his suit, and if they didn't do something about it quickly, Agent Williams would die of cold.

"Explain to me what is going on!" Carl shouted.

It had become so cold in the compartment that the camera lenses cracked one by one. The first camera to go was the one fitted to Williams' suit, and then the two mounted cameras that the team had installed a day earlier. All they had left was the infrared camera that was also moments away from being destroyed.

Then the little girl just disappeared.

"She's gone!" one of the hub controllers said, mystified, while he rewound the infrared camera footage and watched her disappear into nowhere. He looked through all the compartments, but still nothing. Only the General walked the train.

Everybody in the hub was using every resource available to them to find the girl; not that she was a danger. The fact of the matter was that she was the key; if she changed from her school clothes to a red dress then they knew it would begin.

They continued with the hunt, as they used every bit of technology they had, however looking through twenty cameras was taking time. With no digital signature it would be impossible to find her. Peter felt a chill run down his body giving him a warning that something was wrong, and his instincts were right.

Out of the line of their camera views, she appeared, not in the dining area, and not in any corridor...but she appeared in a place where none of them would have expected, smack bang in the middle of their hub! She was still in her little black shoes and school uniform. She looked around in bewilderment, confusion and uncertainty as to why these men were on the train. Then she saw her doll, and like a child, was distracted by needful things. Unbelievably nobody was aware of her presence in the hub.

Their time was beginning to run out; the tunnel was approaching fast. Finally the team was ready for phase two. This was a phase that most of them weren't happy about, but it needed to be done.

"It's time for happy gas..."

They flooded the corridors with the calming gas; they couldn't have frantic people running wild on the train.

Out of their line of sight, the little girl happily played with her doll. And then something started to happen, the very reason why they had needed to find the girl.

In a brief instant, her school uniform turned bright red, and her smile turned to disappointment.

She knew exactly what was about to happen and she was clearly not in the mood for revenge. She looked up and saw Peter still sitting in his chair as he looked at two men that were operating the monitors; Carl and his assistant doubled their efforts to find the little girl.

Then another power surge rippled through the entire train; this one however knocked out all the cameras on the train. It had been slightly stronger than the previous power surge, but it took ages to reboot all the cameras.

"Where are they?" Carl wondered, but this time he wasn't talking about the General. He was talking about Jones and Frederick. Carl and his assistant walked into the next room of the hub and closed the transparent door behind them, as they left Peter in the concealed soundproof room alone with the saddened looking girl. She walked a bit closer to Peter and then in the silence of the room, she spoke.

"You shouldn't be here!" These few words almost made him dislodge from his chair. It had been a while since his heart had almost jumped out of his chest, but in the same sentence she thanked him for the doll and what he had done to try and save them.

Peter couldn't say anything; his heart was still trying to recover from the fright. The only thing that came to mind was the red button Carl had been eyeing since he'd stepped on the train.

She also saw the red button as she followed his eyes; fortunately for them it was covered with a bulletproof cover.

"What is this?" she asked. He had forgotten she was still a little girl and curious to find out everything and red was certainly an inviting colour.

Still Peter couldn't get any words out.

And then finally…"It wasn't me who helped." He stopped abruptly.

At that moment they were both confused; she thought he had helped her and he didn't understand how it was that she couldn't distinguish between him and his grandfather.

She saw Carl and his assistant walk towards the door.

"You need to get off…" she insisted, as she tried hard to repay the favour his grandfather had bestowed on them. Peter understood something. Although she was a little girl, he couldn't negotiate with her. So he tried to make her understand that they were on a moving train and if he jumped off he would die.

"I'll stop the train for you!"

Peter was quiet; he couldn't find the right words to reply. He reminded himself that he was speaking to a ghost, but there were those words she'd said, *"I'll stop the train for you!"*

Those few words were so powerful that he almost gasped, but realised that an open gaping mouth wouldn't be the best way to reply. He thought for a moment, getting more and more confused. How was it possible for her to stop the train?

According to what they knew, her father was in control.

"How?" he asked. He needed to know what she was capable of and how she could stop the train.

But at that exact moment Carl opened the door. He looked at Carl and when he looked back, she was gone.

Carl saw Peter almost halfway up the table and he knew something was wrong.

"She was here!"

Carl wasn't surprised and his reaction made Peter uncomfortable; it was almost as if he knew it would happen, and if he knew that, then he knew their lives were in danger.

This was it for Peter. Before Carl knew it, Peter was on top of him. Two other members of the team saw the onslaught and ran to try and help, but Peter saw them, pressed the door lock button and continued with the assault, as he punched Carl with everything he had.

Outside the door, all the hub crew members tried to shoot the door open, but it was a lost cause, as this was an impenetrable bulletproof door.

It was only when Carl collapsed, and dropped to the floor, that Peter stopped punching him. Then he pressed the button so that the crew could enter. It took two shots to the chest to take Peter down to the floor. The assistants helped Carl up, and when he saw they'd killed Peter he was not happy, at all.

He knew the mission was over, *and it was time*. Peter was their only hope; he was their protection.

Carl took out the key that hung around his neck, unlocked the hardened transparent cover and all around the room small red lights began to flash. He turned around and looked at Peter's lifeless body on the floor. With a barely perceptible nodding of heads, they all agreed.

The maths was easy; press the red button and the train would implode in three seconds. The explosion would take the General and his family down, but it would also take over a hundred innocent people with it.

"May He forgive us" Carl sighed and slowly readied himself. Then he pressed the tempting red button.

But nothing happened. Not even a twitch in the lights.

Then they heard movement behind them and the trigger happy assistants pointed their guns towards Peter's lifeless body. They were sure the noise had come from there.

Then a hand rose from the wall. It was Peter's hand, as he held a piece of computer with a few wires.

Now they knew why the bomb didn't ignite. Carl ordered them to lower their weapons and told them to help him up.

Carl was curious how Peter had survived the shots, and they didn't have to wait long to find out. Carl recognised the bulletproof vest that Peter was wearing with the wolf insignia on it.

"Your grandfather's…" Carl said. He knew where his grandfather had got it; it was a gift from the only angels he knew, Jones and Frederick.

Back in the South of France, the cabinet Peter had opened held a few surprises, and there was that one thing he thought would come in useful, a bulletproof vest. And he had been right, seeing as though he'd never got one from Carl.

"Someone said that was made in heaven," Carl said as he laughed and wiped the blood from his lip.

Peter apologised for his attack. It wasn't like him. He hadn't been in a fight since Angola. Carl didn't seem too worried; he knew something else.

"They are going to nuke us anyway…" Carl said, as he looked for a reaction, but not even the assistants could say anything.

They didn't know about this.

Carl showed them on the satellite map where the line was.

"If we cross there, we all burn."

Carl wanted to save everybody from pain and Peter understood that. If Peter hadn't pulled out the plug, they all would have died painlessly and quickly.

It gave them less than half an hour to live, irrespective of what the General did; they were behind schedule and it was better to accept it and wait for the end.

In short, all the planning and all the efforts were not going to work. The train couldn't reach the tunnel. Carl made all the required calculations, and there was no way for them to survive.

Peter was clearly upset. He was reminded of what the assassin had said; they would not let him leave the train.

Carl mumbled something.

"What did you say?"

Carl repeated it, not that it meant anything. There was no way for them to survive.

"If only we could stop the train..." Carl said again.

Peter smiled; he then remembered what the girl had said, *"I'll stop the train for you!"*

Chapter 23

WHERE'S THE LITTLE GIRL

They only had twenty minutes to stop the train; time was ticking by.

Back at the Vatican City, preparations were being made to target the train. As had been agreed, if the train crossed the designated line, it needed to be disintegrated. A British Typhoon fighter plane would do the trick.

"Get me the British Prime Minister!" barked the man in the white coat, and that's all he had to do. The bomb would be dropped as soon as the train crossed the line. They were all pleased and went along with their daily duties. After they'd checked the perimeter of the city, they took some time to relax; they knew it would soon be over.

The old antique phone rang again in a safe-guarded room, but nobody answered this time. Everyone was too busy looking at the satellite feed, in anticipation of when the train would cross the line. The person who'd made the call on the other end placed the receiver back down. For him it had rung more than enough, but he wasn't in an office or a room of any sorts. Behind him were trees, bushes and a tree trunk. Perched on the half cut off tree trunk was the old antique phone. The man was mysterious; he hid his face in the shade of the bushes and then turned towards an open field across from where he was. He looked at something far away. In the distance he could see the bullet train snaking towards him; it wasn't even ten minutes away. The mysterious man was the one who'd been following Peter around.

"They've had their chance..." he said and poured a noxious liquid over the phone, and watched as it ignited. The smoke was so potent he had to move away from the fire. Shortly after, just when he was a safe distance away, the phone exploded. The force of the explosion was phenomenal, leaving a dead burnt area on the side of the forest, the size of a football field. But those in the Vatican City didn't notice the huge hole that appeared on the satellite; all of them were too busy celebrating the end of the *evil*.

There were two, however, who reacted to the explosion. The two angels acknowledged each other. When it happened, they were standing with their backs to the satellite pictures.

They turned around and saw exactly what had happened and before the men in white coats could say anything, they were gone; just a door was left swinging at the back of the room. The Italian-speaking man instructed them to inform the fighter pilot to ready his weapon. The other man in the room was concerned about the two who'd just left, however the man in the white coat reassured him.

"They are not allowed to intervene…." That is all he said, and no other questions were necessary. He too didn't enquire about the large crater that had formed not too far from the rail track.

Carl sat quietly and looked at the ripped cord that was connected to the red button. Something bothered him. "How the hell did he rip it out of the steel table?" The cord was bolted into the steel, and he knew he wouldn't have been able to remove it. But then he remembered. A few days ago, Peter had come into his office with the redness on his neck. "Impossible…" Only one name popped into his head; 'David Thomas.'

Meanwhile, Peter struggled to find the girl. She had said she could stop the train, but he'd been looking for her for more than ten minutes now and came up with nothing.

Carl called Peter over the radio, and casually let him know that they were only five minutes away from crossing the line at the current speed.

He understood, but if he couldn't find her, he wasn't sure what to do?

When he turned around, there she was standing behind him. She had been following him the entire time. He just couldn't see her as she didn't want to be seen. Even with all their fancy equipment and technology, she could still make herself invisible to them.

She had the power to elude them, and that wasn't all. She *could* stop the train.

He was relieved and wasted no time and asked her whether she could indeed stop the train.

"But why now? We are about to begin...." She paused and turned around; Peter could see she was confused. "He is almost here!" she said, as she scanned the carriages for her father.

But by the time she uttered the words, the radio communications were off the charts. Everyone spoke at once.

The General had become aware of what was going on. He had already sliced up one of the agents, although he'd been unaware of what he'd been doing as he couldn't see him; however the agent had been between the General and the door to the next carriage. Back in the hub, they'd had no idea what had happened until the monitors flat-lined. At that point they realised that the General was in his Nazi uniform, and he was extremely angry.

"How angry? Like in New York?" Special Agent Josh Williams asked. He knew one of his agents was dead, so he needed to know *exactly* how angry the General was.

"No; off the charts," the agent in the hub reported. With every step the General took, the more unstoppable he became.

"Don't make her stop the train!" Carl shouted over the radio, as he rambled on about David Thomas. He was right. When he turned around there was Peter's grandfather.

"Hi there Carl, it's been a long time."

Carl thought he was going to kill him, but he was spared. David Thomas just whispered something in Carl's ear and walked out the back door, and climbed onto the roof of the speeding train.

Carl didn't move. Only the radio on which he'd been talking fell to the floor. He sat back, and looked at the image of the plane on the monitor that was being streamed to him on the train. There were only a few minutes left until the train crossed the line. He saw Peter, and the bleeping sound displayed on the monitor in the hub indicated that the General was merely metres away from him.

"What a shame!" Carl declared, as he knew that Peter was only seconds away from being ripped apart. Carl had given him the opportunity to wear the suit, but Peter had declined. Peter knew it would be difficult to find the girl if he wore one of the 'spacesuits' that the other guys were wearing.

But it was all over now...well, Peter would die before the bomb hit the train. It was probably best; he didn't need to die at the hand of the Company's fire-imploding bomb.

By now Peter could see the raging 'poltergeist' heading straight towards him, but he couldn't understand why he was displaying so much hate. According to the little girl, they were indebted to his grandfather, who had tried to help them.

First Peter just looked; then he sighed. He knew he was going to die; seeing General Ferdinand Schultz dressed in his Nazi uniform was incredible and scary at the same time. The General moved so fast that Peter's eyes could barely keep up. He closed his eyes; he certainly didn't want to see himself die. But after a few seconds had passed, the little girl spoke up: *"NO..."*

It was dark, but he could feel a pain alongside his neck.

It was an intense feeling of something unknown. And then he felt nothing. All the cameras in the hub shut down in an instant, like a power cut.The girl's two letter word was so intense; it ripped through Peter's mind, echoing. He thought he was dead, but he clearly wasn't as he could still hear his heartbeat.

He built up the courage to open his eyes and he saw the General standing in front of him with his arm extended almost against his neck; it was the General's nail. Peter looked into his solid dark eyes, and just stood there, like a statue. He took a step back and saw the little girl smile; not a normal smile, but a truly happy smile. He felt his neck and looked at the small amount of blood from the wound. Moments later, all the power on the train cut off, leaving them with only the natural light from outside. The train slowly decreased its speed until it came to a halt in the middle of, quite literally, nowhere.

"You don't have much time...I'll give you until the train restarts," she smiled. She thought Peter would be delighted that she had stopped the train; after all, he had asked her to. Peter knew this wasn't the time to question her; he was reminded of the conversation he'd had earlier with Carl about restarting the train. "It will take one minute twenty five seconds..."

Peter didn't have much time for conversation, but he had devised a plan. After ten seconds, the power came back on, and the internal lights ignited one by one. The people on the train became restless and tried to force themselves into some of the carriages. Back in Europe twenty eyes stared at the satellite images and the approaching fighter plane, confused about how they'd stopped the train. One of them quickly tapped into the security feed from the Company's hub on the train, but only two cameras worked, one in the hub and one in the carriage where the General was. All three of them were clearly visible. Then all of a sudden Peter ran towards the next carriage.

"What is he doing?" one of them asked, surprised, and moments later Peter called over the radio to all the Company's men on the train. His instruction was short and direct. Some of them doubted him and didn't comply...

Eventually they understood his plan and got out of their spacesuits, all except one of them, Special Agent Martin Davis.

He wasn't convinced it would work. In his mind he was reminded of the word Carl had once spoken to him, "For your life..." It practically drove him to insanity as he spoke to himself in riddles. Then he just stopped. The only thing he had on his mind was killing Peter. He walked down the carriage still dressed in his suit. This made it impossible for him to be seen by anybody, and that included Peter.

Then in the space between, the two angels, Jones and Frederick, suddenly appeared. They could sense the intense hate the Major was feeling, and it wasn't a good sign. His intention was clear; he was going to kill Peter for no reason.

"Payback!" he kept repeating, shooting anybody that looked like Peter.

Jones, the younger of the angels, took a step forward. Frederick stopped him; he was the older and wiser of the two. He reminded Jones that they weren't allowed to interfere, and Jones reluctantly agreed. They were here to guide, never to interfere; although Jones had interfered twice back at the hotel where Peter had stayed, and where Peter's friend Charles le Roux had died. Jones still had to answer for what he'd done, but he was sure his 'Boss' would let this one slide for dispersing the half-human!

Chapter 24

ONLY ONE WAY

Major Davis had now killed four Peter lookalikes. They hadn't even seen it coming; the violet lights, the cooled air and the Company's advanced technology made it impossible for others to see them, and it looked like his rampage wasn't about to stop.

Then he saw Peter - the real Peter - and laughed so hard that a person on the carriage heard him through his almost soundproof suit.

He pointed his firearm at Peter, aimed and squeezed the trigger slowly until the shot went off. Luckily for Peter, the bullet hit him in the back of his bulletproof vest. The last shot was followed by a thumping sound. Peter turned around and saw two large openings in the carriage and the wind blew through his hair slightly. He had no idea what had happened, but there were two people who did know. Their names were Jones and Frederick. However, it wasn't these two who had intervened, it was the man who had set the phone alight, and scorched the side of the forest, making a hole big enough to build a skyscraper in - *the real David Thomas.*

"Replay the images," the man dressed in the white coat ordered. He wanted to see who it was, who had taken care of their problem called 'Special Agent Martin Davis.' They knew he was dead; as the moment the 'thing' had made contact with Davis, his heart monitor flat-lined.

"Show me," he said in Italian and then paused. He recognised the person.

"Isn't that guy supposed to be dead?" an operator of the monitor questioned. He was right; the man they now saw in front of them had been killed in *Chernobyl* – it was none other than David Thomas.

Everyone in the monitor room went into a spin; they all wanted to know how he'd survived a warhead explosion!

Then the man in the white coat got up, walked closer to the monitor, squinted and stared intently at the image.

The rest of the crew became very quiet. Something bothered him.

"Mondavians…" he uttered. He didn't look in the least bit pleased.

One of his personal assistants walked into the room. He looked hurried; in his hand was a very important message. It was a letter from the Pope, a sealed letter only to be broken and opened by the intended receiver. He read the letter and ordered everyone to switch to 'code green.'

"He is coming here in two minutes."

All of his crew followed his order and switched the monitors to internal cameras around the Vatican City to 'code green.'

But before they cut communications, there was one other thing they needed to take care of. The white coated man looked at the images that were being streamed from the British Typhoon fighter plane. He had to make a critical decision; 'yes' to go ahead with the extermination of the bullet train, or 'no' to cancel the order.

He thought for a while and just before the Pope walked in he decided, "It's a go…" he said as he switched off the image.

"The tunnel runs deep…" Carl Mario Columbus once said, and so it did. The secretive manner in which the Company was run had kept them out of the limelight. In this case it was the two-headed wolf.

But all this came with a price, millions and millions of Dollars had been spent on deception.

Hiding away from the Pope was not an easy task. He suspected there was something going on with the man in the white coat, Ricardo Savant.

There was no turning back for the Company. They had started it during the Second World War, so it was their responsibility to end it.

Ricardo Savant looked on as the Pope inspected his building. Then they both strolled out to enjoy a cup of tea in the main room.

But before he stepped out he said one thing; "Let me know of our success!"

Peter stepped back when the bullet connected with his bulletproof vest. He saw the large hole in the wall, but this was no time to stop. Special Agent Josh Williams had already begun with the plan. If this didn't work, it was over for all of them.

First they had to increase the flow of happy gas, so when they got out of their suits they wouldn't frighten everyone as they appeared out of nowhere.

They had a mere couple of seconds left! They could hear the fighter jet do a flyby.

Then over the radio, Peter heard the words he'd been waiting for; "It's done!"

When Peter turned around, the little girl was standing behind him. This time she wasn't smiling. The train had started to move, building up speed as they stared at each other.

All three of them said together in unison; "You tricked me!" They sounded like thunder from the beyond... it was him, the devil himself!!

She said it, but not in a little girl's voice; it was as if she, her father and her mother were speaking in one voice and her eyes turned dark and evil. Then the room became cold, the temperature plummeted with every passing second. He knew the radios would stop working soon. He turned around to find that she had closed all the carriage doors.

Over the radio he gave his last instruction, "Cut us loose." He heard the fighter jet doing the second flyby, and then the pilot armed the missiles.

The plan was simple; get the people out of the last three carriages, separate the trains, and let the fighter jet do the rest.

"It's a good day to become a hero." He gulped. He could hear the General starting to move through the carriage, as he ripped everything in his way.

The train had now reached the required speed, and only had Peter, the General, and his wife and daughter on board.

"Aren't you going to do something?" The two angels heard a voice behind them as they stood in the field. They didn't need to turn around. They knew who it was; David Thomas himself.

The train was moving too fast for him, but they certainly could do something.

"No..." Frederick answered; they weren't allowed to intervene.

The two angels looked at each other in confusion; in fact, it was more indecisive than confusion actually.

"What about the favour you owe me," David Thomas pleaded.

He had a point - they did owe him a favour. A few months ago they had contacted him after they'd seen him watching Peter by the roadside in Cape Town. They had stopped Peter to ascertain with certainty that he was the right one. His mission was to steal the old antique telephone from Major Davis and destroy it.

They didn't answer him; they just turned around and walked away into the field. Peter was so cold that he was almost frozen, but the General didn't kill him. First he inspected the soul and then spoke. "You made the list!" Peter could hear the fighter jet approaching and he knew they had crossed the borderline. He was seconds away from being entirely on French soil.

He was supposed to feel sad and cold, but he had a warm feeling that was surging through his body. To a large extent, he felt peaceful, and had no fear of dying.

Both the General and his wife now stood behind the little girl. She was ready to take Peter's head off! And to think that all this time everyone had thought the General was the evil force behind the killings! She turned to her father and said casually and without emotion, "Rip him apart."

As with the previous killings, the General walked closer to Peter, and followed her instruction. After two steps he froze, he stood dead-still. The little 'poltergeist' girl turned around and saw that he wasn't moving.

"No!" She screamed again in all three voices.

"Sorry..." they all heard it, but not one of them had spoken this word. However, the voice sounded familiar to Peter, and he slowly spun around, thrilled to see a familiar face.

It was Jones, his friend from the Company. Peter was confused, and wondered how he had got on the train. At least, he thought, he wouldn't die alone, and that particular comforting thought prepared him for the inevitable.

Then it happened; the fighter pilot launched a tracking missile. As the train moved, so did the missile, only seconds away from its target! The little girl knew what was about to happen; she'd had a vision moments before the missile was launched.

Jones walked past Peter, and Peter instinctively tried to stop him, as he grabbed his arm and warned him of the danger. Then Jones returned the favour, and reassured him of his safety.

"They can't harm you now!" he comforted Peter, as he walked forward until he was right up against the little girl. She was furious, and was protesting viciously against the intervention. The angels had never intervened and that was how it was supposed to be.

"And I will not intervene." He was correct, technically. They were responsible for their own demise and that of Peter Richards.

"This one is mine" the three-voiced poltergeist shouted, concealed within the little girl in her red dress. She appeared so sweet, but those dark black evil eyes told a different story.

The pilot who had fired the missile then fired a second one; he had to be sure. That was the instruction he had received from the man in the white coat; anything that crossed the line must be disintegrated.

"Five seconds to impact," he reported back to the control room as the first missile ate away the distance between the train and missile.

Jones bent down on one knee to get a better view of the little girl, and smiled.

"Remember to wear sun block...I hear where you are going is hot this time of year!" he chuckled. The moment he said his last word, the missile smashed its target, crowded by the screams of the three voices while a hole was seared into the ground where the train had been travelling. The impact of the second missile followed, just to make sure. Even the missile had the wolf insignia on it.

It was official. He reported back to the control room, as he saw a large cloud of smoke hovering in the air. The conversation between the Pope and the man in the white coat was interrupted by one of the control room members with a message, "The plane has made the delivery."

He understood and they continued with their conversation.

The cover up was also successful. According to the newspapers, a train filled with fertilizer had exploded in the countryside.

Peter woke up; he looked around and saw he was back at his

grandfather's villa in the south of France. A maid entered and handed him the morning paper and a cup of coffee. He thanked her, opened the paper, and laughed softly.

"They do cover up well." He read every last detail of the test train that had exploded on a trial run.

He called the maid back and asked her if she knew how he had got here. She answered politely that the man who had brought him here was waiting for him in the garden. "Mr. David Thomas."

He walked down towards the garden area and saw a man facing away towards the beach. He stood next to him. He had always had the feeling that his grandfather was alive, so meeting him felt ordinary, natural.

Then David Thomas turned towards him, "You can stay here, it's yours..."

Peter also turned, and it was like looking at the splitting image of his father, not older than fifty or so. "You look like you haven't aged a day..." His grandfather, though, didn't answer him and continued with his conversation.

"You should change your name..."

Peter thought 'okay the reason is obvious, the deed is in the name of Thomas', but it wasn't that, it was something else.

The explanation was short and to the point. It had started in New York when he had been in the meeting with Carl and the other two men. When he had walked in he had felt unwell for a few minutes. Peter remembered that day; he had felt as if he was about to collapse. But just as suddenly as it had come on, it disappeared, and he felt better. "I bit you...sorry I had to."

Peter laughed, and thought of vampires. Then he stopped laughing. That wine he drank at the Paris airport, he remembered. "Mondavians..." Peter said as he rubbed the marks on his neck.

"Yes... you will live for another hundred years."

Peter thought this was extremely funny and commented that vampires lived forever. "No!" his grandfather corrected him, and told him that those were only myths. The truth was that they loved blood, and that they aged far slower than humans, but they did however die at the human age of 150. Peter certainly didn't revel in the idea of drinking blood, but David Thomas assured him that its taste differed. "Me, myself, I like..." but they were interrupted by Jones and Fredrick.

"I have to go, check the basement...and page two of the newspaper," he said, as he took off a golden ring from his finger and placed it on the table. "It's your time to fight evil." Peter knew it probably would be the last time he would see his grandfather, as he watched him walk away. He put on the ring. "The two headed wolf," Peter marvelled, as he looked at the solid gold ring.

"So you are not human; are you also Mondavian?"

Peter made a joke but he had a feeling that they weren't from earth.

He had never asked this, but finally it felt appropriate, "What's it like to speak to HIM?"

They laughed at his question. "You have also spoken to him."

"When?"

"Every day when you pray."

The two angels walked away and left Peter to relax in the luxurious villa that his grandfather had left him. Jones now thought it would be a good time to persuade Frederick of something, "How about some coffee?"

And so it ended well.

There was just one more thing to do, but first he needed to look at page two in the paper.

But he couldn't read it as it was in French. Then the strangest thing happened; the more he looked at the paper the more he understood the French words. It dawned on him - the gift they had been talking about over the last couple of months. He read that they had found the missing police officers that had been kidnapped by local gangsters; this, too, of course was a cover up, but who better to frame than the local scum?

He descended to the basement, eager to see what surprise his grandfather had left him. He opened a large steel door, and the room filled with freezing air. With this frigid cold, he expected a body or two, but he found something that would accommodate his whole system; everything from sirloin and rump to aged beef.

His grandfather had told him he must fight evil crime, but how? He had no tools, no leads. He spotted a sealed door next to the butchery, but this door had no key or even a door knob.

"No way...!" He saw the door scanner and pressed his palm against it. The door opened slowly. This was precisely what he needed. This room was filled with guns - loads and loads of weapons - and in the corner of the room sat a large TV screen and a sensor that picked up movement. He switched the screen on. They had said his grandfather was a technical wizard; this was going to make it so much easier to see the beacons on the monitor of evil. He saw red, green and blue icons on his screen from nearly all over the world. "What are they?" There was no explanation, so he was going to have to find out for himself. He looked on the side of the table, and saw a portable device.

"He really thought of everything."

After a few weeks he did what his grandfather had instructed him to do and changed his name to David Thomas. He could feel he was getting stronger and faster as the weeks went by.

Even so, every now and again he saw a couple of red burning eyes with a silhouette body that peered at him from the borders of the house.

Rite of Passage

They had accepted him in their country of Mondavia.

For Carl, things hadn't turned out so well; he was locked up in an asylum for the super crazy.

Who would believe all that was out there? And in a few years Peter would be able to see the other things that lurked about in the dark, hidden away from our spectrum. Some lived among us peacefully and others needed to be kept under control. The extremely dangerous were not to be taken lightly; the red, green and blue icons on his screen kept moving.

About the Author

Teno-E (Tinus Etsebeth) was born in 1979 in Upington, in the Northern Cape of South Africa. He writes sci-fi and supernatural stories. He is an ambassador for animal welfare as he believes that not enough is done for our friends. Teno-E attended Charlie Hofmeyr High School in Ceres, Western Cape, after which he travelled to London for two years for a working holiday in 2001, and then returned to South Africa. He has not been back to London since. In 2001, he studied Tourism and Public Relations at Durbanville College in Cape Town. Then, in 2002, he was accepted into the South African Police Services. Currently, Teno-E resides in Cape Town, South Africa.

In 2013 he started a community project reaching across the world, the International Servicemen and Women Day for all Police - Military - Firefighters –EMS.

www.internationalservicemenday.com

Acknowledgement

- Cooltext – www.cooltext.com
- GIMP 2 - www.gimp.org
- CapeTownCopywriter   -
capetownproofreader.wordpress.com.
- Wikipedia, the free encyclopedia
- Shutterstock / Stokkete – Cover Picture
- Proverbs 3:6 ASV – In all thy ways acknowledge him, And
he will direct thy paths.

www.ingramcontent.com/pod-product-compliance
Lightning Source LLC
Chambersburg PA
CBHW071253250626
47159CB00004B/1161